Friedrich Glauser was born i
referred to as the Swiss Simenon, he died aged forty-two, a few days before he was due to be married. Diagnosed a schizophrenic, addicted to morphine and opium, he spent much of his life in psychiatric wards, insane asylums and, when he was arrested for forging prescriptions, in prison. He also spent two years with the Foreign Legion in North Africa, after which he worked as a coal miner and a hospital orderly. His Sergeant Studer crime novels have ensured his place as a cult figure in Europe.

Germany's most prestigious crime fiction award is called the Glauser prize.

IN MATTO'S REALM

Friedrich Glauser

Translated from the German by
Mike Mitchell

BITTER LEMON PRESS
LONDON

BITTER LEMON PRESS

First published in the United Kingdom in 2005 by
Bitter Lemon Press, 37 Arundel Gardens, London W11 2LW
www.bitterlemonpress.com

First published as *Matto Regiert* in serial form in
Der öffentliche Dienst in 1936
This edition published in German as *Matto Regiert* by
Limmat Verlag, Zurich, 1995
This edition has been translated with the financial assistance of
Pro Helvetia, the Arts Council of Switzerland

A CIP record for this book is available from the British Library

ISBN 1–904738–06–0

Typeset by RefineCatch Limited, Broad Street, Bungay, Suffolk
Printed and bound by WS Bookwell, Finland

. . . and so writers can write novels about the conversations that the inmates locked up in institutions have with each other, while what those employed there say serves more to conceal thoughts and promote ambitions . . .

Arnold Zweig, *Education before Verdun*

Contents

A necessary foreword

There is no risk involved in telling a story that takes place in Berlin, London, Paris or New York. To tell a story that takes place in a Swiss town, on the other hand, is risky. I once had Winterthur Football Club object to one of my stories because a fullback appeared in it. I had to assure the lads that no reference to them was intended.

To embark on a story that takes place in a Bern psychiatric clinic is even riskier. I can already see the protests hailing down. For that reason I would like to make the following clear from the outset: there are three psychiatric clinics in the Canton of Bern – Waldau, Münsingen, Bellelay. My Randlingen Clinic is neither Münsingen, nor Bellelay, nor Waldau. The characters in it are entirely fictitious. My novel is not a *roman à clef.*

A story has to take place somewhere. Mine takes place in the Canton of Bern, in a lunatic asylum. So what? Presumably we're still allowed to tell stories?

Rude awakening

It's five o'clock in the morning, a time when respectable people are still fast asleep in their beds, and the
telephone rings. Wakes you up. It's the chief of police
on the line, so of course you dutifully reply, "Sergeant
Studer here, sir." Naturally you're still in bed, you still
have a good two hours sleep left. Then you're told a story
a half-awake brain has problems getting to grips with. So
you have to keep interrupting your lord and master
with "What?" and "Sorry?" until eventually you're told
you're a moron and you should wash your ears out . . .

That wasn't as bad as it sounded; the chief of police
likes to express himself forcefully, and moron, for
goodness sake! . . . What was worse was that he
couldn't quite cotton on to what he was supposed to be
doing. A certain Dr Ernst Laduner, he'd been told, was
coming to pick him up in half an hour, to take him to
Randlingen Psychiatric Clinic, where a patient by the
name of Pieterlen – yes, P for Peter, I for Ida, E for
Edith . . . – a patient by the name of Pieterlen had run
off.

It happened now and then . . . At the same time, that
is during the same night, his boss went on, the director
of the loony bin – the chief of police had no very high
opinion of psychiatrists – had disappeared. He'd get
the details from Dr Laduner, who wanted to make sure
he was covered, covered by the police. And the chief of
police had made a joke involving the word "covered",
not a very good joke, one with a whiff of the cowshed.

Laduner? Ernst Laduner? A psychiatrist? Studer had clasped his hands behind his head and was staring at the ceiling. Surely he knew a Dr Laduner, but where had he made his acquaintance, on what occasion? Because – and that was the remarkable thing about the whole affair – this Herr Dr Laduner had particularly asked for Sergeant Jakob Studer; at least that's what the chief of police had said. And, after he had told him that, the chief of police had added that he could well understand why. It being a well-known fact that Studer had the odd screw loose, it was no wonder a psychiatrist asked for him specifically.

You could take that as a compliment, thought Studer as he got up, shuffled across to the bathroom and started to shave. What was the director of Randlingen Clinic called? Würschtli? No, but something like that, it definitely ended in "li" . . . – The razor-blade was blunt, tedious, since Studer had a heavy beard – . . . Bürschtli? Ah, of course! Borstli. Ulrich Borstli. An old gentleman, close to retirement.

So on the one hand there was Pieterlen, a patient who had run off, on the other Ulrich Borstli, the director . . . And somewhere between the two of them Dr Laduner, whom he ought to know and who wanted to make sure he was covered. Why did he want to be covered by the police, and more particularly by Detective Sergeant Studer of the Bern cantonal police? That was the kind of unpleasant job that was always coming Studer's way. How did you behave in a lunatic asylum? What could you do when the people behind the bars just sat there raving? Carry out an investigation? It was all very well for the chief of police to ring up and issue instructions, but it wasn't going to be much fun, that was for sure . . .

In the meantime Frau Studer had got up, he could

tell by the smell of fresh coffee permeating the apartment.

"*Grüess Gott*, Studer," said Dr Laduner. He had come without his hat; his hair was brushed flat and a strand stuck up at the back, like a heron's crest. "We've met before. You know, in Vienna."

Studer still couldn't remember. Being addressed familiarly as "Studer" didn't particularly surprise him, he was used to it, and he invited the doctor, very politely and slightly fussily, to come in and take off his coat. But Dr Laduner had no coat to take off, so he went straight into the dining room, said good morning to the sergeant's wife and sat down, all with an assurance that amazed Studer, as if it were the most natural thing in the world.

Dr Laduner was wearing a light-coloured flannel suit, and the fat, loosely tied knot of his tie was a shimmer of cornflower blue between the points of his white shirt collar. He hoped Frau Studer had no objection, he said, unfortunately he was going to have to borrow her husband, but he promised to return him in full working order. Something had happened, something complicated and unpleasant. Anyway, he knew the sergeant well, had known him for a long time – Studer gave a bewildered frown – and had decided to treat the sergeant as a personal guest. Anyway, it wouldn't be that bad.

"Anyway" seemed to be Dr Laduner's favourite word. And the way he spoke was odd, a mixture of eastern Swiss dialect and formal German that didn't sound like authentic Swiss German at all. And his smile was a little disconcerting too; there was something of a mask about it. It covered the lower half of his face up to his cheekbones. That part was fixed and only his eyes and his very broad, high forehead seemed to be alive.

No, thank you, Dr Laduner said, he wouldn't have anything, his wife would have his breakfast waiting for him at home. Anyway, they had to hurry, reports were at eight o'clock, and this morning he had to do the round of all the wards; whether the Director had disappeared or not, work still came first, duty called and all that. Dr Laduner made little gestures with his left hand, still with the glove on, then stood up, gently took Studer by the arm and led him out . . . Goodbye . . .

It was a cool September morning. The trees on either side of Thunstrasse already had the occasional yellow leaf. Dr Laduner's low-slung four-seater behaved itself and started without a murmur. The open windows let in a light breeze, which had a faint hint of mist, and Studer leant back comfortably. His black boots looked a little odd beside Dr Laduner's elegant brown shoes.

At first both men held back from speaking, and Studer used the silence to rack his brains about Dr Laduner. He must have met the man somewhere . . . In Vienna? Studer had been to Vienna a few times, in those distant days when he had been comfortably installed in his position as a chief inspector with the Bern city police, the days before that business with the bank that had cost him his job and he had had to start again from the bottom as a plain detective. Things could be tough if you had too strong a sense of justice. It was a certain Colonel Caplaun who had demanded his dismissal, a demand that had been granted. The same Colonel Caplaun of whom the chief of police would say, in his unbuttoned moments, that there was no one he'd rather see in Thorberg Prison. No point in wasting his time going over the same old story; he'd been cashiered and that was that. He'd started again from the bottom and in six years' time he'd retire.

When you thought about it, he'd got off lightly . . . But ever since that business with the bank he'd had the reputation of being a bit dotty, so actually it was Colonel Caplaun's fault that he was being driven to Randlingen Clinic by a Dr Laduner to investigate the mysterious disappearance of the director and the escape of a patient.

"Can you really not remember, Studer? All those years ago in Vienna?" Studer shook his head. Vienna? All he could see was the Hofburg and Favoritenstrasse and the police headquarters and an old and very senior civil servant who had known the famous Professor Gross, the leading light of criminology . . . But a Dr Laduner he could not see.

Then Laduner said, keeping his eyes on the road, "You've forgotten Eichhorn then, Studer?"

"Of course!" Studer exclaimed. He was so relieved he put his hand on Laduner's arm. "Herr Eichhorn! Of course! And now you've gone in for psychiatry? Weren't you going to reform the care of children with behavioural difficulties in Switzerland?"

"Ach, Studer!" Dr Laduner slowed down a little because a lorry was coming towards them and sticking to the middle of the road. "Here in Switzerland they issue more directives than there are holes in a piece of Emmenthal. And they're about as effective, too."

Studer laughed, a deep laugh. Dr Laduner joined in with a laugh that was slightly higher.

Eichhorn! . . .

Studer saw a small room with eight boys in it, twelve- to fourteen-year-olds. It looked like a battlefield: the table demolished, the benches smashed to match-wood, the windowpanes shattered. He stood in the doorway and saw one boy going for another with a knife. "Now you're going to get it," the boy said. And in one corner was Dr Laduner, looking on. When he noticed Studer in the doorway he signalled him not to intervene. And the boy suddenly threw the knife away and started to cry in a sad, long-drawn-out wail, like a dog that's been beaten, while Dr Laduner came out of his corner and said, in a calm, matter-of-fact voice, "By tomorrow morning all this'll be cleared up and the windows replaced . . . OK?"

And the boys chorused, "Yes."

It was in the Centre for Children with Behavioural Difficulties in Oberhollabrunn, seven years after the war. An institution without coercive discipline. A certain Eichhorn, a gaunt, nondescript man with straight brown hair, had taken it into his head to see if it was possible, without priests, or sentimentality or beatings, to make something out of these so-called juvenile delinquents. And he'd succeeded. For once the education authorities had a man on their staff who happened to have a head on his shoulders. It does happen. In this particular case it was a man to whom Eichhorn's simple idea made sense. His idea was as follows: the little villains were caught up in an inescapable cycle of misdemeanour – punishment – misdemeanour – punishment. Punishment aroused resentment, to which they gave vent by committing further misdeeds. But what if the punishment were eliminated? Shouldn't there come a point where the resentment had played itself out. Perhaps one could make a new start there, build on it perhaps, without the humbug or, as Dr Laduner had put it at the time, "without the religious cod-liver oil".

Eichhorn's experiments had been much discussed in specialist circles and when Studer had gone to Vienna it had been suggested he have a look at them.

He had arrived at the very moment when the

resentment was reaching exhaustion point among the most difficult group. And he had been impressed. As he was a fellow Swiss, Dr Laduner, who was doing a stint as a trainee with Eichhorn, took him to see the director. They had talked together, in slow, measured tones. Studer had told them about Tessenberg, the reformatory in Bern canton, how bad things had been there for a while. By that time it was ten o'clock at night, and there was a ring at the front door. Eichhorn went to see who it was and came back with a boy. "Sit down. Are you hungry?" he asked him, and went to the kitchen himself and brought some sandwiches. The boy was starving. He stayed with them until eleven, then Eichhorn's wife took him to the guest room.

Afterwards Laduner told Studer that it was the third time the boy had absconded. This time he had come back of his own free will, which was why he had been received in such a friendly way. Studer had been filled with genuine respect for both men, for Dr Laduner and Eichhorn.

"What's Herr Eichhorn doing now?"

Dr Laduner shrugged his shoulders. "Completely disappeared."

It kept on happening. A man tried something new, useful, something that made sense, and for two or three years things went well. Then suddenly he was gone, vanished without trace. Well, Dr Laduner had switched to psychiatry. The question was, how had he got on with old Ulrich Borstli, the director who had also disappeared?

For a moment Studer thought of asking about the details of his disappearance, but then let it be; he could not get the image of the young Dr Laduner out of his mind, standing there in the corner of the wrecked room watching the boy go for his classmate with a knife ... To grasp the psychological moment when a situation is ripe! Even at that time he'd shown great understanding had Dr Laduner. And Sergeant Studer felt flattered, flattered that he'd been specifically asked for and that Dr Laduner had invited him to be his guest.

There was one thing that was strange. All those years ago in Vienna Dr Laduner had not worn the smile that looked like a mask stuck on in front of a mirror. And, too – perhaps he had got this wrong, there was no way of checking – he had the impression there was fear lurking somewhere in his eyes.

"There's the clinic," said Laduner, pointing out of the side window with his right hand. A red-brick building, U-shaped as far as Studer could tell, with lots of towers and turrets. Surrounded by pine trees, lots of dark pine trees. It disappeared for a moment, then reappeared; there was the main entrance and the rounded steps leading up to the door. The car stopped. The two of them got out.

Bread and salt

Dr Laduner pointed at the window to the right of the entrance and said, "The Director's office."

There was a hole the size of a man's fist in the lower left-hand pane; splinters of glass were scattered over the window-ledge and the flower-bed separating the entrance from the red-brick wall.

"It looks pretty gruesome inside. Blood on the floor, the typewriter's bitten the dust by the window, the office chair's had a fainting fit. There's no hurry, we can have a look at the mess later, then you can pursue your criminological studies in peace and quiet."

Why did the jokey tone sound so forced, artificial? Studer had a quick glance at Dr Laduner, as if he needed to capture an image that would look different the next moment. His grey suit, the shimmering corn-flower-blue of his tie and the strand of hair that stuck up like a heron's crest. His smile: the teeth in his upper jaw were broad, well-formed, yellow as old ivory. Dr Laduner obviously smoked a lot of cigarettes.

"Come on, Studer. If we stand around here much longer we'll start putting down roots. But there's one thing I will tell you before we pass through this door. You're paying a visit to the subconscious, to the naked subconscious, or, as my friend Schül puts it in his rather more poetic manner: you are being taken to the dark realm where Matto rules. Matto! That's the name Schül has given to the spirit of madness. Poetic? Surely." Dr Laduner put the stress on the second syllable.

"If you want to make sense of the whole affair – and I have a suspicion it'll turn out to be more complex than we think at the moment – if you want to make sense of it, you're going to have to get inside a lot of people's psyches, mine for example, the nurses', various patients' – you'll note I say 'patients', not 'lunatics'. Then perhaps an understanding of the link between the disappearance of the Director and Pieterlen's escape will gradually begin to dawn on you. There are imponderables . . ."

Imponderables! Psyche! And sure-ly stressed on the second syllable. It was all part and parcel of the personality that went by the name of Laduner.

"Anyway," said Dr Laduner as he slowly mounted the steps leading to the door, "you might initially be somewhat disconcerted by the discrepancy between the world outside and our realm. You'll feel uncomfortable, just as anyone does who's visiting a lunatic asylum for the first time. But then you'll get over that and eventually you won't see much of a difference between an eccentric clerk at your office and a catatonic picking wool in O."

On the wall to the right of the entrance was a barometer, its mercury column gleaming red in the morning light. A clock in one of the towers struck the four quarters with a sharp clang then, scarcely sweeter, came the hour. Six o'clock. The last stroke was more of a tinny rattle. Studer turned round. The sky was the colour of the wine they call rosé; birds were calling in the pines that grew behind iron railings either side of the drive. The black spire of the church in Randlingen village was a long way away.

Beyond the door through which they entered there were more steps. On the right was a kind of offertory box with a sign, *Remember the sick.* Above it was a green marble tablet recording for posterity the names of the clinic's benefactors. The His-Iselin family, one learnt, had given 5,000 francs and the Bärtschi family 3,000. The tablet had space left for the names of future benefactors.

There was a medicinal smell combined with dust and floor polish, a strange smell that was to haunt Studer for days. A corridor to the right, a corridor to the left, both closed off at the end by solid wood doors. A staircase led to the upper storeys of the central block.

"I'll lead the way," said Laduner over his shoulder. He took two steps at a time and Studer followed, gasping for breath. On the first floor he had time to look out of a window in the corridor onto a large courtyard with lawns divided into geometrical shapes by footpaths. There was a low building squatting in the middle and a chimney rising into the sky behind it. Red-brick walls, the roofs covered in slate and embellished with a multitude of towers and turrets . . .

They'd reached the second floor; Dr Laduner pushed open a glass door and called out, "Greti."

A deep voice replied, then a woman in a red dressing-gown came towards them. She had short, blond, slightly wavy hair and a broad, almost flat face. She screwed up her eyes slightly, the way short-sighted people often do.

"Studer, this is my wife. Is the coffee ready, Greti? I'm hungry. You can have a good look at the sergeant while he's eating his breakfast. Show him to his room now. He's staying with us, it's been agreed." And then Dr Laduner was no longer there, a door had swallowed him up.

The woman in the red dressing-gown had a pleasantly warm, soft hand. She spoke in the dialect of Bern as she greeted Studer and apologized for not being dressed. No wonder with everything that had been going on: her husband had been woken by the phone ringing at three in the morning because Pieterlen had run off; then they'd discovered traces of blood in the Director's office and the Director nowhere to be found, vanished . . . All in all it had been a very short night; the previous day they'd had the harvest festival (harvest festival? thought Studer. What do they harvest here?) and hadn't got to their beds till half past twelve . . . But Herr Studer would want a wash and brush up, if he would just follow her . . . The long corridor was floored with brightly coloured, ribbed tiles. From behind a door came the crying of a child and Studer shyly ventured to ask whether Frau Doktor didn't want to go and comfort it first. Plenty of time for that, she replied briskly, crying was healthy for infants, it strengthened the lungs . . .

This was the guest room . . . and that the bathroom next door. Herr Studer should make himself at home . . . There was soap and a clean towel, she'd call him when breakfast was ready.

Studer washed his hands, then went into the guest room and crossed over to the window. He was looking down into the courtyard. Men in white aprons were carrying large jugs, some balancing trays, like waiters.

A rowan tree on the edge of a square of lawn had bunches of shining red berries, its feathery leaves a golden yellow.

And at the back two men were coming out of a detached, two-storey building. They too were wearing white aprons. They were walking one behind the other, keeping in step, and between them a black stretcher with a coffin strapped onto it swayed from side to side. Studer turned away. He was wondering vaguely how

14

many people died in an institution like this, after how many years, and what it was like to die here, when he heard the voice with the pleasantly deep tone and homely Swiss accent.

"Herr Studer, are you ready for breakfast?"

"Coming, Frau Doktor, coming."

The dining room was filled with the morning sun, the cool light flooding in through a large window that almost came down to the floor. A brightly coloured woollen cosy sat on the coffee pot. Honey, butter, bread, the red rind of an Edam cheese under a glass-covered cheeseboard. The walls were dark green. From the ceiling hung a lampshade that looked like a gold brocade crinoline for a little girl.

Frau Laduner was wearing a light-coloured linen dress. She opened the door to the neighbouring room. "Ernst!" she shouted. The reply was an impatient grumble, then the creak and screech of a chair being pushed back.

"Right then," said Dr Laduner. He was suddenly sitting at the table. You couldn't really keep tabs on his comings and goings, he moved so quickly and silently. "Well, Greti, how do you like our Studer?"

"Not bad," his wife replied. "He's got a soft heart, he can't stand children crying. Apart from that, he's a quiet one, you hardly hear him. But I'll have to have a closer look at this Herr Studer."

She took a pince-nez out of a case lying beside her plate, clamped it onto the bridge of her nose and scrutinized Studer with a faint smile on her lips, her forehead slightly wrinkled.

Yes, she continued after a while, it was just as she had thought. Herr Studer didn't look like a cop at all, Ernst had been quite right to bring him. "And please, Herr Studer, do help yourself. Eggs? Bread?"

"Sure-ly," said Dr Laduner. "And I think it was very sensible of me to ask specifically for Studer." He cracked the top of his boiled egg with a silver teaspoon.

Fried eggs appeared on Studer's plate, with browned butter poured over them. Then there was a strange little incident. Dr Laduner suddenly looked up, grasped the bread basket in his right hand, the hexagonal salt cellar in his left, and held them out to the sergeant, saying softly – it sounded like a question – "Bread and salt. Will you take bread and salt, Studer?" As he spoke he looked the sergeant straight in the eye and the smile had gone from his lips.

"Yes ... with pleasure ... *merci* ..." Studer was somewhat confused. He took one of the slices of bread and sprinkled salt over the fried eggs on his plate. Then Dr Laduner took a piece of bread and let some of the white grains trickle onto his egg, murmuring as he did so, "Bread and salt ... the guest enjoys the sacred protection of hospitality."

The smiling mask reappeared round his mouth and it was with a different voice that he said, "I haven't told you anything about our vanished director yet. His name was Borstli, as I presume you already know, first name Ulrich. Ueli, a nice name – and that's what the ladies called him."

"Ernst!" said Frau Laduner in reproachful tones.

"What's the objection, Greti? That's not a judgment, it's a plain statement of fact. Anyway, every evening, at six on the dot, the Director used to go to the village to see his friend Fehlbaum, the butcher and landlord of the Bear, one of the pillars of the Agrarian Party. Once there he would have a half-pint carafe of white wine, sometimes two, now and then three. Twice a month he would have one too many and get drunk, but not so's

16

you'd notice. He used to wear a large loden cape and a black broad-brimmed hat, the kind you see artists wearing. He was usually the one who wrote the reports on the chronic alcoholics, by the way; he was certainly very competent in that field ... Though that's not quite true. He'd start writing them, the reports that is, but then he'd get bored and I was allowed to finish them off. I didn't mind, I got on well with the Director.

"You must excuse me, Studer, if I don't seem to be treating the matter with proper seriousness. You see, the Director had a penchant for pretty nurses, and the lassies were flattered when he showed it, for example by a gentle pinch on the cheek or a little fondle to express his admiration for the fullness of their curves ... At ten o'clock yesterday evening, for example, our Herr Direktor was called to the phone during our little celebration, and he hasn't been seen since. *Cherchez la femme?* Perhaps. There would be no real cause for concern if it weren't for the patient, Pieterlen, running off from his room next to O dormitory, leaving behind a nightwatchman laid out on the floor. Bohnenblust's his name, he's got a lump the size of an egg on his forehead, the result of a clash with our freedom-loving Pieterlen. You'll want to cross-examine him, Bohnenblust I mean. And, as I said, there's one thing you mustn't forget: the Director liked pretty nurses. But remember, discretion's the order of the day. Directors of clinics are taboo: they are little popes, and therefore condemned to infallibility."

"Ernst!" Frau Laduner admonished her husband again, but then she had to laugh. "He has such a comical way of putting things," she said apologetically.

That wasn't true. Dr Laduner's way of putting things wasn't comical at all. And his wife's remark was a feint too; she must have realized his jokey tone sounded

17

false. She wasn't stupid, Frau Doktor Laduner, he could see that. Also, the fact that the word "comical" wasn't usual in the Swiss dialect confirmed his impression that something wasn't quite right. But what? It was too early for deductions. Perhaps Dr Laduner's advice that he should settle in first, get to know the place, was genuine. He could ask harmless questions, which would at least help him to familiarize himself with the atmosphere in which he was going to be operating.

"You mentioned a harvest festival, Herr Doktor. What was that? I mean, I know what a harvest festival is, but I find it difficult to imagine that in an institution like this . . ."

"We have to keep the patients occupied. The clinic has a large farm attached, and when the corn has been gathered in ("the corn has been gathered in!" thought Studer. The way the fellow talks!) we have a celebration. There's a chapel here; it's normally just used for the Sunday sermon, but for festivals tables are set up with ham and potato salad. There's music, the patients dance, men and women together, the nurses are there, male and female, the Director makes a speech, tea is served, sexual tensions worked off . . . Yes . . . We had our harvest festival yesterday, 1 September. The dignitaries, that is the Director, the hospital manager and wife, Dr Laduner and wife, the farm manager, no wife, and the other doctors, were all sitting up on the stage – our chapel has a stage as well – watching the dancing. Pieterlen was there too, he provided the music, he gets a good tango or waltz out of his accordion. At ten Jutzeler–"

"Who's this Jutzeler?" Studer asked, taking out his notebook. "You'll have to excuse me, Herr Doktor, but I haven't got a very good memory for names. I have to get things down in my notebook."

"Sure-ly," said Dr Laduner, glancing impatiently at his watch and yawning. Frau Laduner started to clear the table.

"That means," said Studer, speaking in measured tones, well aware that he was putting on a bit of an act, but this seemed the right thing to do for the moment, "that the people connected with the case are: Borstli, Ulrich: Director – disappeared.

Pieterlen . . . er, what's Pieterlen's first name?"

"Peter – or Pierre, if you prefer, he's originally from Biel," Dr Laduner replied patiently.

"Pieterlen, Peter: patient – run away," Studer dictated slowly to himself, writing it down.

"Dr Laduner, Ernst: consultant, deputy director!"

"I don't need to write him down, I know him already," said Studer dryly, ignoring the little dig. "Then we have the nightwatchman . . ."

And Studer wrote: *Bohnenblust, Werner: nightwatchman, dormitory in O Ward.*

"Another one for you to note down," said Laduner. "Jutzeler, Max, staff nurse, O Ward, we usually just say 'O'."

"What does O stand for?"

"O is the Observation Ward. That's where the new patients go, though we leave some there for years. It all depends. P is the ward for placid patients, T is the Treatment Ward for those suffering from some physical illness. Then there are the two wards for disturbed patients, D1 and D2. D1 contains the isolation units. It's easy to grasp, just remember what the initials stand for. Anyway, you'll like Nurse Jutzeler, one of my most capable staff. The general run of nurses, though . . . You can't even get the useless crowd organized in a union."

Organized? thought Studer. I wonder what the old

director thought about unions? But he said nothing, just asked, with the point of his pencil hovering over his notebook, "What was actually wrong with Pieterlen?"

"Pieterlen?" Laduner asked, and the smile disappeared from his lips. "I'll tell you all about Pieterlen this evening. Pieterlen . . . To explain Pieterlen takes time, Pieterlen wasn't a director, nor a nurse, he wasn't any Tom, Dick or Harry. Pieterlen was a classic case . . ."

What struck Studer was Laduner's use of the past tense. "Pieterlen was . . .". The way you talk about someone who's dead. But he said nothing. Laduner suddenly shook himself, stood up, stretched and turned to his wife. "Has Kasperli gone off to school yet?"

"Yes, he's left already. He had his breakfast in the kitchen."

"Kasperli's my seven-year-old son, if you want to note that down, Studer," Dr Laduner said, with his fixed smile. "Anyway, I have to go to hear the reports now, you can come down with me and have a look at the office. The Director's office – the scene of the crime, if you prefer. Although we don't know yet whether there's a crime to go with the scene."

At the door out into the corridor they were further held up by a young man, who insisted he had to talk to Dr Laduner.

"Later, Caplaun, I've no time just at the moment. Wait in the sitting room. I'll talk to you between reports and my rounds."

With that Laduner started to leap down the stairs, taking them three at a time. But Studer did not follow him. He stood outside the door, staring at the man Laduner had addressed as Caplaun. Caplaun? Caplaun had been the name of his old enemy, the colonel who had been involved in pulling strings over that business with the bank, the business that had cost the then Chief Inspector Studer of the Bern city police his job. There weren't many Caplauns in Switzerland, it was an uncommon name . . .

Well, it certainly wasn't the Colonel. The man who entered Dr Laduner's apartment and slipped into a room as if he knew his way around was young. Young, skinny and blond, with a hollow chest. Pale as well, with wide, staring eyes. Caplaun?

Studer caught up with Dr Laduner on the ground floor. The doctor was pacing up and down impatiently.

"Herr Doktor," said Studer, "that young lad who went into your apartment just now, you called him Caplaun. Is he related to . . . ?"

"To the colonel who put a spoke in your wheel? Yes. The colonel's his father. Young Caplaun's undergoing treatment with me. As a private patient. Analysis. Anxiety neurosis, typical case. Not surprising with a father like that. He has a drink problem as well, does Herbert Caplaun. Yes, Herbert's his first name. Perhaps you should put him down in your notebook."

Again Studer deliberately ignored the irony. Putting on his most guileless expression, he asked, "An anxiety neurosis? What's that, Herr Doktor?"

"God, I can't give you a lecture on the typology of neuroses just now! I'll explain later. Anyway, there's the Director's office. I'll be busy for the next hour; if you need anything, just ask the porter. His name's Dreyer, you'd better write it down in your notebook."

A door slammed, and he was gone.

The scene of the crime and
the casino

The bush outside the window had white berries that looked like balls of wax. Two sparrows were hopping about on the window-ledge, among the splinters of glass. They kept bobbing up and down, their heads appearing over the bottom of the window frame, then disappearing, only to reappear again after a brief interval. When Studer set the desk chair back on its legs they flew away.

First of all he sat down, took out his oilcloth-bound notebook and wrote, in his tiny handwriting that somehow recalled Greek letters: *Caplaun, Herbert: the Colonel's son, anxiety neurosis, Dr Laduner's patient.*

Then he sat back, a satisfied expression on his face, and had a look at the devastation.

Blood on the floor, that was true. But only a little, a few separate drops that had dried to dark scabs on the gleaming parquet. They went in a line from the broken window-pane to the door. Perhaps someone had put his fist through the glass and cut himself.

The little table to the left of the window was presumably intended for the typewriter, while the desk – large, wide, ornate – took up all the space in the corner to the right of the window. Studer stood up, went over and picked up the typewriter. Surely there was no need to look for fingerprints here. For the moment they didn't even know whether there had been a murder, or whether the Director had just gone off on a little jaunt.

If that were the case, you would have expected him to inform the other doctors, but old men sometimes got these fancies . . .

On the wall above the desk was a group photograph: surrounded by young men and women in nurse's uniform was an old gentleman with a broad-brimmed, black hat on his head, a rampant, curly grey beard on his chin and cheeks, and a pair of steel-rimmed spectacles on his nose. Written in white ink underneath the photograph was: *To the Director, with the respectful good wishes of all the participants on the first course.*

Hmm, they looked like a class of overgrown model schoolboys, all those young men in their black suits and stiff, high collars with ties slightly askew. *To the Director* . . . No date? Oh yes, there it was, in the bottom corner: 18 April 1927.

On the green blotting pad underneath the picture was a letter folded in the middle. Studer read the first few lines: *We would most urgently remind you that it is over two months since we requested a report on the mental condition of* . . .

Hm! He certainly took things at his own pace did Herr Direktor Borstli with his loden cape and broad-brimmed hat. Bet he wore a swallowtail coat . . . Yes, got it in one! There it was on the picture, a grey one as far as he could tell, and the trousers were baggy at the knees. An old man, a gentleman of the old school. How had he got on with someone as businesslike as Dr Laduner, though? He still didn't know that much about Herr Direktor Ulrich Borstli, apart from the fact that he liked pretty nurses and got them to call him Ueli. And why ever not? He was answerable to no one, a little king in – what had Dr Laduner called it? – yes, that was it, in Matto's realm. He really ought to get to know that Schül who had thought up the spirit of madness. Matto! Brilliant. *Matto* meant crazy in Italian. Matto – it had a ring to it.

Had he been married, the old director? Must have been! Widowed? Probably . . .

There was nothing for him in the office. Why then had Dr Laduner sent him here? The man did nothing without reason. What was he afraid of? Studer felt slightly inhibited. He liked Laduner, genuinely liked him. Above all he could not forget that scene, the scene in the Oberhollabrunn reformatory. And then he had offered him bread and salt, too. *Chabis!* A load of nonsense really, but then things usually were.

Where could the Director be hiding? The best idea would probably be to have a word with the porter. Porters were usually chatty people, not to say downright gossipy. At least they always knew what was going on.

And so Studer, to the sound of a monotonous voice trickling through the closed door to the neighbouring room, the doctors' room, slipped out of the office like a schoolboy trying to keep out of the teacher's way. The teacher? In this case Dr Ernst Laduner, senior consultant, deputy director.

Dreyer, the porter, wore a waistcoat with sewn-on sleeves of some shiny material with an apron tied over it. He was busy sweeping the corridor. Studer stood in his way, arms akimbo.

"Now then, Dreyer."

The man looked up with a vacant stare. His left hand, still resting on the brush handle, was bandaged.

"Yes, Sergeant?" So the man knew who he was. All the better.

"Cut yourself?"

"Nothing serious," said Dreyer, lowering his eyes.

Drops of blood on the office floor, the porter with a cut – on his hand! Now then, Studer, he told himself, don't go jumping to conclusions. Just note: Dreyer, the porter, has a cut on his hand, and get on with it.

"Was the Director married?"

The porter grinned. Both his eye-teeth had gold fillings. It bothered Studer and he looked aside.

"Twice," said Dreyer. "He was married twice. And both of his wives are dead. The second started as his cook – housekeeper, that's what they called her. Quite a family she came from, too. She was very good at finding positions in the clinic for her relations, her brother as mechanic, her sister in administration as bookkeeper – and her brother-in-law, the husband of her other sister, is one of the consultants."

It was just as Studer had expected. Porters really did know everything that was going on. And they liked to talk. Not as wittily as Dr Laduner, for example, but more to the point.

"Thank you," said Studer in a matter-of-fact tone. "Did the Director receive a sizeable sum of money yesterday?"

"How did you know that, Sergeant? Between May and August he was ill. He took leave, but he was insured, and the money came yesterday. A hundred days at twelve francs per day, that makes exactly 1,200 francs."

"Aha," said Studer. "Presumably he also took his salary on the first, that was yesterday too?"

"No, he always leaves that with Accounts until there's a decent amount built up, then he has it sent to his bank. He hardly needed any money: board and lodging free. He didn't want to employ another housekeeper, so the kitchen sent up something from the first-class menu every day."

"How old was the Director?"

"Sixty-nine. Next year he would have been seventy."

Then, as if that was it, Dreyer set off, pushing the black brush in front of him. For a moment the smell of floor polish and pharmaceuticals was overlaid with the smell of dust.

"Did he keep the money on him? I mean the 1,200 francs."

The porter turned round to answer his question. "One 1,000-franc note and two 100s. He stuffed all three into his wallet. He told me he was going to put the money in the bank tomorrow – that is today now. He had to go to Bern anyway, he said."

"Where was the harvest festival held?"

"Go out by that door at the back there and the casino will be right in front of you. The door's open. You won't be disturbed."

The "casino"! Just like in Nice or Monte Carlo! And here he was in Randlingen Psychiatric Clinic.

It looked like the aftermath of an office party: cigarette ash on the floor, torn streamers festooning the walls, white tablecloths strewn with pieces of bread. The air smelt of stale cigarette smoke. At the back was a stage with a table on it, wine glasses . . . The "dignitaries", as Dr Laduner had put it, had not been drinking tea, then. Windows with pointed arches and cheap coloured glass gave the room a churchy look, an impression that was strengthened by the pulpit fixed to one of the side walls, a little above floor level. Perhaps that was what churches had looked like during the French Revolution when the Feast of Reason was celebrated in them.

Studer took a chair and sat down facing the stage. He lit a Brissago and started making little gestures with his right hand, like a director giving actors their places at the beginning of a scene.

The Director . . . He was probably sitting in the middle of the table, in that armchair that wasn't quite straight, as if someone had got up in a hurry. To his right would have been Dr Laduner, to his left the hospital manager, then the junior doctors. The other consultant was the husband of the sister of the Director's second wife . . . Complicated family connections. That meant the doctor was a kind of brother-in-law to the Director. What was his name? He really ought to have asked what his name was, even if it meant extending the list in his notebook.

There was an old piano in the corner. Who had accompanied Pieterlen when he played his accordion? And then they'd been dancing. Here, in the free space between the tables, men and women together, male and female nurses. And the patients had – how had Dr Laduner put it? – oh yes, "worked off their sexual tensions".

Next point: at ten o'clock the Director was called to the telephone. By Staff Nurse . . . what was his name? Jutzeler. Was called to the telephone by Staff Nurse Jutzeler. Must make a note to ask Staff Nurse Jutzeler whether it was a man's or a woman's voice asking for the Director . . . The telephone? . . . Where was the telephone?

Studer got up, went over to the piano and picked out a few notes. The thing was pretty out of tune. Then he climbed up onto the stage – it was a bit of an effort – and began to go round the table, bent down. Stooping like that, in his black suit, he looked like a gigantic Newfoundland dog following a scent. He lifted up one corner of the tablecloth and reached down. A card, blue, very grubby. Neat handwriting, like something out of an exercise book. A schoolgirl's handwriting: *I'll give you a ring at ten, Ueli, and we can go for a stroll.* Stroll with only one 'l'. No signature. Even if he hadn't found the card under the armchair, it would not have been difficult to guess whom it was intended for. Where was the telephone? Studer climbed down from the stage and had a look round. The phone was in a cubby hole off the "casino".

It was black and had a white disc with the numbers one to nine on it. Just like any telephone in the city. In the middle was the number 49. Hanging from the wall beside the phone was a list, with, written in small block letters at the bottom: ALL NUMBERS PRINTED IN RED HAVE AN EXTERNAL CONNECTION.

12 – Director was in red, of course, also *13 – Deputy Director, Administration Office,* etc. But the numbers of the various wards were in black. O dormitory (male side) had the number 44. And the casino, with the number 49, was also in black.

So the logical deduction was that the call for Herr Direktor Borstli had come from within the clinic. If it had come from outside, it would have been the porter, Dreyer, who had come to fetch him and the Director would have had to take it in his office or his own apartment.

It was a lassie who had rung him. *I'll give you a ring at ten, Ueli* . . . If it was ten, it would be a girl he was going for a stroll with. Perhaps the "stroll" had been longer than originally planned, perhaps they had not come back, but taken the early train to Thun, to Interlaken; it must be very nice in Ticino, too, now that autumn was coming.

And the mess in the office had nothing to do with a crime. Pieterlen's running off was a coincidence, there was no link to the Director's disappearance, not to mention Dr Laduner's "imponderables".

Perhaps the chief of police had interrupted his

beauty sleep for nothing – though there was still Dr Laduner's odd request "to be covered by the police" . . .

There might well be something behind it. Especially if you took into account the fact that the infamous Colonel Caplaun was hovering somewhere in the background too. His son . . . anxiety neurosis. All well and good, but once bitten, twice shy, and Sergeant Studer had been bitten by Colonel Caplaun.

The handwriting! he thought. The lassie's not been out of school that long. And he smiled, a rather simple smile, as he pictured the old Director, in his cape and black broad-brimmed hat, arm in arm with a girl. The young girl was looking up, full of respect, at the man she regarded as a person of consequence, surely dreaming of becoming Frau Direktor in the near future.

Dr Laduner would want him to accompany him on his rounds. Probably. In the course of that he would presumably meet Staff Nurse Jutzeler and could ask him what the voice on the telephone had sounded like. He could cross-examine the nightwatchman, Bohnenblust and find out how Pieterlen had managed to escape.

Then everything would be sorted out and he could get Dr Laduner to drive him back to Bern with a clear conscience, back home to his flat in Kirchenfeld. Studer took out his notebook, placed the blue card in it then started to whistle "The Farmer from Brienz", softly, but very artistically. He was just starting on the second verse as he left the casino, but then he broke off.

A strange vehicle was going past. It was a two-wheeled cart and there was a man trotting along between the shafts at the back. A long chain was attached to the other end of the cart, with four wooden crosspieces. Each of these crosspieces was held by two men, so that eight men were pulling the two-wheeled cart by the chain. Alongside the cart was a man in a blue overall. He greeted Studer with a smile and called out, "Whoa. Whoa, I said." The man between the shafts stopped his trotting and the eight men stood still. Studer, in a voice hoarse with astonishment, asked, "What's all this about?"

The man in blue laughed. "The Randlingen Express!" he said. Then, in confidential tones, he explained that it was part of the occupational therapy, in order to give the patients some exercise. "Of course," he added, "we can only do it with the complete cretins. But they're much quieter afterwards. So long for now!" Then he shouted, "Gee up, you lot." Obediently the "Express" moved off.

Occupational therapy! thought Studer, shaking his head. A cure through work! Those draught animals were beyond cure. Still, he wasn't a psychiatrist, just a simple detective sergeant . . . Thank God!

The *éminence blanche*

The door next to the Director's office burst open with a crash of wooden panels against the wall, then the ground-floor hall of the central block was filled with the low murmur of voices, from which a squeaky, up-and-down voice emerged, asking, in the thickest of Swiss accents, "How about it, Herr Doktor, shouldn't we be preparing a lumbar puncture?"

Then came Laduner's voice. "For old Schmocker, you mean? If you like." In comparison, Laduner's Swiss sounded decidedly odd. Studer moved closer, almost colliding with Dr Laduner. He was wearing a white coat, his chest thrust out, still with the strand of brown hair sticking up like the crest on a heron's head.

"Ah, there you are, Studer. Good thing you're here. You're accompanying me on my rounds, of course. I'll just introduce you quickly, then we can get on."

There were four figures in white coats behind him. Laduner stepped to one side.

"Sergeant Studer, who's going to play the detective in our little comedy of disappearances – Dr Blumenstein, consultant, distantly related to our missing Director . . . Delighted to meet you – Me too. No need to say anything, I'll speak for everyone." Dr Laduner was clearly worked up.

So the Director's brother-in-law was called Blumenstein. Studer looked at him. Well over six feet tall, a pink baby face and – those hands! They weren't hands, they were small tennis rackets. And he was married,

Herr Doktor Blumenstein. Hmm, he didn't look married. He looked a bit like those giant children they exhibit at fairgrounds.

"One moment," said Dr Laduner. "Introduce yourselves – or Blumenstein, you see to it . . ." And Dr Laduner was gone. Up the stairs.

He has to talk to Herbert Caplaun, the anxiety neurotic, as he calls him. If I could only listen in on what those two are saying, Studer thought to himself, not really concentrating on the names he was being given. The second white coat was obviously Swiss French, since he said "*Enchanté, Inspecteur,*" and then the two others, they were – my God, it couldn't be true! – women! He had a decided distaste for working women. These two didn't look interesting, anyway. Colourless, if anything. Wearing heavy shoes with rubber soles and cotton stockings over their skinny calves.

They stood around and waited. Someone had been ignored and now this someone introduced himself. It was the possessor of the voice with the thick Swiss accent that had talked of the "lumbar puncture".

"Ah, so you're this Sergeant Studer, very pleased to meet you. I'm Weyrauch, senior nurse." He had a red face, his cheeks covered with jolly little veins, and wore horn-rimmed spectacles, the lenses of which concealed intelligent little piggy eyes. His white coat was open, revealing an apron, also white, and his belly protruded, protruded in such a majestic curve that the apron stretched tight and the watch chain adorning his waistcoat stood out in relief under the cloth.

Putting on his most official expression, Studer took out his notebook and made an entry in his tiny writing.

"Hey, what's that you're writing, Sergeant?"

"Your name."

"So I'm going to get into police records after all,"

Weyrauch said, laughing long and loud until he was forced to cough.

"A real treasure is our 'ead nurse, our Weyrauch," said Neuville. He had a centre parting, very white hair, and beneath it a small, pale face. He reminded Studer of a weasel.

"You'd better put Dr Neuville in your book, too," said Weyrauch. Studer followed his suggestion.

Weyrauch, senior nurse.

Blumenstein, consultant; brother-in-law of the Director.

Neuville, junior doctor.

If it went on like this, he'd have to buy another notebook. He wasn't interested in the two women doctors. One was tall, the other short, what did their names matter?

Then Dr Laduner returned and the group set off. No one seemed to object to Studer joining them. With long strides, Dr Laduner led the way, the ends of his white coat fluttering up in the air when his knees pushed against them. Weyrauch waddled along beside him. Now he was putting the key into the wooden door that closed off the central block on the right-hand side. "If you'd be so good . . ." he said, and the group filed past him.

Studer was at the back, wearing his grimmest expression. He felt superfluous. The two women were walking in front of him. They walked with a very stiff gait, they didn't swing their hips. Their hair was kept short, shaved at the neck. They seemed sexless.

A long corridor. A fourth element joined the smell of pharmaceuticals, floor polish and dust: the smoke of cheap tobacco. On the left a row of tall windows. But their construction was odd: they were divided up into tiny panes held together by iron bars. Studer had a surreptitious look at them and glanced out. The courtyard. The sergeant was standing opposite the rowan tree with its red berries and bright yellow leaves. He found the tree comforting . . .

Studer had always imagined a lunatic asylum as an infernal place, but there was really not a trace of the infernal about it. Here was a room painted a rich orange colour, with benches round the walls and tables in front of them. Outside the windows, with their tiny rectangular panes, were pine trees swaying in the gentle breeze. Men were sitting at the tables. The only noticeable thing about them, perhaps, was that they had stubble that was at least a week old. Their eyes were a little strange, but not really any stranger than those of people Studer had visited in Thorberg Prison.

Men in white aprons were standing around. They had no collars on, the buttonholes at the top of their shirts were held together by brass collar studs. Nurses, apparently.

Dr Neuville appeared at Studer's side. "We are in P," he whispered, full of self-importance, "the ward for placid patients. Dr Laduner do not like the nurses here, 'oly Joes the lot of them."

Yes, Dr Laduner had gone up to one of them and was giving him a ticking-off in a low voice, at the same time pointing to a corner of the room where a man was sitting slumped, doing nothing. The others, those at the tables, were busy sticking paper bags together. There were bowls of glue standing around.

"The old Director, he like the 'oly Joes very much because they never complain. Only Jutzeler! He want to organize the workers in a union. Last week we have almost a strike. Jutzeler get the sack, but Dr Laduner, he protect him. I call Dr Laduner *l'éminence blanche.* You know that in French history there was the *éminence grise* who pull the strings in the background? Dr

34

Laduner, he too pull the strings in the background . . .
The old Director? Beuh!" And the junior doctor
(Neuville, wasn't it?) made a dismissive gesture with
his hand.

One of the woman doctors was trotting along beside
Laduner, who was shaking hands, asking people how
they were. The fixed smile never left his lips. Studer
was convinced Laduner thought his smile was heart-
warming, encouraging. He patted a shoulder here,
leant down there over a silent patient who wasn't
answering. One got overexcited and started shouting.
Dr Laduner turned round and whispered something
to one of the white aprons . . . He went across to the
overexcited patient and – and the little group left the
room.

Another wooden door, a long corridor, the parquet
floor gleaming. And a little manikin with bandy legs
and a big fat cigar in the corner of his mouth strolling
towards them across the gleaming parquet. The manikin looked very pleased with himself.

'What's Schmocker doing in T Ward?" Dr Laduner
asked in a loud voice. The shorter of the two women
doctors went up to him and whispered something in
his ear. The only word Studer managed to catch was
"isolate".

"But, my dear girl, that's impossible," Dr Laduner
said, showing his irritation. "The man has to work,
like other people. Even if he did share a room with
Pieterlen, that's no reason . . ."

By that time the fat manikin had reached them. He
started to make a speech in a booming, soapbox voice.

He demanded, he declared, to be handed over to
the federal authorities, his crime was political and
he should not be in a lunatic asylum, surrounded
by madmen and murderers, he had always been

respectable, had earned his bread by the sweat of his brow, and if they refused to listen to his justified complaints, then he would resort to other measures. Politically he had always been a loyal citizen, conservative, he believed democratic government was the best of all possible systems, but if they insisted on treating him like this he would put his weight behind the dictatorship of the proletariat. Then certain very important people would be in for a big surprise . . .

Dr Laduner stood there before him, stiffly upright, his hands in the tiny pockets of his white coat. He spoke in formal German when he replied. "What you are telling us, Herr Schmocker, is beside the point. You will return to P and glue paper bags together. Otherwise I will have you put in the bath. Goodbye."

The little man went red and swelled until Studer was afraid he was about to burst. His voice quavered as he said, "On your head be it, Herr Doktor." He took a pull at his cigar, but it had gone out during his speech.

"Sure-ly," said Dr Laduner, heading off through the next door, which Weyrauch was holding invitingly open.

"If you would be so good . . ." he said.

"Otherwise there's nothing special in T is there, my dear?"

"No, Herr Doktor." A gracious gesture and the young lady was dismissed. Dr Laduner waved Studer over. Weyrauch closed the door gently.

They were in an empty corridor, which was rather dark – presumably the end of one of the arms of the U-shaped building since the corridor ended in a wall. A window in it was open.

"Anyway, come with me for a minute," said Dr Laduner, then abandoned Studer to turn to the shorter of the women doctors. "Didn't Schmocker say anything? I mean about Pieterlen's escape?"

"No, no, Herr Doktor." The woman blushed, her ears were burning. "He just refused to work this morning, so I thought it was better to isolate him a little ." She started to gabble, then fell silent. She, too, spoke formal German, but with the harsh accent of the Baltic coast.

"Good, good, my dear girl, there's no need to get worked up. Take a note, Weyrauch. We'll give Schmocker an hour in the bath after all, perhaps that will help him get over his manic state more easily . . . No, no injection . . . Were you going to say something, Studer?"

No, no, Sergeant Studer wouldn't dream of such a thing. He shook his head vigorously.

"You see," said Dr Laduner, walking up and down the long corridor, his hands clasped behind his back, "we do not regard the bath as a punishment, but as a means of accelerating the patient's adjustment to reality and its demands. We have few ways of maintaining a basic level of discipline as far as work is concerned. We are not in a prison, we are in a sanatorium. But we can only heal the sick mind by activating the healthy aspects of the psyche, the desire to work, the willingness to adapt to a community. Even the most confused minds have a part that— Anyway, Studer, you must know about Schmocker? I'm not revealing any professional secrets in telling you, it was in all the papers at the time."

"Schmocker?" Studer vaguely recalled something about an assassination attempt, but could not remember the details, so he asked what the story was. Since he had shared a room with Pieterlen, it would certainly be of interest to know how he should view the said Schmocker's attitude to truth.

"Sure-ly." Dr Laduner took Studer by the arm, drawing him with him on his perambulation. He strode up and down the corridor, the four white coats following him in a line, quietly fooling around, like schoolchildren when the teacher's out. Right at the back the chubby senior nurse waddled along.

"Herr Schmocker's crime was as follows: he stopped one of the revered members of the Federal Council and stuck an unloaded revolver in his face, at the same time saying, in a quavering voice, 'I'm going to kill you.' The said council member immediately started leaping around in the middle of the street. He wasn't to know the revolver wasn't loaded, and he feared for his precious life – perfectly understandable, given that he was both a human being and a politician. Our good Herr Schmocker watched the Council member jump up and down for a while, then put the revolver away, went home to his wife and tucked into a large plateful of cold sausage. Please, Studer, don't laugh. It's all there in the files. The Bern city police are very particular in these matters. They're quick off the mark, too. They interrupted Herr Schmocker in the middle of his cold sausage, took him down to the station and locked him up. He could prove the revolver was unloaded, true, but he had made a federal dignitary jump about – and in the middle of the street at that – a heinous crime in a peaceable democracy such as ours. Making a member of the Federal Council jump up and down! Since, however, there were doubts as to whether Herr Schmocker was responsible for his actions, he was sent to us for psychological assessment. Actually, he's rather a bore, otherwise I'd find his way of going about things amusing. He used to deal in grain, you see, before the state monopoly was introduced. It was the monopoly that ruined him. The gentlemen of the

Federal Council, in their wisdom, were kind enough – no, stupid enough – to pay him compensation. For three years Herr Schmocker received 500 francs a month without having to do a stroke of work. Just because he had the gift of the gab and was good at making threats. He was offered posts – he rejected them. He refused to take a subordinate position, he said. Eventually our lords and masters lost patience with him. So Herr Schmocker was filled with rage and went and bought a gun in a junk shop. But he didn't buy any ammunition. There you have it, the story of a grain dealer who saw himself as William Tell and a member of the Federal Council as Gessler."

Laduner fell silent. He was still gripping Studer's arm, just below the elbow. The two of them stopped by the open window.

"That two-storey building over there, that's D1," Laduner said, "and the lower building behind it contains the isolation units for D2. Things are worse there than here in O . . . Weyrauch," he shouted.

'What is it, Herr Dokt'r?"

"Is Bohnenblust waiting in the dormitory?"

"Yes, Herr Dokt'r. I ordered Bohnenblust to wait till you'd seen him, sir . . . Herr Dokt'r, sir."

Dr Laduner let go of Studer's arm and went over to a door.

"Pardong . . . Ekskewsay, Herr Dokt'r," said Weyrauch, hurrying over to put the passkey in the lock and flinging the door open. He stood beside it like a well-trained, very obese butler. "If you'd be so good . . ."

Laduner went out to the stairs.

O dormitory

Studer estimated the dormitory at about fifty feet long, twenty-five feet wide. The room was painted white. Twenty-two beds in two rows. At one end a raised cubicle with two bathtubs. The window behind them was open. It had narrow iron bars and it, too, provided a view of the two storeys of D1.

Beside the cubicle with the bathtubs was a door, with glass in the upper half, leading into a side room. A wall with a small table fixed to it projected out from the middle of the dormitory, forming a cubby-hole. And in front of it the nightwatchman, Bohnenblust, was sitting. He was in late middle age, with a bushy moustache, and wore a grey pullover full of darns. There was a bruise on his forehead. Standing beside him, ramrod straight, was Staff Nurse Jutzeler in a white apron and a white coat with a white cross on a red background sewn onto the lapel.

Dr Laduner went over to him and asked if everything was all right, which Jutzeler assured him it was. Jutzeler spoke with the lilting accent of the Bernese Oberland. He had brown eyes, large and gentle as a deer's.

Bohnenblust stood up with the ungainliness of a man who spent too much time sitting down. When he took a deep breath a wheezing noise came from his chest.

"Stay in your seat," Laduner snapped. The nightwatchman stared, gasped and sat down again. Laduner sat down at a larger table, waved Studer over to sit on the bench beside him, then leant his elbows on the table. Bohnenblust was sitting to the right, the small table behind him.

"Right, then, Bohnenblust, tell us all about it."

The two women doctors were leaning against the wall, Neuville was practising his tap-dancing and Dr Blumenstein was standing on one leg. In his white coat he looked like a stork. A bumblebee buzzed in the silence, came closer and hovered for a few seconds right in front of Studer's nose, its belly a shimmering velvety brown.

"The Herr Doktor will know," Bohnenblust said.

"The Herr Doktor knows nothing. What the Herr Doktor would like to know is how you came by that bump on your noddle." The word "noddle" sounded very odd coming from Laduner's lips.

"Well," said Bohnenblust, standing up, then sitting down again, shifting backwards and forwards on his chair, as if he were sitting on the top of a hot stove. "It was one in the morning, I'd just done the time clock—"

"He has to clock in every hour," Laduner explained to Studer.

"At one o'clock I heard noises coming from the side room. Shouts." Bohnenblust pointed to the door with glass in the upper half. "I went in—"

"Did you switch on the light?"

"No, Herr Doktor. Schmocker always complains if I do."

Laduner nodded, the two assistant doctors nodded, the two women doctors nodded, even fat Weyrauch nodded. There was no doubt about it, a man who could threaten a member of the Federal Council would have a natural talent for complaining, and plenty of practice, too.

"So I went in," Bohnenblust said, blowing a gust of air through his moustache. "And that's all I can remember until I woke up again. That was about half past two. Then I pressed the alarm bell and Jutzeler and Hofstetter and Gilgen came. Through the middle door, which was still locked, as were the other two. And my passkey and my triangular key were still in my pocket."

Once more Laduner turned to Studer with an explanation. "To open the doors, our nurses have a passkey and a triangular key. When they leave they hand in their keys to the porter – at least they're supposed to. But half the time they just keep them in their pockets, so they can get in if they happen to come back late because they've been playing a few too many rubbers of *jass* down in the village ... Isn't that so, Jutzeler?"

The litany he has to go through every time! thought Studer. We'll never get anywhere like this. Five medics – the two assistants, the two women, Dr Laduner – were they all blind? Had they never seen the marks caused by a blow to the head? Without wanting to boast, he, Sergeant Studer, only had to glance at the bump on Bohnenblust's head to know what he was dealing with. He'd bashed his "noddle" against something, the edge of a table, a door, a cupboard, a projecting wall even. But he had certainly not been hit.

Should he keep his head down and let the oh-so-clever Dr Laduner get on with his game of question-and-answer in peace?

"And the noise didn't wake Schmocker, then?" Dr Laduner asked. "You lay there unconscious in the next room for two hours and Herr Schmocker did not wake up? No one in the dormitory noticed anything? You know there are a few patients there who don't sleep well – they didn't notice anything?"

Studer decided to intervene. They were never going to get anywhere like this. "I think we can leave that for the moment. If you're agreeable, I'd like to try and form an overall picture of the affair. Could I see the room Pieterlen shared with Schmocker?"

"Yes, of course, Studer, off you go, there's the door . . ."

Studer got up and went into the next room. Two windows. One looked out into the garden, the other onto the two storeys of D1. Two beds. A dozen charcoal sketches on the walls: heads, male, strangely stiff, obviously drawn from photographs; ghostly looking trees; a large head, like something out of a dream, with a wide mouth, froglike. And the head of a girl . . .

The head of a girl. Chocolate boxy, like those postcards people like to send to their boy- or girlfriends. But it was clear that it hadn't been drawn from a photograph. One by one Studer pulled out the four drawing pins, folded up the picture and put it in his pocket. Then he lifted first one mattress, then the other. Underneath the second he found a square piece of some tough, grey material. He picked it up, feeling the texture between his fingers. It was firm. Studer shook his head and put the piece of cloth in his pocket. There was nothing else of interest in the room. One drawer he pulled out contained pencils, sticks of charcoal, chalk, a bottle of fixative . . . He went back into the dormitory.

The others had not moved an inch, apart from Neuville, who was practising a difficult tango step, turning and going forward at the same time. He couldn't quite master it, his weasel face was screwed up in an earnest frown.

43

"This piece of cloth," Studer said, "can anyone say where it comes from?"

It was Jutzeler, the slim staff nurse, who answered first. He was surprised, he said, that the sergeant had found that scrap of cloth. Did he consider it significant? It came from one of the linen sheets they used in D1 for patients who liked to tear everything up. Pieterlen had been given part of one – quite a large piece, by the way – to dry his paintbrushes. Why was the sergeant so interested in it?

No reason, Studer replied, apart from the fact that he had found it underneath the mattress, in the middle, fairly well hidden. Perhaps there was nothing to it.

"But let's get on. Pieterlen was at the harvest festival yesterday?"

"Yes."

"How long did it go on for?"

"Until midnight," Jutzeler said, crossing his arms over his chest as if to say: I'm here to give information. There was definitely a similarity between him and Dr Laduner.

"And did Pieterlen dance?"

"No. At first he was looking forward to dancing, then, suddenly, he refused to. He sat down in a corner and it was only with great difficulty that we managed to get him to play the accordion . . . for a few dances. He was in a bad mood – probably because Irma Wasem hadn't come to the festival."

Wasem? Studer pricked up his ears.

"Who is this Fräulein Wasem?" he asked Dr Laduner, putting on a guileless look. He saw Dr Neuville suddenly pause in the middle of a dance step, balance on the ball of his foot, wink and grin, while Dr Blumenstein, still standing on one leg like a stork, blushed. The two ladies stared at the floor.

Dr Laduner cleared his throat. Jutzeler was about to answer, but the deputy director cut him short.

"Pieterlen had been assigned to the decorating unit," he said in a matter-of-fact voice. "The group's most recent task was painting the walls in the female O Ward, in the course of which Pieterlen fell in love with Nurse Wasem. It does happen. There are imponderables . . ."

"Imponderables," said the woman doctor from the Baltic coast with a sage nod of the head; Dr Neuville gave an audible snigger.

"Wasem . . . Irma Wasem," said Studer dreamily. "And did the lassie reciprocate?" As he spoke he subjected his fingernails, which were short and flat, to a detailed inspection.

Embarrassed silence. Embarrassed? No, not only that. Studer sensed that the silence was also intended to express displeasure: displeasure at the lack of respect his line of questioning showed. What concern of a simple detective sergeant were the internal affairs of a medical establishment, that was what the silence was meant to express. And the displeasure that was being expressed was also directed at Dr Laduner, which was presumably the reason why he answered.

"At first certainly . . . Definitely . . . I was kept informed . . ."

But then Dr Laduner's halting explanation was interrupted by a squeaky, singsong voice. It was the senior nurse, Weyrauch, fat, at ease with himself and the world, his little piggy eyes glinting behind his horn-rimmed spectacles, reminding them of his corpulent presence.

"With your permission, Herr Dokt'r, I have some information," he said. "Recently Nurse Wasem has quite often been seen going for a walk with the Director in the evening—"

Dr Laduner waved Weyrauch away, so violently that it looked as if he were being attacked by a swarm of midges. Studer smiled to himself. A blue card with schoolgirlish handwriting: *I'll give you a ring at ten and we can go for a strol.*

But Dr Blumenstein, consultant and distant brother-in-law of the Director, said angrily, "That's just gossip, Weyrauch. You should be ashamed of yourself, reporting things like that to outsiders."

The fat man was not so easily embarrassed, however. He answered with the lack of concern of a man whose position is much more secure even than that of a consultant. His thick Swiss dialect boomed round the dormitory, as he laughed and said, "But everyone in the hospital knew the Director wasn't averse to a kiss and a cuddle."

Dr Laduner blinked, but his smiling mask did not change. Studer took the charcoal drawing with the chocolate-box girl's face out of his pocket, showed it to the senior nurse and asked, "Is that Irma Wasem?"

"I should say so!"

Turning to Jutzeler, Studer asked, "You answered the telephone yesterday and called the Director. Who was it asking for him? I mean, was it a woman's voice?"

"No, no," said Jutzeler, "it was a man's voice."

Studer was astounded. "A man's voice?" he asked in disbelief.

"Yes. I'm quite certain of it." The staff nurse clearly felt his word was being doubted.

Studer thought. There was something wrong there. He needed to continue his questioning, but it was difficult under these circumstances. When there were so many others listening, people refused to come out of their shell. He ought to take each of them separately, then he could give them a real grilling. He looked from one to the other. Blank faces. Behind them, at the small table, Bohnenblust with the darned pullover and bushy moustache was sitting, a contented expression on his face, glad that he seemed to have been forgotten. He was breathing so gently the wheezing from his chest was no longer audible. Don't worry, thought Studer, your turn will come. Perhaps, however, it won't be necessary. He was still hoping things would turn out all right. Though the fact that it was a man's voice . . .

"Tell me, Jutzeler, were you still in the vicinity of the telephone while the Director was talking?"

"Yes."

"You didn't listen, of course. But you might have noticed something? A change of tone in the Director's voice, say?"

Jutzeler thought, then nodded. "At first he was very curt; he seemed to be furious and slammed the receiver down. But it rang again straight away and the Director answered. He smiled . . ."

So Ulrich Borstli had spoken to two people on the phone. It was starting to look as if this might be a murder investigation, even though at the moment it was only the disappearance of a patient – Pieterlen – that was on the agenda. Wasn't it still possible the Director had simply taken himself off, gone on a trip somewhere? But there were so many things that contradicted that. Studer walked up and down the dormitory, several pairs of eyes following him.

Three doors in one of the longer walls. He tried the handles – they were locked. To open them you needed just a passkey, not a triangular key.

"We have to get on, Studer," said Dr Laduner, standing up. "I'll get the senior nurse . . . Weyrauch, give the sergeant a passkey and a triangular key so he can go where he likes. I assume you don't need to go to the female ward, Studer?"

Studer shook his head. "Just one more question. Is Irma Wasem in the building?"

It was the corpulent senior nurse who answered. "It's her day off," he said, with a wink from behind his horn-rimmed spectacles.

So they'd discussed the case during the morning reports, thought Studer, going over to the last door, the one next to the raised cubicle with the bathtubs. It was less than three yards from the side room. From the other side came the hum of voices.

"By the way," Studer asked, "do you happen to know where Pieterlen's accordion is?"

Jutzeler blushed, which looked rather odd, and stammered a little as he answered in a low voice that the accordion was not to be found.

"Then I suppose Pieterlen will have taken it with him, wherever he's gone," said Studer, shaking his head. He simply could not picture this Pieterlen in his mind, whom Laduner had described as a classic case. A classic case! Why?

"If you're going to stay in O, Studer," said Dr Laduner, "then I'll introduce you to my friend Schül. A poet, is our Schül. Not the most beautiful sight; a hand grenade exploded right in front of him during the war. Made quite a mess of his face. But he's a very intelligent man, I think you'll get on well with him. Also, he was a great friend of Pieterlen, the vanishing patient."

With demonstrative thoroughness, Studer took his little notebook out of his pocket and wrote down: *Wasem, Irma, nurse,*

"How old was she?" he asked, and when Weyrauch told him, he added: *22 years old.*

Matto and the redhead

Like all the corridors in the clinic, the main corridor smelt of floor polish and dust. A narrower one branched off to the right, leading to the kitchen. This was painted a light blue and wasn't really a kitchen, just a large room for washing up. There was a sink in one corner, with hot and cold taps over it, and two huge windows at right angles to each other, one looking out onto the central block, the other onto a lower building in the middle of the courtyard with a chimney rising up at the end of it.

"Hey, Schül," said Gilgen, the red-haired nurse who had been delegated to show Studer round.

A man in a blue apron, who had been busy stacking soup plates on a large tray, looked round. His face was one big scar. His nose had been flattened and in place of nostrils the ends of two silver tubes stuck out; his mouth looked like a poorly healed cut.

"I've brought someone to see you, Schül," said Gilgen, rolling up the sleeves of his blue shirt even further. "Greetings from Dr Laduner, and you're to keep the sergeant company for a while."

The man with the scarred face dried his hands on his apron, then held one out to Studer. It, too, was covered in scars. And he had protuberant eyes. Bloodshot.

He spoke rather stilted, formal German that had little of the Swiss dialect about it. In fact, it sounded more French, which was hardly surprising since Schül, as he told Studer, had spent twelve years in the Foreign Legion and had fought in the Great War with the *Régiment de Marche* under Colonel Rollet.

He told him – little bubbles of spittle formed at the corners of his mouth – that he had been seriously wounded in the war (*"un grand blessé de guerre!"* as he put it). A hand-grenade – Dr Laduner had presumably told him? – yes, a hand grenade had exploded in front of him, ripping apart not only his face, but his hands and his whole body as well. He pulled up his trouser leg to show him, and Studer just managed to stop him pulling his shirt up over his head to bare his torso.

"Look at the way they treat heroes," Schül complained. "You give your all for a country's freedom, I'm a *chevalier* of the *Légion d'honneur*, I've been awarded the *Médaille Militaire* and I'm paid the full pension. And who do you think pockets it? The Director!" Schül bent down to whisper in Studer's ear and the sergeant had to make an effort not to draw away. "Who pockets my pension? The Director! But that blasted money-grubber will get his comeuppance! Matto will teach him a lesson. You cannot torture a man who stands under the protection of an important spirit and get away with it."

He suddenly grasped Studer by the sleeve and dragged him over to the window that looked out onto the central block.

"Up there, do you see?" Schül whispered. "The attic window? Above Dr Laduner's apartment? Can't you see him darting out and in, out and in? That's him, that's Matto. He dictated a poem to me, I'll show it you, I'll write out a copy for you so you'll have a souvenir of him, of Matto."

Studer couldn't help feeling a little disconcerted.

Even with his poor sense of direction, he had no difficulty establishing that the window Schül had pointed out was right above the guest room Frau Laduner had given him.

Schül continued to chat away while he looked for the poem in a cupboard crammed full of papers.

Matto had cried out last night, he said, cried out again, a long-drawn-out, plaintive cry. In the corner between T Ward and P this time. He interrupted his search for a moment to show Studer the place.

There was a good overall view from the window that looked out onto the central block. Firstly, of all the central block itself, with the doctors' apartments – in the afternoon Studer would learn that the Director's apartment lay immediately beneath Laduner's – then P, the ward for placid patients, and, at right angles to it but in the same wing as O, where he was at the moment, T, the Treatment Ward for those suffering from a physical illness. And in that corner, where a door led to the basement, someone had cried out. When Schül went back to rummaging around among his papers, Studer asked the red-haired nurse whether he could believe him.

Gilgen shrugged his shoulders, as if he had been put on the spot. In general, he said, Schül was quite observant, and it wasn't impossible he might have heard something, since he slept directly above this kitchen, in a room whose windows had bars on the outside, so was left open all night.

"Schül," Studer asked, "what time was it you heard the cry?"

"Half past one," Schül said in a matter-of-fact voice. "The clock in the tower struck immediately afterwards. Here's the poem."

It wasn't a poem in the usual sense, rather a passage

of rhythmical prose, written out in Schül's neat handwriting.

Sometimes, when the Föhn spins the mist into soft threads, he sits by my bedside, whispering and telling me things. Long are the green, glassy nails on his fingers, and they shimmer as he waves his hands in the air . . . Sometimes he sits on the top of the clock tower, casting threads, coloured threads, far and wide over the villages and towns, and over the houses that stand alone on a hillside . . . His power and glory stretch far and wide, and no one can escape him. He waves and throws his coloured streamers and War sails up like a blue eagle; he flings a red ball and Revolution flares up to the heavens and explodes. But I committed the murder in Doves' Gorge, at least that's what the police say, I know nothing about it. My blood was spilt on the battlefields of the Argonne, but now I am locked away and if I did not have my friend, Matto the Great, who rules the world, I would be alone and might perish. But he is good to me and he digs his nails of glass into the brains of those who torment me, and when they groan in their sleep, he laughs . . .

"What's all this about the murder in Doves' Gorge, Schül?" Studer asked, that being the one sentence that fell into his own area of expertise. The rest sounded quite good, especially the bit about Matto being responsible for the war breaking out, but he also felt it was rather overblown.

It was Gilgen, the nurse with the rolled-up sleeves, who answered. It was just an idea Schül had, he said. Old Schül never hurt a fly. Then he asked Studer if he would like to go with him to the day room, it was eleven o'clock and he had to relieve a colleague, lunch was at half past, did the sergeant fancy watching a few rubbers of *jass*, or even joining in?

Studer shook Schül's scar-covered hand and thanked him for the lovely poem; the patient promised him a copy for the following afternoon. Then Studer followed his guide.

As they were going out of the door, Schül called after them in his hoarse voice, "Matto looks after his own, you'll see. He freed Pieterlen. And he came for the Director . . ."

So what, Studer thought. The only thing he found slightly disturbing was Schül's claim that Matto had set up his headquarters in the very attic that lay above the guest room.

The wide corridor ended in a glass door, which led into the day room, in which everything was painted a dark orange: the tables, the chairs, the benches with the high backs on which were fixed wire-mesh holders with pot plants – asparagus fern – interspersed with vases of dahlias. Although two windows were open – they looked out onto D1 – the room was filled with thick smoke. As Studer looked round, he thought about the nurse accompanying him, Gilgen, the first person he had met in the clinic to whom he had felt unreservedly attracted.

He couldn't have given a reason. The front half of Gilgen's head was a bald, shiny sphere, the red hair behind it was cut short and gleamed like copper that had just been polished with Brasso. His neck was brown and his face covered in freckles. It was a friendly face, despite the lines at the corners of the eyes and across his forehead, presumably caused by worry. He was short, only coming up to the sergeant's shoulder, but there was a warmth about him which the patients in the day room also seemed to feel, greeting his arrival with "Ah, Gilgen" or "*Grüess di*, Gilgen".

The skin of his bare forearms was covered in freckles too . . .

"We're going to have a few rounds of *jass*," said Gilgen, "and I've got a visitor here who has business in the clinic and who'd like to join in. Who's interested?"

Two volunteered: a long, skinny fellow with "alcoholic" written all over him and a short man with an asymmetrical face who turned out to be an extremely pedantic, slow and irritating card player.

Studer partnered Gilgen. There was not much worth saying about the *jass*, apart from one game where Gilgen passed with a run of four to the ace of spades, three clubs and the nine of hearts, forcing Studer to play the game with hearts as trumps. Since he had spades as well, they managed to make all nine tricks, but secretly he found Gilgen's style of play a bit much, though that served only to increase his liking for the red-haired nurse.

Then Gilgen announced he had to go and eat, but first, he said, he'd take Studer down to the ground floor, to get the keys from Weyrauch. Another nurse came to relieve him, but before he could open the door to the stairs Schül came hurrying past with a tray loaded with soup plates.

"Just wait till I catch whoever created the world," he called out to them with a laugh on his scarred lips that revealed his toothless mouth.

And it was with a laugh that the two of them went down the stairs to the ground floor. At the bottom the stairs continued. "To the basement," Gilgen explained.

Another corridor. At the end leading to D Ward some alterations were being carried out. Another day room with brightly coloured furniture, Gilgen explained. Dr Laduner had managed to push through a certain amount of renovation work on the clinic. It was he, too, who had set up the decorating and brick-laying groups, usually a dozen patients with a nurse who had worked at the trade before going in for nursing.

"You liked Pieterlen?" Studer suddenly asked.

Gilgen halted, playing with his bunch of keys. "You'll give Pieterlen time, won't you, Sergeant?" he asked, with an expression like a anxious mouse. "You won't arrest him straight away?"

"Arrest him? Who said anything about arresting him? Pieterlen isn't even on the official wanted list. It's just because he disappeared at the same time as the Director that Dr Laduner asked the police to send me to . . . No, no, an arrest doesn't come into it . . . But what do you know about Pieterlen?"

"Nothing, nothing at all," said Gilgen, putting his keys away again. "But I felt sorry for him. He was a nice chap, much too nice."

They were standing in the middle of the corridor. As on the floor above, here, too, there was a narrower corridor branching off. One voice rose above the babble of conversation coming from it, declaring, "If the cops start poking around all the wards with their grubby fingers, that'll be just great . . ."

It was the voice of Staff Nurse Jutzeler, and it didn't sound half as respectful as it had an hour ago. Gilgen quickly hurried the sergeant on till they came to a door. He knocked. The senior nurse, *Herr* Weyrauch, took his lunch in his own room. He sat there, content with himself and the world; the bacon joint he had just been eating had left a shiny ring round his mouth.

"Oh, the keys for Herr Studer? Of course. Pardong." He got up and rummaged around. "Yes, Herr Dr Laduner gave me instructions . . . Ah, here we are, Sergeant."

On the table by the window, to which Studer had followed him, were some nudist magazines. "Ha-ha-ha," Weyrauch laughed. "Very artistic, eh, Sergeant?" he said, giving Studer a gentle dig in the ribs.

Artistic! Well, if Weyrauch insisted. Studer had nothing against that kind of thing, but that didn't stop him finding Weyrauch a rather unpleasant character. Perhaps he was just prejudiced.

Gilgen was waiting patiently outside. He followed Studer to the door of O Ward that led out into the courtyard, opened it, then stopped. He had his hands inside the bib of his apron, which was like a thin white muff round them.

"By the way," Studer said, "what's wrong with Schül? Has it anything to do with his injuries?"

Gilgen shook his head, like an expert. "No, his mental illness has nothing to do with his injuries."

"What is it then?"

"Skidsoffreenia."

"What?"

"Skidsoffreenia," Gilgen repeated, loud and clear. "We did it on the course."

"And what about Pieterlen?"

"Skidsoffreenia."

"But recently he hasn't been, er, you know" – Studer tapped his forehead – "at all?"

"No, he's been quite normal."

"How long has he been in the clinic, then?"

"Four years."

"Why so long?" Studer wanted to know.

"Before that he spent three years in prison. He cracked up in there."

"Why was he in prison?"

"He murdered his child!" Gilgen whispered, telling Studer to ask Dr Laduner if he wanted the details.

56

There was a pause, then Studer asked one final question.

"And what do you think of the Director?"

"Of Herr Dr Borstli? A randy old goat."

And with that the redhead who had passed with a run of four to the ace of spades walked off, leaving Studer standing in the courtyard.

A free lunch

When he got to the middle of the courtyard, Studer stopped and had a look round. His first impression had been correct, the clinic was built in the form of an angular U. He was surrounded on three sides by two- and three-storeyed buildings, all interconnected. Behind him was the casino, to the right the men's wing, to the left the women's. And in front was a flat-roofed building, long and low, with a chimney at the back corner spewing out sluggish clouds of black smoke.

Through the wide-open door the sergeant could see huge cauldrons heated by steam. They were tipped forward and the kitchen maids were filling large containers with soup and overcooked macaroni, as well as large bowls with lettuce. In the middle of all the commotion, a fat individual of the female sex was waddling silently over the tiles. Silently, that is, in the sense that her footsteps were not audible. Her voice, on the other hand, was; from time to time she emitted a screech that galvanized the girls into action. Studer watched; he found the whole business interesting and it didn't last that long, anyway. Soon two long crocodiles, one on the left, one on the right, emerged from doors that were concealed by the corner of the building. Women to the left, men to the right. Some of the women were wearing white caps, either starched or soft, others were bareheaded; almost all the men wore white aprons: the nurses were taking lunch to wards P to D.

The kitchen maids disappeared, it was impossible to tell where to, and the fat individual of the female sex who could waddle so silently appeared in the doorway and nodded at Studer. Studer returned her greeting with a smile. The woman's cheeks were as red and shiny as a ripe tomato.

Was he the new cop? she wanted to know.

He was, Studer replied. From the criminal investigation department. "Sergeant Studer's the name."

"And mine's Fräulein Kölla. Won't you come in?" she asked. She'd gone out with a gendarme once, she immediately continued, but that was a long time ago. The gendarme had turned out to be a swine who'd dumped her for a rich farmer's daughter.

"I can certainly come in," said Studer, "but Dr Laduner's expecting me for lunch, so I can't stay long."

"Lunch!" exclaimed Fräulein Kölla contemptuously. He should have lunch with her, she'd do him a steak, just they way he liked it. And then they could have a little chat; she knew all sorts of things that might be of interest to the sergeant. Especially about what had gone on the previous night.

Studer thanked her for her kind invitation, but he wasn't sure whether Dr Laduner wouldn't feel . . .

"Oh, don't you bother your head about that," said Fräulein Kölla in her vigorous manner, "I'll give Dr Laduner a ring and that'll settle it. At least here," she added, "you'll get something decent to drink." She didn't seem to have a great opinion of Dr Laduner's wine cellar.

Fräulein Kölla was a real chatterbox. She started talking about her young days, about other men, who . . . He would have to interrupt the unceasing flow of words, Studer decided, so he asked a question.

"Do you remember the harvest festival?"

"Of course."

"Did you see the Director?"

"He came out of the casino at ten."

"Alone?"

"At first, yes."

"And then?"

"And then he met a lassie at the corner of the women's O Ward."

"What lassie would that be?"

Fräulein Kölla's eyes went wide with astonishment. She'd never have thought, she said, a copper could be so stupid.

Studer accepted the remark with equanimity, tucking into his steak, which was so tender his knife went through it like butter. Then he continued his patient questioning.

"So who was it?"

"That Irma Wasem, of course. The girl's" – and the cook used an expression normally reserved for a female mammal at certain stage in its reproductive cycle.

"Aha . . . oh, yes," and Studer conceded that he had heard something along those lines already.

"Why do you ask such silly questions then?"

"We-e-ell, you know . . . So, anyway, the two of them went off for a walk together?"

"Arm in arm!" said Fräulein Kölla. She'd been sitting up there at her window, she explained. There were some arc lamps in the courtyard, it was bright as a sunny day.

She deposited a pile of green beans, liberally flavoured with garlic, on the sergeant's plate, refilled his glass, wished him "Good health" and clinked glasses with him. Then she emptied her tumbler in one gulp.

Studer raised his glass to her. He approved of Fräulein Kölla.

"And when did the two of them get back?"

"About half past twelve. The lassie came with the Director to the door of the central block, then he kept her waiting there for a long time. When he came back down, about half an hour later, he was wearing a loden cape. They walked together to the women's O Ward and Irma Wasem went in, while the Director continued his walk." That was when Fräulein Kölla had gone to bed, so she couldn't say whether the lassie had come down again. But she couldn't get to sleep right away, that's why she'd still been awake when she heard the cry.

"The cry? What cry?"

"There were others heard it too. A cry. It sounded like a cry for help"

"When did you hear this cry?"

"Just before the clock struck half past one."

Studer bowed his head. The curve of his back was like the gentle rise of a dark hill. "Where did the cry come from?"

"From the corner on the men's side, where wards T and P join."

Aha! So Schül had been right about what he had heard.

"A hoarse cry, Sergeant. It sounded like this."

Fräulein Kölla tried to imitate the cry. It sounded like the squawk of a hungry young crow. Some people would have laughed at it, but Studer remained serious. So people in the clinic had been talking about it. Why then had Dr Laduner not mentioned it?

In the corner between wards T and P.

That seemed to put paid to his theory about a

little excursion to Lake Thun or Ticino. No amorous escapade, such as old gentlemen sometimes go in for, even if they do happen to be directors of medical establishments. No one talks about them. Colleagues make their little jokes, but nothing trickles through to the outside world ... The cry! No, the cry was no laughing matter. If you listened carefully, it seemed that everything in this case that sounded funny at first eventually struck a wrong note.

The smashed-up office – a wrong note; the male voice on the telephone – a wrong note; Pieterlen's disappearance – a wrong note; Bohnenblust's bruise – a wrong note.

Everything sounded wrong: Dr Laduner's jokey tone, his offering of bread and salt, the way he played the distinguished physician on his rounds – as if he were already the director – and there was something not quite right about that friendly nurse either, Gilgen, the redhead who passed with a run of four to the ace of spades and who had those worry lines all over his anxious face ...

"In the corner between T Ward and P?" Studer asked, lost in thought. "What's there?"

"Workshops ... a storeroom ... the heating plant ..."

Studer stood up and started pacing up and down the room, from the door to the window and back again. Fräulein Kölla had rested her heaving bosom on the table and was following him with her eyes. He stopped by the window, opened it and leant out: a lawn, newly mown, iron poles with clothes lines stretched between them, sheets waving in the gentle breeze. He could hear the hum of a machine.

"What's that?" Studer asked.

"The laundry's next door," Fräulein Kölla

explained. "One of the machines must be spinning to make that kind of whirring noise."

And Studer thought of all the things needed in a clinic like this: countless shirts, socks, handkerchiefs, sheets, nightdresses, all marked, all arranged in piles, all counted. He caught himself thinking that he wouldn't mind if the investigation took a while so that he could see how such an organization worked. He felt like spending some time here, in this realm that was ruled over by a spirit called Matto, who had been invested with such great power ... Sergeant Studer would quite like to make this Matto's acquaintance ...

He stared out of the window.

"Is that the female O Ward?" he asked, gesturing with his hand at the building opposite.

"Yes."

Studer heard Fräulein Kölla's reply, but by then he was already leaning out of the window, watching a girl who was hurrying towards the entrance to the ward, bent forward, holding her handkerchief over her eyes.

A woman crying. It could mean everything and nothing, but to Studer it suggested that silly young thing Nurse Irma Wasem, who imagined she was soon going to be Frau Director Borstli.

He called the fat cook to come over quickly, pointed out of the window at the girl and asked who it was.

That was the girl they'd just been talking about, she said, that Irma Wasem who ... But Fräulein Kölla's explanation tailed off in a giggle as Studer swung himself up over the window-ledge, ran across the grass, getting entangled in a sheet, and caught up with the girl just as she was putting her key in the lock. He placed his hand on her shoulder and said, in a very gentle, fatherly voice, "What's happened?" Then he asked if she would come for a short walk with him, there were some questions he'd like to ask.

The handkerchief was sopping wet. The tears were still running down her cheeks . . .

More by instinct that conscious reflection, Studer realized that the only way to calm the girl down was a matter-of-fact approach. He abandoned his usual sympathetic tone and asked in a dispassionate voice, "Are congratulations in order, Fräulein Wasem? Is it Frau Direktor Borstli now?"

A stare . . . A look of defiance . . . The tears dried up. "Who're you?"

"Detective Sergeant Studer."

"Lord above! I knew it! Has something happened to Ueli?"

Ueli . . . Dr Ulrich Borstli MD, Director of Randlingen Psychiatric Clinic, was simply Ueli. Lucky old Dr Borstli. Actually, Studer would certainly not have objected himself if Irma Wasem had called him "Köbi" or, even better, "Köbeli". His wife had got into the habit of calling him "Dad". There were times when it got on his nerves . . .

"We don't know yet," Studer said. "Have you spoken to anyone else?"

A shake of the head.

Sergeant Studer came to a decision. "The Director's office looks as if there's been a fight there," he said. "Traces of blood on the floor, the typewriter's bitten the dust . . ." Studer shook his head. Why on earth was he using Dr Laduner's jokey expression? Then he finished with, "The Director's disappeared and–"

"Jutzeler! The men's staff nurse in O Ward!"

That was not at all what Studer had been going to say. "And Pieterlen's run off," was what he had been about to add, so Irma Wasem's interruption took him aback for a moment.

"What's this about Jutzeler?" he asked.

"They had an argument. Ueli ... the Director and the staff nurse."

"When?"

"That's why I had to wait so long, almost three quarters of an hour. I could see them through the glass door in the central block. Jutzeler stopped the Director and started going on at him. He was obviously furious. Then they both went into the office. I saw them. Half an hour later he came out by himself and went up to his apartment. When he came down he'd put his loden cape on and he had a leather briefcase under his arm. I asked him what he was doing with the briefcase, but he waved my question away. 'We're going tomorrow morning,' he said. 'Go back to your room.' He accompanied me to O Ward and then went back."

"At half past one?"

"Yes, it was around half past one. This morning he was going to go to Thun with me. I waited for him at the station for a long time."

"And you didn't hear anything after he left you, Nurse Wasem?"

"No. That is, I did wonder, at around a quarter to three or so, if someone had cried out for help. But we have so many people crying out round here ..."

"You sleep by yourself ... ahem, er ... I mean, do you have a room to yourself?"

"No, there's another nurse who shares the room with me."

"And no one checks up on what time the nurses get back?"

"The others, yes, but me ... no!"

Studer sighed. If you were the Director's sweetheart even the Matron, or whatever title the old trout had, would turn a blind eye to anything you did.

In the corner between wards P and T . . . A cry for help . . . Perhaps Matto, as Schül called the spirit of madness, had been plaguing one of his subjects with a horrible nightmare.

Studer stood in the middle of one of the paths and looked round. An uneasy feeling crawled up his spine. He was surrounded on three sides by the red-brick walls of the clinic, and the fourth side was closed off, too. That was where the kitchen was. He felt as if the many windows, glittering with a multiplicity of tiny panes, were insect eyes observing him. He had nothing to hide, nothing at all. He was carrying out an investigation, it was his right to be with a lassie who might have some information. But he felt uncomfortable all the same. The windows were squinting at him, giving him questioning looks. What was the man doing? What's he going to do now? It would be better if he got away from here and had a look at the corner from where the cry for help had come the previous night; the cry that had sounded like the squawk of a hungry young crow.

The late Herr Direktor Ulrich Borstli

Dr Laduner was playing tennis. The courts were beside the railway line, on the other side of the village of Randlingen.

"Game," cried Dr Laduner. He sounded as if he was in good spirits.

He was playing with a woman. As Studer got closer he saw that it was the assistant doctor who had not said a word during the rounds. Without her doctor's coat she looked slim, agile, only her legs were too skinny . . .

"Herr Doktor," Studer called out, sticking his nose through the the wire-mesh fence.

"Hey, it's you, Studer. What's new?"

Dr Laduner came over, balancing his racket on the ball of his hand. The "doctor-on-his-rounds" smile was on his lips, the half-mask again.

"I've found the Director," said Studer in a low voice.

"Dead?"

Studer nodded.

"Have you told anyone yet?"

Studer shook his head.

"My dear girl," Laduner said to the woman, who was standing at the net, staring at the ground, "I have to go back to the clinic . . . Listen, I told my wife I'd get some sausages, but I haven't time for that now, would you be so kind . . . ?

The woman nodded earnestly, ignoring Studer entirely. He calls her "my dear girl," he thought to himself, and remembers the sausages he's supposed to be getting, while in the boiler room, at the foot of the iron ladder leading to the furnace door, the Director's lying on the floor with a broken neck . . . But perhaps the errand's just an excuse to get rid of the lady . . . ?

"Excellent. Bye then . . . Take my racket too, will you."

A white shirt, white linen trousers, white shoes. Just his face was brown, and a strand of hair was sticking up at the back of his head.

"Let's go then," said Dr Laduner.

They walked down a long avenue of apple trees, the branches covered in pale lichen and with tiny apples hanging from them, green as grass. At the end of the avenue the central block loomed up, crowned by a little tower with a bell in it. The hammer was raised, fell . . . The sound was sharp, sharp as the apples must taste. Studer counted the strokes . . . Three o'clock in the afternoon. All kinds of things were going through his head as he walked along beside Dr Laduner. The first sentence of the report that was still to be written, for example: "In the course of my investigation, at 2.30 p.m. on 2 September, I found the body of a man in late middle age in the basement housing the heating plant below T Ward of Randlingen Psychiatric Clinic. His pockets were empty . . ."

"Where?" Dr Laduner suddenly asked.

"The heating plant of the male T Ward."

"You know your way round the clinic pretty well already, Studer. But you let us down at lunchtime. I like listening to Fräulein Kölla myself, but just you beware. She's more dangerous than a movie vamp."

Another wrong note, but he couldn't quite grasp it . . . You can't grasp a note anyway.

"And he was dead?"

"Dead as a doornail," said Studer.

Dr Laduner stopped. He breathed in deeply and stretched until the material of his white shirt was tight across his chest.

In a low voice Studer said, "Yesterday night, quite late, Staff Nurse Jutzeler had an argument with the Director. In the office . . ."

"Jutzeler?" Dr Laduner's surprise was genuine, but then he waved the matter away as being of no interest. "Oh yes, that's quite possible. But it will have been a difference of opinion about politics. Jutzeler wanted to get the staff organized in a union, the Director was an arch-conservative."

At the foot of the stone steps leading up to the main entrance, in the same spot as that morning, Dr Laduner halted. Studer kept his eyes on the ground. When the silence remained unbroken, however, he glanced discreetly at the other man. Dr Laduner had his jaws clamped so tightly together the muscles stood out like cords under the skin of his cheeks.

"Now presumably we'll have to look for Pieterlen . . . won't we, Herr Doktor?"

"Pieterlen? Sure-ly. We'll get on the telephone. You think it's murder?"

The sergeant shrugged his shoulders and waggled his head from side to side. "I don't know," he said.

But he said nothing about his find. On the landing, at the top of the iron ladder leading down to the furnace door, he had found something that looked like a huge salami: a good fifteen inches long, twice as fat as a man's thumb, made of coarse linen, filled with sand and sewn tight. A handy cosh. And the cloth was the same as that he had found under the mattress in Pieterlen's room.

Nor did Studer say anything about the envelope in the breast pocket of his jacket. It contained dust, dust he had combed out of the thick, white hair of the corpse. Perhaps a microscopic examination would reveal some tiny, glittering grains of sand among all the ash that would doubtless be there . . .

Why did he not mention his find, and the precautionary measure he had taken, to Dr Laduner? Studer could not have said, at least not at that moment. Sometimes he had the feeling there was a fight to be fought out between himself and the slim, intelligent doctor. A fight? . . . No, not quite that. Wasn't it more a trial of strength? A friendly way of getting his own back? Dr Laduner had "particularly asked" for Studer in order to be "covered by the police". Was it not a matter of honour to prove to the doctor that he was more than a convenient shield? Or, to put it better, more than an ordinary umbrella you opened when it started to rain?

The hall of the central block was cool, the gilt letters shimmered on the green marble of the benefactors' plaque. Dreyer, the porter, was nowhere to be seen.

Down the steps into the courtyard they went, the two unequal companions: the sergeant in his off-the-peg suit beside Dr Laduner, white, clean, with a spring in his step and still determinedly brisk, as if to say, "Come on, come on, I've no time to spare, I've got things to do. Even if the Director's been killed ten times over, what's it to do with me?"

But perhaps he was mistaken in imputing such thoughts to the psychiatrist?

They passed the casino on their left and crossed over to the corner between P and T wards. The sun was still high in the sky, reflecting off the windows, which dazzled like tiny spotlights.

Studer hunched forward a little and squinted up at the window above his guest room from which, according to the war invalid Schül, Matto darted out and in, out and in. A superstitious belief, definitely. That morning Studer would have laughed if anyone had told him he would come to fear Matto. But now, after what he had found in the boiler room? It put an entirely different complexion on the situation.

They went through the door to the basement. A corridor, long and echoing, with a vaulted roof, a cement floor ... A door painted with grubby yellow gloss paint ...

"Give me your passkey, Studer," Dr Laduner commanded. He put the key in the lock, turned the handle, pulled the door open and went in. His movements, his steps, were as swift and precise as they had been that morning. He went down the iron ladder. On the fifth rung from the bottom, he stopped. The feet of the corpse were in his way. Resting his right hand on a rung at shoulder height, Laduner balanced on the balls of his feet, jumped off and landed with a perfect knee-bend. Then he straightened up, tall, broad shouldered and white in the grey dust. Studer stood at the top, following the slim man's every movement. He could see the dead body, too, and the thought that came to him was that in a report he would never be able to convey the impression the dead Director made.

The old man was lying on his back because he had fallen down backwards, and his legs were stuck up against the iron ladder. His trousers had slipped back to the middle of his calves ... grey woollen socks, linen long johns, the white tapes at the bottom holding his socks up ...

Not a man for elegant suspenders, old Director Borstli, despite his penchant for young nurses. His face was covered with a dusting of yellow ash and his eyes had rolled up under his half-open lids.

Dr Laduner was standing over the body, arms akimbo, his hands on his grey leather belt. Then he bent down, put out one hand and gently lifted one of the Director's lids.

"Sure-ly," he said softly. "He's dead. Do you want to photograph him?"

He spoke with a pronounced hiss, presumably because he was having difficulty getting the words out through his clenched teeth.

"No," Studer replied, "I don't think that will be necessary. If . . ." he paused, "if someone really did . . ."

" . . . knock the Director down," Laduner finished for him, "then it happened up there, where you're standing. In that case it's really unnecessary to record the position of the corpse."

That consciously matter-of-fact tone! Studer couldn't help shaking his head slightly. After all, Dr Laduner had worked together with the old Director for years, which made his "record the position of the corpse" sound a little odd. There was something about Dr Ernst Laduner MD that irritated the sergeant – though he wouldn't have found it easy if he'd been asked to explain what it was. He both repelled and attracted him. He repelled him in the way masked faces sometimes repel us. But that wasn't the only thing about it: there was also the desire to see the real face hiding beneath the mask. The mask: Laduner's smile. How could he see behind the mask? Above all it called for time, it called for patience. Well, patience was one thing Sergeant Studer had plenty of, he'd had to learn the hard way . . .

Laduner lifted the Director's legs off the ladder. He did it gently, much to Studer's approval. Finally the body was laid out on the dusty stone floor. Then Laduner picked up the loden cape that lay crumpled beside the body, rolled it up and pushed it under the Director's head. He nodded as he weighed the head in his hand for a moment, as if confirming some suspicion. Then he picked something up. It was an old pair of spectacles, with oval lenses and steel rims. He handed them up to the sergeant, who had to kneel down to reach them. The smile playing around the doctor's lips as he did so was no longer the "consultant-doing-his-rounds" smile; on the contrary, it was a tender, slightly wistful smile, the kind of smile people have when they're thinking of past times they feel nostalgic about because they imagine things were different then, and better . . .

The sun-filled courtyard again, the staring windows, dazzlingly bright, like the eyes of nightmare monsters, the steps and the hall of the central block . . . Dr Laduner's white linen trousers were dirty, there was a smudge of rust on the left shoulder of his shirt.

"His pockets were empty?" the doctor asked. "You did check them, Studer?"

"They were empty," said Studer.

"Aha . . . empty . . . odd . . ."

Silence.

Then: "Blumenstein can do the autopsy. It would be nonsense to bring in a pathologist from outside."

Studer shrugged his shoulders. It was all the same to him. But Blumenstein? Who was this Blumenstein? He needed to consult his notebook, there were just too many names in this clinic . . . Blumenstein? Wasn't that the tall doctor, the one who'd been standing on one leg like a stork in O dormitory this morning? The Director's brother-in-law? . . . Why should Dr Blumenstein perform the autopsy?

They were standing outside the door of the doctors' room. From inside there came a loud crack, followed by voices raised in laughter. Studer was beginning to get to know Dr Laduner's idiosyncrasies: thrusting the handle down, flinging the door open . . .

Dr Neuville was standing by the window. He was lifting up a cardboard file in order to bring it crashing down again with all his might on a small typewriting table, at which the little doctor from the Baltic was sitting, the one who had been given the ticking-off that morning because of Schmocker, the would-be political assassin. She was flushed, a look of apprehension on her face.

"Neuville! That's enough of this childish behaviour!" said Dr Laduner sternly.

Dr Blumenstein was sitting close to the door, with his feet on the desk. Despite the fact that he was leaning back comfortably and smoking a tipped cigarette, he still looked like a huge baby.

There was a telephone on the shelf that divided the desk in two. Dr Laduner picked up the receiver, dialled and waited. In the silence the click of the receiver being lifted at the other end could be clearly heard.

"Laduner here. Yes, Dr Laduner. Call Jutzeler to the telephone."

They waited in silence. Dr Blumenstein didn't dare take his feet down off the desk. Only after Dr Laduner had fished a packet out of his pocket with his left hand and gestured at him with his cigarette did he tuck his long legs under the desk and hold out a lighted match to his superior.

"Yes?" Laduner said. "Is that you, Jutzeler? Find Gilgen and Blaser and get a stretcher. Take it to the boiler room under T Ward, you'll find the Director there . . . What? . . . Yes, he's dead . . . You'll cover him up, won't you? . . . I know it won't make any difference, it'll be all

74

over the clinic in a quarter of an hour, but still . . . Yes, take him to M, Dr Blumenstein will perform the autopsy, you can assist him, Jutzeler . . . Oh, and tell Weyrauch he's to come to the office . . . Yes, that's all." Laduner replaced the receiver and said, turning to Studer, "M's another section. It's not the last letter in the alphabet, but it's the last stage for some of our patients – the Mortuary. I presume you'll be able to remember what the letter stands for."

After a pause, during which no one spoke, he slipped down from the desk. "Blumenstein, you'll determine the cause of death. Bring the report to me . . . An accident, the Director fell down a ladder in the heating plant."

Silence again. The windows were open. Somewhere outside they were playing croquet. It sounded like someone dreamily picking out the same low note on a xylophone again and again . . . Then an accordion started up . . . The leaves on the bushes outside the window were such a dark green that in the shade they looked almost black . . .

"My dear," said Laduner to the little doctor from the Baltic, who was sitting by the window, looking vacant and slightly distraught, her fingers still hovering over the keys of the typewriter, "would you get Pieterlen's medical history out for me. And write out a description of him. You can bring the files up to my flat. We'll have a talk about Pieterlen this evening, Studer . . ."

He fell silent.

Then: "About Pieterlen, Pierre, the classic case . . ."

Dr Ernst Laduner MD, Deputy Director of Randlingen Psychiatric Clinic, went over to a cupboard, put a doctor's coat on over his tennis gear and, deliberately tapping the palm of his left hand with his stethoscope, said in an emphatic voice, looking up on the last three words, "And remember, in all things you will – come to *me*." He sounded like a major telling his troops, "Battalion – you will – take – your orders – from me!"

Short intermezzo in three parts

1

"Just go up to my apartment and wait for me, you don't need to ring . . ." Dr Laduner had said.

So now Studer was standing in the cool corridor. Someone was playing the piano, a simple melody. Studer crept closer. The sounds were coming from the door opposite the dining room. Studer listened. The notes were as cool as the song of the blackbird on an April morning. Then the piano fell silent and a boy's voice said, "Right, Mummy, now sing something."

"But I can't sing, Kasperli."

"Of course you can, Mummy . . . you know, the French song."

The sound of chairs being moved. A short prelude.

> *Plaisir d'amour ne dure qu'un moment*
> *Chagrin d'amour dure toute la vie . . .*

An alto . . . Suddenly Studer was far away, although he was leaning his head against the panel of the door. Randlingen Clinic and the old man who had broken his neck receded into the distance, and with them Pierre Pieterlen, whose description was to be circulated, and Dr Laduner with the smiling mask, to which he would have to give some serious thought.

In his mind's eye Studer saw a jungle of towers and roofs from which there rose a dull hum, interrupted now and then by short, shrill sounds. Trails of mist swirled and a glittering river wove its way through the houses below. Beside him sat a woman, accompanying herself on the guitar as she sang:

J'ai tout quitté pour ma charmante Sylvie . . .

Her voice was untrained, dark and full of sadness . . .

There was a sharp crack and Studer was back in the apartment corridor. The wood of the panel his head was leaning against had sagged a little.

Steps were approaching; the door opened.

Frau Laduner wore her pince-nez. She peered strenuously out into the dark corridor, her eyes came to within a hand's width of Studer's face, then she laughed.

"Herr Studer! But you must come in and sit down, instead of standing out there in the corridor. There's still some tea left . . . a dash of kirsch with it? Yes? . . . And Kasperli, say 'Good afternoon' to the gentleman. This is Herr Studer, who's staying in the guest room."

He was Herr Studer again. He could forget the detective sergeant, condemned to solve crimes. He was shown to an armchair, a serving trolley suddenly appeared before him, the tea being poured into his cup was mahogany brown, a shot of kirsch was added, and then he had to take a slice of toast, warm, with the butter melting – just like they ate in England, perhaps.

Would Frau Doktor be so kind as to sing a song for him, Studer asked. The wallpaper was a dark yellow, but above the black piano there was a patch of sunlight on the wall that shimmered like white gold. Frau Laduner replied that she couldn't sing, though there was no affectation or false modesty about it. It was like the reply she'd made that morning when she'd been asked how she liked "our Studer": "Not bad." It cheered him up.

Kasperli was getting impatient. "Come on, Mummy."

And Frau Laduner sat down at the piano. Her hands were short and stubby, the bottom joints of her fingers had a cushion of fat. She sang one song; she sang two songs. Studer drank his tea.

Frau Laduner stood up, saying that was enough. Was there any news? she asked.

He'd found the Director, Studer replied.

"Dead?"

Studer nodded silently and Frau Laduner sent her son out of the room.

"Well, well," she said. "It was inevitable."

Studer agreed, yes, it was inevitable.

She wasn't sure, Frau Laduner went on, whether Studer could appreciate what this would mean for her husband. Did he have a picture of Ernst? Of his character? Of the way he was? Ernst had found it very tough to have to do all the work. God, Studer could have no idea what the clinic looked like before they came to Randlingen.

"The patients just sat around all day in the wards. In O they played cards all day, T looked like a museum of Gothic statues. The sick patients just stood there, all contorted. One spent the whole day sitting on the radiator in the corridor, like a gargoyle. And the stench! The baths were occupied all day by the disturbed patients. The ward with the isolation units was overcrowded . . . and at night they screamed; the echoes were so loud in the courtyard, I was frightened. Do you know what occupational therapy is?"

Studer could not help smiling at the thought of the "Randlingen Express" he had seen that morning.

"What are you smiling at?" Frau Laduner asked, and Studer told her.

"That's only one part of it, and I can well understand why you find it funny. They try to keep the patients occupied. My husband is very gifted in practical matters, he literally invented occupational exercises himself. He put on courses for the warders – in those days we still called them warders – and he used to visit all the wards five, six, ten times a day. He's a man who usually swears and curses when something goes wrong, but he was patient . . . And every evening the Director went off to the Bear for his half pint of wine, married his cook and was a father again at sixty . . . Then when everything was working, when the clinic was running smoothly and people came to see it, when the patients were quiet at night and the wards, which used to look like a madhouse, were just workshops where paper bags were stuck together, mats woven – when patients who had been considered incurable could be discharged, who was it who got all the glory? . . . I once happened to see a letter in the office. Some German professor had written to tell the Director how surprised he had been at the modern way the clinic was run and congratulated the Director on introducing recent advances in psychotherapy into his establishment."

Frau Laduner had become quite heated. Now she fell silent. Her hands were resting in her lap and her linen skirt had rucked up almost to her knees. Frau Laduner's feet looked good-natured, Studer thought. Good-natured and energetic.

He thought, "Battalion – you will take – your orders – from me," and concealed a smile under his moustache.

"And now the Director's dead!" said Frau Laduner.

80

She breathed in deeply and the material of her blouse stretched tight over her breasts. It was the same kind of deep breath that Dr Laduner had taken, in the avenue under the apple trees with the tiny, grass-green apples hanging from their branches, apples as sharp as the bell that rang the hours from the turret on Randlingen Clinic.

A door-handle was thrust down, a door flung open.

"Frau Doktor, I think Herr Dr Laduner is back," said Studer, standing up.

Somewhere in the apartment a door was slammed shut. She'd go and have a look, said Frau Laduner, and with that she took her leave of the sergeant.

2

On the doorpost of the first-floor apartment was a tin nameplate, the kind you could emboss yourself on those machines that had sprung up on all the railway stations at one time: Dr Ulrich Borstli MD.

Cautiously, Studer tried the door. It was not locked and he found himself in a corridor similar to the one in Dr Laduner's apartment. He felt slightly uncomfortable but, he thought, it was after all his job to investigate any link there might be between the disappearing patient and the death of the Director.

He called out in a loud voice, "Hello," and "Anyone at home?" . . . Silence. It smelt of stale cigar smoke.

Studer went into the first room. A grand piano, a music stand, a small table with a full ashtray. Chairs, a dilapidated leather armchair drawn up in front of the fireplace. On the wall above the piano was the enlarged photograph of a woman. Studer went over to it. A thin face, big eyes, heavy plaits piled up elaborately on the back of her head . . . An old picture . . . His first wife?

The piano was locked and covered in dust. There were red velvet curtains hanging at either side of the windows and through the glass the pale trunk of a silver birch shone. Withered leaves quivered on the slender branches.

In the next room was a desk and on the desk a bottle of brandy with a dirty glass beside it. Studer remembered that it was the Director who wrote the reports on the chronic alcoholics and could not repress a quiet laugh. Beside the glass a book lay open. Studer turned to the title page: *The Memoirs of Casanova*.

An odd choice of reading! Still . . . But he must search the desk drawers. They weren't locked. No money in them. The 1,200 francs the Director had received the previous day were nowhere to be seen . . . So he'd had them on him? But his pockets were empty . . . And what about that cosh?

The bedroom. Two beds; one had no sheets or blankets, the other had not been slept in – there was no depression made by a head in the pillow. The coverlet was smoothed out.

There was something about the whole apartment, though he couldn't quite put his finger on it. It wasn't just the stale cigar smoke, nor was it the faint smell of brandy, although both were part of its essential atmosphere. It wasn't just the open volume of Casanova or the unmade-up bed or the dust or the locked piano or the velvet curtains or the silver birch with the withered leaves . . .

Studer stood in the middle of the apartment, by the open bookcase with just a few books lying haphazardly on the shelves. On the desk was a triple photograph frame: girls, men, newly weds, children ... The Director's grandchildren?

"Aha!" exclaimed Studer out loud. Now he could see what it was that filled the whole apartment.

Loneliness.

An old man who escaped to the Bear because he couldn't stand the loneliness any more. Two wives dead, the children far away, the grandchildren only coming during the holidays ... And the young nurses he went for walks with? An old man fighting against his loneliness, and it was a hopeless struggle.

Studer slipped out of the apartment, hurried up the stairs and into the second-floor apartment. Frau Laduner came to meet him. A nurse was asking for him, she'd taken him to the guest room.

When Studer opened the door he saw Gilgen sitting on the edge of a chair. He looked pale and anxious.

3

Gilgen scratched his bald head. He was wearing a jacket that had been patched several times. Out of one of the pockets he took a sheet of paper, folded in four, and handed it to Studer. The title was written in a beautiful hand; it was a dedication.

Dedicated to the very respected, very kind and very wise Inspector Jakob Studer by a great war invalid on behalf of Matto, the great spirit whose realm is spreading ever wider over the world.

There followed the strange passage of prose Studer had read that morning, only the beginning was a little different: *When the mist spins the rain into thin threads . . .* and so on, and so on. Then came the passage about the coloured streamers fluttering all over the world and war flaring up and the bit about the red balls and revolution blazing up to the heavens . . . It was similar and yet different. This time Studer found it strangely moving, and he shivered. So much had happened in the meantime. He had found the Director at the bottom of the iron ladder, he'd seen his apartment and understood the loneliness of an old man. He had seen Laduner breathe a sigh of relief, he'd seen his wife breathe a sigh of relief . . .

And Sergeant Studer read the last section of Schül's unrhymed poem:

Matto! He is powerful. He can take on all shapes, now he is short and fat, now slim and tall, and the world is his puppet theatre. Men do not realize that he is playing with them, like a puppeteer with his marionettes . . . And his fingernails are as long as those of a Chinese scholar, glassy and green . . .

Poor old Schül! He certainly had a thing about Matto's fingernails . . . But what was that? Studer felt uneasy, but it wasn't Schül's "poem" now, it was something else . . .

"Who's that playing the accordion?" he asked in irritation. It was impossible to work out where the music was coming from. He'd heard it already, down in the doctors' room, far off and quiet; up here it was louder, it seemed to be coming out of the walls, or dripping down from the ceiling.

He glanced at the red-haired nurse and saw that the little man had turned pale. It looked odd, the freckles stood out so clearly, like spots of rust on dull steel.

"What's wrong, Gilgen?" Studer asked.

"Nothing, Sergeant . . . Do you really need to know who's playing? It'll be impossible to tell, there's so many in the clinic who play the accordion, it could be coming from any of the wards."

Studer acquiesced, though the accordion playing still irritated him. He couldn't have said why. He was trying to remember something that had struck him that morning. It was something connected with accordion playing, but he couldn't quite bring it back to mind.

"Sergeant," said Gilgen, then paused. Only when Studer had given him a nod of encouragement did he continue with a request that Studer should ask Dr Laduner not to dismiss him.

"Dismiss you? Why should he dismiss you?"

It was a sad story Gilgen had to tell. He'd bought a little house, four years ago . . . 18,000 francs. He'd made a down payment of 7,000 francs, the rest was a mortgage. At first it had gone well, but now his wife was ill. She was up in Heiligenschwendi, it was her chest. And they were in debt! On his days off he'd always stood in for Jutzeler, and a few times he'd had to speak sharply to the young nurses to get them to treat him with due respect, so they'd become a bit obstreperous. They'd made an official complaint, claimed he was wearing underwear and boots belonging to patients. The Director had investigated the matter and had believed the others. He'd been going to sack Gilgen, but Staff Nurse Jutzeler had threatened to call a strike if Gilgen was dismissed. The Director had just laughed, and he'd been right to laugh, there wasn't much unity among the nurses, hardly a dozen of them were in the union. The rest were glad just to have a job nowadays, when things were so difficult . . .

"So what's the problem now?" Studer asked. He felt sorry for him.

He'd been home at lunchtime, Gilgen said, and found the final demand from the building society. Now if they got his wages paid straight to them, he'd be in a complete mess. His wife didn't belong to any insurance scheme . . . He'd tried everything, he went on, he'd done tailoring work for colleagues in his free time, even though it was officially forbidden to earn a double income. At least it was forbidden to the nurses. The fact that Dr Blumenstein's wife taught at the village school while her husband had his salary from the clinic didn't count, of course . . .

Studer nodded. The world was an unjust place. He could have told Gilgen about the 1,200 francs the Director had received from the insurance company, but he didn't want to stir things up even more.

Still, it was remarkable how the little man trusted him. Gilgen, a nurse he hadn't even known the previous day.

He'd played *jass* once with him, that morning, and it was probably pure chance that Dr Laduner had got him to show Studer round O Ward.

Studer offered what sympathy he could, promising he'd do his best. For the moment Dr Laduner was running the clinic so he'd put in a good word for Gilgen with him.

Gilgen left feeling a little more hopeful.

Studer noticed that as he did so he shot an anxious glance at the ceiling – but immediately forgot about it. The accordion had stopped . . .

He accompanied Gilgen to the apartment door and stopped outside the study on his way back along the corridor. He remembered he'd been going to phone his wife.

He gave a firm knock, opened the door and started back.

Lying on a couch, facing the door, was a young man, eyes wide with fear. He had his hands clasped behind his head and tears were running down his cheeks. At his head Dr Laduner was sitting in a comfortable armchair, smoking. When he saw Studer, he leapt up, came over to the door and said, in an agitated whisper, "In half an hour, I'm busy just at the moment," then closed the door.

Studer stood there for a while, thinking. The young man on the couch was Herbert Caplaun, the colonel's son.

Why was Herbert lying on a couch, crying?

Frau Laduner came rushing along the corridor. Her husband was not to be disturbed just at the moment, he had a private patient in analysis.

Analysis? What was that? he asked.

Frau Laduner waved the question away. It was difficult to explain.

Just as difficult, Studer thought, as the expression anxiety neurosis.

He went quietly back to his room and started to empty out his pockets. His dilapidated old leather suitcase had been brought and was on the table. In it, beneath his underwear, he put the little sandbag, the envelope with the dust he'd combed out of the Director's hair and the piece of coarse cloth he'd found beneath Pieterlen's mattress.

Then he took out his notebook, opened it at the page with the names and started to learn them off by heart, like a schoolboy learning his Latin vocabulary.

"Jutzeler, Max: staff nurse; Weyrauch, Karl: senior nurse; Wasem, Irma: nurse, 22 years old . . ."

Then it occurred to him that he'd forgotten to put

Gilgen in, and Schül, Matto's friend, nor was Fräulein Kölla from the kitchen in his notebook. But he left those three out, they didn't seem to be involved in the case.

He whispered softly a few times, "Pieterlen, Pierre: child murderer," and, "Caplaun, Herbert: anxiety neurosis."

Then he shut his notebook, folded his arms across his chest and closed his eyes. He was still memorizing while he was half asleep *"Dr Blumenstein, consultant, performing the autopsy, the brother-in-law of the Director, husband of the sister of the second wife of the Director . . ."*

But all the "ofs" were irritating him, like a fly buzzing round, about to settle on his nose, and he shook his head to chase it away. Then he fell asleep.

He dreamt that Dr Laduner was forcing him to write down the names of all the patients, all the nurses, all the kitchen maids, maintenance and office staff and all the doctors in a huge book.

"When you know all the names off by heart," Dr Laduner said, "then you can be Director instead of me. Sure-ly . . ."

In his dream Studer broke out in a sweat.

Pieterlen, the classic case

"Read that," said Dr Laduner, handing Studer a sheet of paper across the round table. Then he leant back, his elbows resting on the arms of his chair, his chin on his knuckles.

The lamp had a parchment shade painted with transparent, coloured flowers. Studer leant forward and read out loud.

"Ld: Not a single look to interrupt the police officer's questioning; when we look at him, an oddly unmotivated smile flits across his face. Asked what day it is, he ponders, then says, looking past us strangely, 'Thursday,' and apologizes, saying he had to think about it first, he'd been in prison since February and he quite often had a fever. To the question 'Since when?' he replied, again with that strange look that went right past us, 'Four years,' by which he meant that for the last four years he had suffered from high temperatures in the spring. He had come, he added, because of a murder. Here, too, he smiled, quite unmoved and certainly completely uninvolved. He also shook hands with the policeman when he took his leave. Pupils normal, tongue coated, hands steady, patellar reflex brisk . . ."

"Until then," said Dr Laduner, taking back the sheet. "Just a minute, have a look at the date."

"16. 5. 1923."

Laduner was silent for a while, then he said, "That was when I got my first dressing-down from my boss.

He said my initial assessment was poetic instead of factual and scientific. You saw the two letters at the beginning of the paragraph? Ld? That was Ernst Laduner, thirty years old at the time. Old? He was young, very young. That was when young Laduner first met Pierre Pieterlen. It was his first report . . ."

Laduner lit a cigarette, then held the flat, red match between his thumb and index finger, like a tiny, coloured conductor's baton. "Pierre Pieterlen, twenty-six years old at the time, accused of murder because he had suffocated his baby at birth. I can still repeat by heart the questions the district prosecutor's office asked, even with their abstruse German.

"1. Was the mental condition of the accused at the time of committing the act disturbed to such an extent that he was not in possession of the ability to control his actions, or of the judgement necessary to understand the criminal nature of the act he was committing?

"2. If question 1 is answered in the negative, please state whether the accused committed the act in a state of diminished responsibility and, if so, to what degree?

"Two splendid questions. Would you believe it if I told you I once sat there from ten o'clock at night until one o'clock in the morning thinking about them, trying to work out exactly what the legal gentlemen meant? That's how stupid I was in those days, so stupid that after that case I was ready to abandon psychiatry. But it seems there are certain arguments one cannot avoid. I was to meet Pieterlen again.

"'Diminished responsibility, and to what degree?'

"How can one know that, Studer? Do I know whether you possess 'judgement'? I can observe how you work when you're investigating a crime, I might even be able to form an opinion as to whether you think logically, see how you establish facts and fit them together. But your 'judgement'? Just imagine, for the legal eagles you have to express the possession of judgement, or the lack of it, in percentages! 'His judgement was fifty per cent, or thirty per cent.' Just as we say Standard Oil stands at twenty or thirty per cent below or above par. It's a funny old world we live in."

Silence. Then the clatter of plates from the kitchen. Out in the corridor Kasperli asked in a loud voice whether he could say good night to Daddy; Frau Laduner answered that he should wait a while longer. Laduner took another sheet of paper out of the file and handed it across the table.

"Look at the date first."

Studer did so. "2. 9. 26. The second of September nineteen hundred and twenty-six."

Then he read on.

"TW: Initial assessment. Bearded and in prison dress, holding his cap behind his back, he stood there stiffly, but he was concerned about his possessions, particularly his pencils, he wouldn't like to lose them, he said. The Governor of R. Prison could keep the money, he added with a forced smile. When asked, he said he had no complaints, though he had written a letter to his legal guardian, Dr L. He didn't want to say any more about it. Stiff, inhibited, he refused to shake hands with the doctor from R. Prison when he left. Asked why, he said that in his opinion that wasn't a doctor, though such things could be a matter of personal feeling."

Studer put the sheet of paper on the table. He waited. Laduner didn't speak, didn't move; his face was in shadow.

"It all revolves round the second of September," he said eventually. "It's strange. Pieterlen's baby died on

91

the second of September; the next year Pieterlen was convicted of murder and sentenced to ten years in prison on the second of September. Despite the fact that our, that is my, report was favourable; simply because the district prosecutor thought his behaviour was insolent.

"I did try to get the prosecutor in charge of the investigation to understand my conclusions, namely that Pieterlen was suffering from a latent mental disorder. We have decent public prosecutors here in Switzerland, and we have others for whom, if I had to write a report on them, my – perfectly objective – conclusion would be: moral debility. They are people who, it is quite obvious, only deal with crime professionally so as not to become criminals themselves. An abreaction, we psychologists call it. Perhaps you've come across people like that yourself. Anyway, the public prosecutor in that town was one of that type. Fat, with curly hair on a pointed skull, plenty of hair cream – I can still smell the brilliantine – a collector of copper engravings, more active in his erotic than his professional affairs. With every person who came before him, no matter what they were accused of – a thief, a woman who'd been shoplifting, a pickpocket, an embezzler – his first question was about their sexual experiences. Fat lips, permanently moist.

"If anyone had expressed surprise at the interest he showed in what went on between the sheets, he would have replied that it was purely psychological. All kinds of things have seeped through to the general public from one of the modern schools of psychological thought. Nowadays lawyers go to lectures on psychiatry as well – you can easily imagine with what results. A public prosecutor like that, for example.

"I realized straight away that he was ill-disposed

towards Pieterlen because he had refused to answer any of his bedroom questions. His wife, on the other hand, was in the prosecutor's good books – she was presumably intimidated, put up less resistance and divulged all sorts of things he found more interesting than her husband's snub. 'What do you expect, Herr Doktor,' he said to me, 'this Pieterlen's an insolent fellow, but we'll wear him down. You should have seen the merry dance he led us at first. And you fell for it too, of course.' What could I say? I tried to explain that Pieterlen was sick, that my honest opinion was that in this particular case a custodial sentence with hard labour would have a detrimental effect. A complete waste of breath. The prosecutor just laughed at me. He'd show Pieterlen what's what, he said, and immediately went on to tell me about a particularly pretty waitress in the second class station buffet and a collection of risqué engravings from the end of the eighteenth century he'd got for a song. Then he spoke about an illustrated edition of the memoirs of the Marquis de Sade. That tallied . . . I don't want to generalize, there are some very decent men among the public prosecutors, but sometime they are like that. What was it my old boss always used to say? 'Don't go holding me responsible for the fact that the world is full of nonsense. Believe me, even if you can manage to understand different points of view, that won't get rid of them.' He was a wise old bird, was my boss.

"As I told you, it all revolves round the second of September. Three years later to the day, on the second of September, Pieterlen was sent, as insane, from the prison to the psychiatric clinic of the canton where he had been sentenced. Before the trial he had told me he hoped to get away with three years, and I hoped so too. The conclusion in my report was manslaughter committed while emotionally disturbed. And three years later . . . Another doctor wrote the initial assessment, but I was still involved. Yes, I had become Pierre Pieterlen's legal guardian, I was the Dr L. he had written to from R. Prison."

"And today is the second of September," said Studer.

"Five and three is eight plus one year on remand. He's been locked up for nine years."

Studer sat there, leaning forward, his forearms on his thighs. He glanced up at Laduner's face and was surprised to see that the mask had fallen. Sitting in the chair was a youthful-looking man with soft lips and a voice that neither sounded like "Battalion – you will take your orders from me," nor recalled the tone of "My dear girl". The look on his face was gentle, the curve of his lips soft, his voice warm.

The change was even more pronounced when the door opened and Kasperli came in to say good night. He shook hands with Studer as well.

Then it was quiet in the room again. The cigarette smoke curled up under the parchment shade and billowed out of the top, like smoke from a chimney.

Laduner said, "At first Pieterlen had to work as a carpenter in the prison; he made coffins in his cell. Don't imagine I'm making all this up, I can show it you in the files. After he had spent a year all alone in his cell making coffins, he was allowed to sew buttons and buttonholes on army coats. For two whole years. Then . . ."

Laduner searched in the file for a document, then read it out in the same gentle voice: "Prison report no. 76: Pieterlen . . . striking changes in his behaviour: he has suddenly started carrying out tasks, which he has previously performed satisfactorily, in a negligent manner, the results being unusable, for example, he

94

sewed buttonholes on the right-hand side of coats, instead of the left, and made parts of articles of clothing with the reverse side of the cloth, which is clearly different, on the outside. In response to complaints, he said he would alter the clothes, but did them again with the same mistakes. In the evening he made his bed underneath the table where he worked and slept there . . ."

A rustle of paper. Laduner lit a cigarette from the one he had just finished, stood up, went over to the window and looked out into the night, which lay, heavy and sultry, over the land.

"He crawled away to hide, he sewed buttonholes in the wrong place . . . after three years – the second of September again. Believe me, Studer, I'm not particularly soft-hearted, but this Pierre Pieterlen he's . . . he's a classic case." Laduner made an unsuccessful attempt at a laugh.

Studer listened, listened carefully. If he were honest, it wasn't the story of Pierre Pieterlen that interested him so much as the tone in which it was told.

"How long have you been in harness, Studer? Twenty years? Yes? Well, you'll be looking forward to your pension soon. But in those twenty years you'll have read lots of files, won't you? Written lots of reports? And all this time you'll have been wondering, Studer, wondering why I'm being so open with you, wondering why I invited you to stay with us. Admit it, you found it rather odd, didn't you? But I've followed your career, I've heard about the struggle you had with Colonel Caplaun, and I've also read five of your reports, all on the same case. The case is neither here nor there, but I was struck by the reports, by their tone, it was different from that of your colleagues. There was something that crept in between the set formulae of official phraseology. It sounded as if you were always trying to understand, and once you'd understood, you wanted the reader to understand. Am I making myself clear? That's why I'm telling you about Pierre Pieterlen, because I think he's a classic case, and because I know you won't laugh at me. Years ago people could quite justifiably laugh at me, and my old boss did so, he laughed me to scorn when I wrote that first report. And he was right. You see, I had this idea I could get the gentlemen who sit in judgement to understand something, but all that counts for them is . . ."

Laduner picked up a sheet of paper and read out, "The accused has been found guilty of murder as defined in paragraph 130 of the Swiss Penal Code in that on the second of September 1923 in his apartment in Wülflingen he did, wilfully and with malice aforethought, unlawfully kill his child, that had been born live to his spouse, Klara Pieterlen, by placing a towel over its face, pressing it down with his hand and strangling it with his hands, thereby causing it to die of asphyxiation . . ."

The document fluttered to the floor. Studer picked it up and put it on the table. Laduner went out and spoke to his wife, then came back and asked, standing in the doorway, "Red or white?"

"White," Studer growled without looking up. He knew he was being impolite, but he couldn't help it.

"Getting sleepy, Studer?" Laduner asked as he poured the wine. He clinked glasses with the sergeant, his thoughts clearly elsewhere. He didn't wait for Studer to reply, but started walking up and down between the plain desk and the other corner of the room, where the bookcase was.

"Pieterlen was a conductor on the Lötscher mountain railway, his wife a waitress in Sitten. They'd known each other for four years when they decided to get married. But Pieterlen lost his job. He'd had the flu. When he felt better, he went out dancing with his fiancée, was seen by some of his workmates, they told on him and he was fired. He wasn't popular with his colleagues, Pieterlen, they said he was arrogant. After that he went to an industrial town in eastern Switzerland and worked as a labourer in an engineering works. They got married four weeks before the child was born . . .

"I've got two children. Pieterlen hadn't wanted a child. He said it loud and clear. He told the district prosecutor; he told me. 'Wilfully and with malice aforethought'. A splendid ring to it, don't you agree?

"Nineteen hundred and twenty-three. Five years after the war. How many people died in the war? Do you know? Ten or twelve million, something like that? So Pieterlen didn't want to bring a child into the world. Not for ideological reasons, though Pieterlen had read all sorts of books . . . Reading can make you arrogant, and Pieterlen was arrogant. His workmates said that, and so did his superiors. If they read at all, his workmates read the tabloids, not even detective stories, and they played *jass*. But Pieterlen read Schopenhauer and Nietzsche, and thought about things, about the world and mankind. He did drawings in his free time . . . He was learning English, French he spoke well already; his father originally came from Biel, though he later became a dairyman in the Oberland. He never knew his mother, she died when he was born.

"Pieterlen didn't want to bring a child into the world, because as a labourer he earned too little. He'd rented a room-plus-kitchen in Wülflingen because accommodation was cheaper out in the village than in the town. As a labourer he earned a good deal less than one franc an hour . . .

"You'll object that there are any number of labourers who don't earn any more than that and still have a wife and children. You'll object that things are even worse in the other countries around us. We've got welfare bureaux and poor-relief officers and marriage-guidance counsellors and rehabilitation centres for alcoholics and homes for the physically and mentally handicapped and hostels and clinics and workhouses and orphanages. We're very humane. We have trial by jury and a supreme court, even the League of Nations meets here . . . We're an enlightened country, Studer – so why did a labourer called Pieterlen not want to have a child?

"The simple answer is: because he wasn't normal. It's easy to say. In my report I wrote that . . ."

Laduner picked up a sheet of paper and read from it.

"His action springs from a psychological abnormality. For months he has been labouring under a strong emotion, which, at the crucial point, provided the final impetus for his crime. It would be entirely wrong to call him a criminal type. Rather he is a person with a definite, congenital psychological abnormality, namely a schizoid psychopathy. It would not be in the least surprising if at some later date it turned into a full-blown mental illness, namely schizophrenia."

"Schizophrenia . . ." Studer muttered. "Tell me about it." The words were muffled because he had his chin resting on his hands and his fingers over his mouth.

"Etymologically it means split, being split," said Laduner. "Look at it in geological terms. You have a mountain, it seems calm, solid, it rises up from the plain, it breathes out clouds and brews storms, it's covered in grass and trees in leaf. Then there comes an earthquake. A tremor goes through your mountain, there's a yawning gap, it's split in two, it doesn't look calm and solid any more, it looks terrible, you can see inside it, yes, its insides are suddenly on the outside. Imagine a disaster like that happening in someone's mind. And just as the geologist talks about the causes of the rift in the mountain, so we can talk about the psychological mechanisms that can cause a mind to split. But we are cautious, Studer, and when I say 'we' I mean the few people in our profession who don't think you can solve the mystery of the human mind with a few bastardized Graeco-Latin compounds.

"The mountain, Studer, remember the mountain, its insides suddenly becoming visible. I'll take you round O Ward tomorrow and some things will become clear to you. Among others, the strange embarrassment many people, even the healthiest, feel when confronted with the mentally ill.

"Someone once said the reason for that is that we are literally visiting the subconscious. The subconscious – now you'll be asking me to explain the subconscious to you. All the things we don't allow to come to the surface, the things we push to one side as quickly as possible the moment they attempt to show the slightest sign of life, that's the subconscious. You show me one single person who has never at some time in their life, either as a child or as a grown-up, committed murder in thought, who has never killed someone in their dreams. You won't find a single one. Do you think that otherwise it would be so incredibly easy to get people to go to war? Bring me the kindest of fathers, the most caring of mothers and they would both have to admit, if they were honest, that they had said to themselves, 'How much easier life would be without children.' And not just once, no, many times. But once a child is there, how can you get rid of it without killing it? You have a child, Studer, now come on, tell me true, didn't you often feel it was a burden, a restriction on your liberty? Well?"

Studer grunted. It was an angry grunt. He didn't like being forced into a corner. Of course he'd harboured thoughts like that when his daughter was still little and he'd not been able to sleep at night because the child was crying. Perhaps he'd even said out loud the damned kid could go to hell for all he cared. But from saying something like that to killing a child . . . Although . . .

"They can't arrest us for our thoughts – fortunately," said Laduner, and his smile was sad. "As long as they remain thoughts, wishes we don't give way to, then everything's fine and society is happy.

"A man can write in his books that 'property is theft', and nothing much will happen to him, at least not nowadays. But you just live by that principle and you'd have to arrest yourself, wouldn't you? Try writing in all the newspapers: 'It's madness to bring a child into the world today' and then acting on it. You don't even have to kill a child, just perform an abortion. You'll find yourself with a few years in Thorberg Prison to reflect on what it means to break a law. Pieterlen didn't have the law in mind at all. He just spent months pondering over the fact that a child was coming into the world and he wouldn't be able to bring it up properly on his pay of eighty rappen per hour. He proposed to his wife that they should go to Geneva and . . . but she didn't want to do that. Then one night he comes home – it's after midnight, he's been working overtime – and sees the light on in his apartment . . .

"During the case I went to Wülflingen; it's a tiny village, hills all round, and the house Pieterlen lived in was a little way out of the village. I had to see the room, and I had to see his wife. Of course, I could have got the wife to come to me, but I wanted to see her in the environment where she had lived for four weeks with Pieterlen. I wanted to see the lamp, the lamp that . . ."

Laduner scrabbled among the papers until he found the one he was looking for. Holding it by the lower edge, he tapped it twice, briefly, and read out: "Frau Pieterlen could not see into the basket, there was paper wrapped around the light, which had been pulled down to the floor, so it was very dark in the room. Afterwards he took a shovel and buried the child in the woods. To make sure he was not burying it alive, he tied a cord round its neck. His wife knew nothing of all this . . ."

Silence.

Studer stared at the lampshade. He was grasping the arms of his chair tightly with both hands. He felt the same as he had the time he had flown over the Alps: the plane went into a dive, unstoppable, and he got a funny feeling in his stomach, nothing was firm any more, everything was shaky. During that experience, too, he had clung on desperately with both hands, even though he knew it would make no difference. And now . . .

Letters typed on white paper . . . Words, words, sentences . . . A man reading out the words and sentences until the room appeared, and the woman in bed, and the lamp with the long flex, and Pierre Pieterlen, who had murdered a child, "wilfully and with malice aforethought".

"His wife was in his power," Laduner read on in a monotonous voice, yet with such strange emphasis it made Studer wonder. "He had such a strong influence over her that she never tried to oppose him. She agreed not to call in a midwife or an obstetrician . . ."

Laduner cleared his throat. Studer was distracted and a few sentences passed unheeded before he heard the doctor say, " . . . to suffocate it. It only made a little sound and he did not think it could have been heard by his wife, because it was muffled by the towel . . . He showed her the child without her being able to see whether it was a boy or a girl. In fact, it was a girl, born live . . ."

Laduner put the document back in the file, stood it on end and tapped it on the table to arrange the papers, then carefully replaced it on the table, adjusting it until the edge of the file ran parallel to the edge of the table. Putting his hand over his eyes, he continued.

"The room . . . A double bed. The plaster grubby, crumbling in places. Three chairs; a table and a lurid green cloth with fringes . . . The woman looked weary. Of course, she'd been arrested as well, but then she'd been released since her husband had taken everything on himself. A simple woman, disturbed. She didn't look me in the eye even once. Among other things, she said that her husband had only really been happy with her, mostly he kept himself to himself, he hadn't had any friends. 'Such an educated man,' she said. When I left, I knew that the woman had been in agreement with the murder. She made that pretty clear – to me. In court she denied everything. She said, 'My husband had me in his power . . . '

"What would you have done, Studer? Put it in the report? Made another person unhappy? I know that my eminent colleague, for example – the one who looks like Albert Bassermann when he played the mysterious doctor in that film – is always ready to support the judicial authorities, to say what they want to hear. Doctor and judge rolled into one. Fine, if you can double up like that. I can't. I'm a modest man, Studer – though if I tell you I'm modest then it's a sign that I'm not really. But I still believe a cobbler should stick to his last. I'm a doctor, a head doctor as people sometimes call us with a somewhat mocking smile, they think we're a bit funny with all our long words. But that's beside the point . . ."

All of a sudden Laduner got up. He wasn't wearing a jacket, so as he faced Studer, arms akimbo, his hands stood out dark and brown against the white of his shirt.

"Before I go on, let me point out that we have three cases of chronic alcoholism in the clinic. One, a man in his forties now, lost his job because of his drinking. He's fathered seven children, all of them living; the state has to provide for his wife and children, the state has to pay to keep the man here. Second case: a labourer earning the aforementioned eighty rappen per hour. Since he wanted his share of what we nowadays call life – a place to call home, a wife who was part of it – he got married. You can't do much on eighty rappen an hour, but he led an orderly life at first, his wife too. Three children. Not enough money. The man went out drinking, the woman took in washing. Two more children. Rotgut schnapps is cheapest, twenty rappen a glass – you can't expect a man like that to drink blanc de Vaud at five francs a bottle, can you? The man had a home, but the burden became too great, he wanted to forget. Can you force people to face up to their misery all the time? I don't know. The gentlemen from the welfare services are convinced you can, but then that's what they're paid for. As for myself, I'm not so sure. But cheap schnapps is not a healthy drink, it can produce a splendid delirium tremens, and that's what it did. The result? The man's in here, the woman gets a small allowance from the local council, the children are placed with foster parents. And the third case is even more tragic . . . We'll not go into that, however, it would just be a repeat of the other two. Suffice to say it involves three children. The council – the taxpayer – looks after them. Tot them all up, Studer: seven children in the first case, five in the second, three in the third. That makes fifteen children, all of whom have to be provided for. Plus six adults . . .

"And Pierre Pieterlen was sentenced to ten years hard labour because 'he did, wilfully and with malice aforethought, unlawfully kill his child that had been born live to his spouse, Klara Pieterlen, by placing a towel over its face, pressing it down with his hand and strangling it with his hands, thereby causing it to die of asphyxiation . . . '"

Laduner smoothed his hair with his hand, pressing the recalcitrant strand down on the back of his head, but it just sprang up into a heron's crest once more.

"I know, I know, Studer," he said, after a while, "they're just idle thoughts, we're not going to change the administration of justice, we're not going to change people, but perhaps we can make some adjustments to circumstances. With schizoid personalities in particular – and I include Pieterlen in that group, although I have to admit that the term is an equivocation, a mental convenience – with schizoid personalities there is the possibility that the illness will never fully develop. Imponderables . . ."

Studer smiled. That is, factors you can't precisely gauge, he thought to himself.

" . . . play a significant part in that. What I call imponderables most people usually call fate. If the man had been in reasonable circumstances, if he'd had a decent income, no one might have noticed anything odd about him. He might perhaps have become pedantic, a bit of an eccentric who collected postage stamps or ideologies, it's impossible to say for sure. What we do know for sure is that he got married, or, to put it in more cautious terms, he found a woman to help him escape from his loneliness. His wife did say, you'll remember, that he kept himself very much to himself, except when he was with her . . . Loneliness, Studer, loneliness!"

Was it surprising that Studer's thoughts went to the apartment that he'd been to look at on the floor below? There, too, the loneliness had been almost palpable, the loneliness of an old man abandoned by his children.

"Loneliness," Laduner repeated for the third time. "Labourers on eighty rappen an hour can experience it just as much as those on a comfortable salary, and it's just as much of a torment . . . Pieterlen felt he was faced with a moral dilemma. With eighty rappen an hour, was it right for him to bring a child into the world? People in a well-paid position will point out that in the old days he would only have been getting thirty rappen an hour, and people then were happy with that. That's all well and good, but we're not living in the old days. It's not our fault if our expectations are higher today. And Pieterlen wasn't suited to the role of a labourer with eighty rappen an hour and a large family. Perhaps he wasn't suited to the role of father at all. If, consequently, he believed he had the right to kill his child, then it was an act that, although difficult to comprehend and horrifying, was determined by certain facts: the fact that Pieterlen had a particular personality, that he had acquired a twisted philosophy from reading books, that he was incapable of conforming to the rules of society and looking for a less tragic way out of his dilemma.

"What you must understand, Studer, is that I have been moved by the things that have happened to this man. Despite his schizoid personality, which, in my diagnostic wisdom, I recognized, Pieterlen was a decent fellow. And when he asked me to be his guardian, I agreed. Perhaps one of the reasons was that I could not for the life of me understand why a deed with a perfectly obvious explanation, which, unless I was completely wrong, ought to make sense to the legal mind, even when expounded by someone of my limited intellectual capacity – why such a deed (you remember: his wife in bed, the light with paper wrapped round it, pulled down to the floor, the towel) – why such a deed, which only took a few minutes, must be atoned for by being locked up in a six-by-ten-foot cell for ten whole years . . . A certain sense of balance within me refuses to accept that. The punishment end of the scale sinks down, while the end with the crime shoots up in the air. A punishment for what? For killing the child he himself had fathered, perhaps because he was afraid of the responsibility? Because he thought more of himself and his own well-being than of his offspring? But – if you'll allow me the question, Studer – what about a drunkard who beats his child up so badly that it dies? That's not murder, committed wilfully and with malice aforethought, but grievous bodily harm with fatal consequences. Isn't that so? A maximum of two years in prison. But the child the drunkard beat to death already had feelings, felt pain, was frightened, suffered. God knows, if a person like that was put behind bars for ten years or life I'd have no objections. You will probably argue that the man is a victim of his personality and background, but it's an argument that leaves me cold. We don't want to start getting sentimental. Anyway, I've come to terms with the Pieterlen case, you can believe me ... Until this evening, that is, and now everything's coming out again ...

"You read that second initial assessment? Well, Pieterlen arrived here two months later because he had been declared incurable and was being shunted back to his home canton. I saw him during my evening rounds the day he arrived. It was a scene I'll never forget. He recognized me, but he didn't say hello. There was a frozen smile on his lips. He was sitting on a bench in the long corridor of O Ward – the day room hadn't been built then – staring into space, when I suddenly appeared before him. He stood up, put his hands behind his back and gave me a ceremonial bow. He looked in a bad way. The next day I examined him. His lungs were a bit the worse for wear, nothing serious. For three days he didn't say a word to anyone, he just sat in a corner, looking through magazines or staring at the floor. And when I came by on my rounds he stood up, hands behind his back, to bow to me. On the third day he had an argument with a warder, he became incredibly abusive. I think it was about a pair of socks that didn't fit. The next morning – they're particularly touchy at that time of the day – he smashed a window. I had him transferred to D. During the night he was so agitated he had to be put in the bath. We don't use straitjackets, as you know, so what else can we do with with someone who is worked up? Warm water is calming. Two nurses were left on watch – and they knew I keep a sharp lookout for bruises. That's always the first thing I check up on when I do my rounds in the morning and I know that an

107

overexcited patient has had to spend the night in the bath.

"Another digression, Studer. I'm sorry, but it's necessary. Have you ever thought about this? We or, to be more precise, I, can describe the mental state of a murderer at the time of the murder in a report, I can analyse his motives, his emotions, the mechanisms . . . Fine . . . And I know, as I've told you, that we are all murderers in our dreams, in our thoughts, but there is something holding us back, we don't actually go from thought to deed. But what happens if we do cross the barrier and become murderers? Does the act have such an effect on the murderer that his whole outlook on life collapses? I'm not talking about murder committed under orders here . . ."

Again there was the strange emphasis, just as when he had read out "his wife was in his power", but Laduner went on quickly, as if he wanted to blur something.

" . . . as in war or during a revolution. In those cases it is the leader, whoever he is, who bears the whole responsibility. What I'm talking about is the one-off murder, a murder committed under the influence of some strong emotion. Don't you think that after the deed the murderer thinks, feels, acts, sees, hears differently from before it? Unless there is remorse, which is a rarer response than people generally think. It's on a different plane, on the religious plane, if you like, and today religious people are as rare as people with a sense of responsibility. What passes for religion is at best, as I told you all those years ago in Vienna, something like cod-liver oil. It's supposed to strengthen us, but it's unpleasant to take and it doesn't help much. Nausea is definitely the dominant effect and the nausea is stronger than the positive effect on our health.

"Someone's whole outlook on life collapsing! When we discuss schizophrenics, we talk of an apocalyptic mood. The mountain splitting open, a disaster for the mountain world . . . a murder, a disaster for the whole of humanity. We psychiatrists assume – and everything seems to point to this being correct – that schizophrenia has an organic origin. A disorder of the glandular system, to put it in layman's terms. Can't be diagnosed in the early stages, at best just the predisposition. The most we can do, as in the Pieterlen case, is to say that a mental illness is likely to occur later on. No more than that. But if we're so ingenious, then we ought to be able to get the legal gentlemen to understand that in a case such as Pieterlen's they're not dealing with a criminal, but with a sick man; that Pieterlen killed his child for reasons that we can just, if only just, understand psychologically, but that show that the barrier I mentioned was not there.

"Well, I did try to get the public prosecutor to understand. So it was the public prosecutor's fault, at least to some extent, that Pieterlen was handed over to us in such a sorry state. Pieterlen the child murderer had fled to a realm where I could not follow him. You see, my metaphor is not entirely accurate. With schizophrenia we don't always think of a mountain that has been split open, sometimes we think of a pond that is fed by a spring within it, but has no supply from outside. Sometimes it looks like flight to an alien realm, and we are left knocking at the gates (very poetic, don't you think, Studer?), and sometimes it looks like a common-or-garden obsession, and we start thinking about the witch trials of the Middle Ages and the Franciscans' exorcisms, and we wish we had a herd of swine handy so we could cast out the evil spirits into them.

"In Pieterlen's case the symptoms were pretty extreme: stiffness of facial expression, of gesture, of affective rapport, if you understand what that is. It meant that the bridge between him and me was broken, and not only between him and me but between Pieterlen and the whole of the outside world. What there was instead of the outside world I can only guess at. There were coffins there, his child was there, the prosecutor was there – Pieterlen said there was a smell of brilliantine – quotations from books emerged . . . But all of this didn't exist like memories, which we are able to keep at a distance; for him this past was present, it was there, it spoke to him, it was alive: a nurse could became the prosecutor, and Pieterlen would fly into a rage, a patient could become his wife, and Pieterlen would caress him. And sometimes the devil was there, a very literary devil, not unlike Goethe's Mephistopheles, and Pieterlen resisted the devil's suggestions, and sometimes he listened to them, rapt, like a saint in an ecstatic trance. There was no order there, it was illness . . . I'm a doctor; it was not my business what would be done with Pieterlen if I could cure him. My sole concern as a doctor, and I say this in all humility, was to bring Pieterlen back from the realm he had fled to and silence the voices that were tormenting him . . .

"A course of so-called sleep treatment seemed indicated. There were things that spoke against it, but I still decided to try. I stuffed him full of sleeping pills, which put him into narcosis for ten days. The idea was to stop the images running through his mind, the voices. I wanted to drown the images in sleep. Talking to you, I'm putting things in quite simple terms; if colleagues were to hear me talk like this, they'd find it funny. The only one who might not grin would be my old boss. He looked like an elderly gnome with a long white beard and his arms were so long that when he bent a little as he walked, his hands knocked against his knees.

"During this long narcosis – Jutzeler helped me, you know, the staff nurse in O Ward, none of the others would have been capable of it, conditions in the clinic in those days were as chaotic as before the earth was divided from the waters – during the narcosis Pieterlen lost weight. That was to be expected. When he woke after ten days of sleep he spat in Jutzeler's face and bit my hand. Not a serious bite, he was too weak. . . . Jutzeler had to be there all day to look after him, to play with him, to go for walks with him, to encourage him to draw. I had great hopes of his drawing. A mind like that, returning from another realm, surfacing again, it's like a retarded duckling, you want to give it swimming lessons . . .

"To put it briefly. it was a fiasco. I tried to fatten him up. He went on hunger strike. Force-feeding, a tedious business. I thought he was going to die on me."

A sigh. A match flared. Laduner took a long pull on his cigarette.

"Then, suddenly, he started to eat like a horse, stopped coughing and put on weight, over a stone in ten days. His favourite occupation was smashing windows. Perhaps in his disturbed state of mind he imagined he could get rid of the glass wall separating him from things and people. And the voices continued to torment him. He had a whole repertoire of bizarre, obscene nicknames, all of which referred to the public prosecutor, whom I had the dubious honour of representing.

"After three weeks Pieterlen was glistening with fat and, despite all precautions, the bill for repairing

111

windows was still rising. The carpenter who fixes windows for us here was spending all his time in O. So I tried another course of sleep. I didn't want to put Pieterlen in the bath; actually I was quite pleased he was smashing windows. At least he was doing something, even if it was destructive. How can you go about rebuilding, Studer, if you don't destroy things first? Window-panes or other obstacles?

"And the sleep treatment worked. He woke up and looked round, like Tannhäuser emerging from the Venusberg, but it was a real awakening, and he stayed awake. That was four years ago.

"I see that my psychiatric disquisition has not had too soporific an effect, Studer, so I will permit myself another little digression: a murderer has been found guilty by a number of 'good men and true', who have sworn on their honour to give a fair judgement, and condemned to ten years hard labour. Fine. In prison the aforementioned murderer goes mad. In these humane times a sick man isn't punished any more. He's handed over to us and we make him well again, if our psychiatric skills are up to it. Make him well? Let's say we try to straighten him out. So he's put into our power, the power of the much-maligned psychiatrists. In prison he really has gone mad, so it's no longer the case that he might go mad. The verdict has been quashed. Fine. We decried psychiatrists believe that he is resocialized, that is, he could be released; the probability of him committing a similar crime – in this case infanticide – is, let's say, one per cent. But we are not allowed to release the man. We cannot make a formal application for him to be released until the time is up that he would have spent in prison. We have to keep him here until then. Logical, yes?

"Now you're going to object . . ."

Studer had no intention of making any kind of objection whatsoever. He was still clutching the arms of his chair and his only thought was, when are we going to come out of the dive? But he clenched his teeth and clung on bravely; he felt sick.

"You're going to object that there are cases more deserving than murderers who are in prison for killing a child. Agreed. We don't help everyone who deserves it. It's not our fault, we do what we can, it's the circumstances that are beyond us, the circumstances – or should I say the authorities? You can't hold me responsible for the fact that the world isn't ruled by logic . . .

"What I did was to try and make things easier for Pieterlen. He was allowed to draw, I talked with him a lot, sometimes I invited him up here to my apartment, I lent him books. When he asked to be allowed to work – that was after last year's New Year dance – and said he would like to join the decorating unit, I gave my permission, even though I knew why he wanted to join that particular unit. Pierre Pieterlen, the classic case, had fallen in love. Yes . . . And even though I did not approve of his taste – I believe you've already made the acquaintance of Nurse Wasem, so you'll understand why – despite all that, I thought it would do him good, he wouldn't run off into his dark realm any more, the mountain wouldn't split open again.

"It was touching, it really was. I was kept informed, of course, rules are rules. The nurse in charge of the decorating unit duly reported to me, the staff nurse in the female O Ward turned a blind eye and the idyll went on its merry way. And why shouldn't we have an idyll within these red walls, once in a while? Of course, there were some people who complained. 'Laduner's encouraging immorality,' that kind of thing. It was narrow-minded people who said things like that, especially those our Gallic colleague calls 'oly Joes. On Sundays Pieterlen was allowed to go out for a walk with a nurse. I usually sent Gilgen, you know him, the jolly one with the red hair . . ."

Studer's voice was a little hoarse when he interrupted the flow of words with, "I should say I do."

Laduner looked at his watch. "It's late. Time for bed?" He yawned.

Studer asked, "I presume Pieterlen was jealous of the Director?"

"Clearly. Pieterlen's wife had obtained a divorce while he was in prison. It was his first love affair since his illness."

Silence again. Then Laduner said, almost as an afterthought, "Perhaps now you can understand why I haven't officially reported Pieterlen missing so far. But I'll do it tomorrow. Tomorrow? Today, to be exact . . . It's one o'clock. Shall we close the meeting, Studer? Unless there's something else you want?"

Studer cleared his throat. His stomach still didn't feel quite right. The dive! He tried to answer in as matter-of-fact a voice as possible, but didn't quite manage it.

"Yes, Herr Doktor . . . I wouldn't mind a kirsch."

114

Reflections

Back in his room, Studer switched on the bedside light and sat down at the window. The courtyard was black and quiet. Perhaps the arc lamps had been on the previous night in honour of the harvest festival. From time to time a tiny moon peeped out from behind the clouds, then disappeared again, but even when it was there its light was so weak it was hardly worth mentioning.

He could feel the fire of the kirsch in his stomach. Studer had drunk three glasses and now he was wide awake. Strangely enough, though, he didn't feel like smoking. He wanted to think, to think clearly. But isn't it always the case that when you specifically require your mind to think clearly, your thoughts are vague, hazy and very, very disjointed? . . .

The situation had changed markedly since the morning, of that there was no doubt. It was all very well for Dr Laduner to talk of an accident. Sure-ly, as he would say, a murder in the clinic would cause an outrage, especially if it could be connected with Pieterlen, the classic case . . . But didn't everything seem to point to Pieterlen? The grey square of cloth underneath his mattress, the sandbag made of the same material, his escape just before the moment when cries for help had been heard . . . And then his motive! Jealousy. A powerful motive . . .

Cherchez la femme. It was an old rule for detectives and not even Dr Locard from Lyon had dared to mock it.

115

Dr Locard, his old mentor, who, in a memorable article, had cast doubt on the reliability of all witness statements . . .

Pieterlen, then? Let's assume it was Pieterlen . . . though he had nothing to gain from the murder . . . Perhaps it would be a good idea to think back to the reformatory in Oberhollabrunn where he had first become acquainted with Dr Laduner . . .

In particular to think back to that memorable scene in which one boy had gone for another with a knife in his hand and Dr Laduner had played the interested spectator . . . What had Eichhorn's rule been? The resentment must be allowed to play itself out. All well and good, as long as a murder wasn't committed. Dr Laduner could go on at great length giving reasonable psychological explanations for the murder of a child, so reasonable it made you feel queasy, just as if you were flying over the Alps . . .

But the murder of an old man who had perhaps come to a rendezvous all unsuspecting – didn't that put the matter in a somewhat different light? And what had been the point of Laduner's long lecture. He had got carried away, sure-ly, it hadn't all been an act, he had become fond of Pieterlen, you could feel that, but still, you don't go on at a detective sergeant for three hours without some kind of ulterior motive. That's the way people are – especially people as complex as Dr Laduner – they never have just one single motive for the things they do. A young examining magistrate might be stupid enough to imagine that, or a prosecutor like the one in Pieterlen's story, but not a sensible person such as, for example, an old detective. Of course, he might look naive, sure-ly, but he'd been around enough, he'd got to know about people. Now all that about the subconscious, there was a lot to it, though he wouldn't have been able to formulate it like that . . . But then the attack . . . An attack, yes, that's what it was. "Haven't we all at some time murdered a child in our dreams?" Oh brilliant! Very clever, this Dr Laduner . . .

Into line! he commanded his thoughts . . . Pieterlen the murderer? Only one fact spoke against that: the telephone conversation. Pieterlen couldn't have rung up at ten since he was at the harvest festival and it had been established that the call came from inside the clinic. That staff nurse from O Ward – what was his name now? All the memorizing during the afternoon hadn't been much use, he still had to consult his note-book – Jutzeler! Jutzeler, who had waylaid the Director at half past twelve, he was ruled out, too. He was the one who had answered the phone, so he couldn't have been talking at the other end at the same time. What was pretty clear from the witness statements was that the Director had gone to fetch the file to talk to someone . . .

The file? . . . That had disappeared, just as the wallet with the 1,200 francs had disappeared . . . Why had Gilgen (funny how he could remember that name without difficulty), why had Gilgen had such a worried look on his face? Why had he come to see Studer? It had been pointless, really, Gilgen must have known the sergeant's influence was minimal . . . Had Gilgen been at the harvest festival? Had there been something in the file that could endanger someone?

Gilgen, the redhead. The one person he had liked from the very start. What he felt for him was nothing at all like the somewhat tentative attraction he felt towards Dr Laduner. It was more like one of those friendships between men that are so strong because they cannot be explained. These things exist, it's

117

difficult to asses them objectively . . . Gilgen . . . Right, Gilgen was a trail he had to follow up. But in that case he would have to start by clearing up Pieterlen's escape, that was essential . . . Bohnenblust, the asthmatic nightwatchman with the wheezing lung was on duty now, a chat with him seemed advisable . . .

And then there was the fear in Dr Laduner's eyes. In the morning it had been pretty clear to see, this evening it seemed to have vanished . . . But there was that long lecture on Pieterlen . . . Suspicious . . .

"Are you asleep, Studer?" Dr Laduner's voice came from outside the door.

Not replying was impossible, the light was on.

"No, Herr Doktor," Studer replied in a friendly tone.

"Do you want a sedative?"

Studer had never taken a sedative in his life, so he said thank you, but no. At this Dr Laduner said the bathroom was free, if Studer wanted a bath, now or in the morning, he should go ahead . . . And Studer thanked him once again. Dr Laduner clattered around in the neighbouring room for a time, then his steps retreated, for a while his voice could be heard in the distance, presumably he was telling his wife something . . . No wonder after a day like this.

Plaisir d'amour ne dure qu'un moment . . .

Why had the song come back to mind? To get rid of it, Studer started to unlace his boots, but then a sentence from Laduner's lecture on Pieterlen, the classic case, occurred to him, a sentence the doctor had spoken with a strange emphasis: "His wife was in his power . . ."

Studer tried to repeat the words the way Laduner had spoken them. He had put the stress on "power".

118

Power! To have someone in your power. Who? . . . Dr
Laduner had had Pieterlen in his power. Anyone else?

Then the blond young man appeared in his mind's
eye. He was lying on the couch and the tears were
pouring down his cheeks. At his head sat Dr Laduner,
smoking . . .

Analysis . . . Fine. He'd heard of that method of
healing minds. But it was all very vague, and above all
rather embarrassing. Embarrassing, certainly! They
cured the sick – no, the neurotics, that was the word!
Studer straightened up.

They cured them by exploring their dreams and all
kinds of obscene stuff came out. Studer's friend
Münch, a lawyer, had a book about the method. There
were all sorts of things in it you wouldn't even talk
about on an evening out with the boys – and what was
said then was definitely not for sensitive ears . . . So
that was analysis . . . The real name was different,
though, there was another word that went with it . . .
psychoanalysis, that was it! Psychoanalysis, if they
insisted, every profession had its own jargon. In criminology they talked of poroscopy, and no outsider had
any idea what it meant – and in Witzwil Labour Camp
they called the warders "screws". That's the way it was,
every profession had its own jargon, and psychologists
talked of schizophrenia, psychopathy, anxiety neurosis
and psycho . . . psycho . . . psychoanalysis. That's
right . . .

But now it was time he was on his way. He put on a
pair of close-fitting leather slippers, which he kept on
tight with a rubber band across the instep, and put the
light out.

Glancing out of the window he saw a light moving
across the courtyard. He peered through the dark
and saw that it was a man in a white apron waving a

119

stable lamp. Obviously a nightwatchman doing his rounds.

Sergeant Studer slipped out on his own rounds. It seemed as if very quiet accordion music was trickling down through the ceiling, but he ignored it.

Conversation with the nightwatchman

Sometimes a block of the parquet floor creaked in one of the long corridors. Then it went quiet again. A lock snapped shut. He went past doors that were so silent you would have thought there was a corpse laid out behind them. Then there were others that were loud, snores came through them, words spoken in a dream, a soft cry. Was it Matto spinning his silver threads? It was stuffy, the windows closed, the small square panes imprisoned in the iron bars. Another floor that creaked, another lock that snapped shut ... A long corridor, an eternity ... Stairs, a short corridor ... Now there was a shimmer of blue light coming through a keyhole. A door handle. Carefully Studer pushed the passkey into the keyhole, feeling with the wards, like a burglar who wants to avoid making noise ... The wards engaged and carefully – carefully! – Studer turned the key, concentrating so hard on not making a noise that he sucked the skin of his cheeks in between his teeth. At the back of his mind was the thought of Dr Laduner wanting to be covered by the police – the police, whose representative was at that moment making his furtive way round the sleeping clinic ...

The dormitory. In the middle of the ceiling was a bulb swathed in blue paper, spreading blue light over the white beds and transforming the sleeping faces into those of drowned men. It stank: of bodies, of medicaments – and of floor polish, of course.

A few more steps. There was the projecting wall. Bohnenblust, the nightwatchman, was sitting at his little table in the cubby-hole, his head against the wall, his eyes half closed and his moustache undulating like water-weed on the bottom of a stream.

Studer had come across many types of startled response: The shoplifter as you gently grasp her arm with a quiet, "Come with me, please, Fräulein." The tears appear in the corners of her eyes and roll down, drawing tracks across her powdered cheeks ... The shock of the man as you place your hand on his shoulder in the street. "Come along with me now, and don't give any trouble." His eyes open wide, his lips are pale and thin. You can tell his mouth is dry, his throat too; he'd like to cry out, but can't. Then there is the startled surprise of the swindler you wake from a deep sleep. His hands are trembling so much it takes him five minutes to tie his tie – and even then it's not straight ...

But the nightwatchman's shock at Studer's sudden appearance was completely different. For a moment the sergeant was afraid the man was going to have a stroke. His face flushed deep purple, his eyes were bloodshot and his lungs produced a wheezing noise. He tried to stand up, then sank back, leaning his head against the wall again, precisely where there was a large greasy patch. How many hours had the nightwatchman spent with his head resting on that spot?

"Come on, man," said Studer in a friendly voice. Then he was just in time to catch Bohnenblust's hand, which was getting ominously close to a row of bell-pushes. He was about to sound the alarm! "It's me, Sergeant Studer."

"Er ... Yes ... Herr ... Doktor ... Herr ... Sergeant ... Herr ..."

"It's all right to call me Studer."

"Have you come to arrest me, Herr Studer? Because – because it was my fault Pieterlen escaped and murdered the Director?"

Studer was silent. He sat down beside the fat man and gave him a few reassuring pats on the sleeve of his woolly sweater. After a while he said he had no intention of arresting anyone. As far as he knew, the Director's death had been an accident.

"You're only saying that," said Bohnenblust as the purple slowly cleared from his face. "Surely Pieterlen killed the Director, everyone in the clinic says so."

"Who, for example?"

"Weyrauch and Jutzeler and the others on P, T and D wards. And Jutzeler said it was my fault . . ."

Aha, so that was the version going round the clinic, was it? Interesting.

It looked as if old Bohnenblust was going to cry. His eyes went moist, he screwed up his face . . . But the last thing Studer needed was another man in tears; he still couldn't get the fair-haired man on the couch in Dr Laduner's study out of his mind.

"How come it was your fault?"

"I only did what I did all the other nights. Pieterlen slept badly and when he got too restless he came out here and read the newspaper, at this table, with me."

Studer saw that there was a lamp at head height fixed on the wall of the cubby-hole. Its metal shade was arranged in such a way that the light fell only on the table. The rest of the dormitory was bathed in blue murk.

"And then?"

"And then he said, as he did almost every night, 'Hey, Bohnenblust, let me into the day room, I fancy a cigarette.' He liked a smoke, did Pieterlen, and it's forbidden here in the dormitory. So I let him out by that door there; I even gave him a light. Then I locked the door again. Usually he knocked when he'd finished his cigarette; sometimes he smoked another and walked around a bit in the day room. Yesterday it was longer, so I went to see what was going on, and there was no one there."

"And your bruise?" Studer's grin was broad.

"I bashed into something while I was stumbling around in the dark, a door or a wall, I don't know. So that gave me an excuse to say I'd been hit on the head in the side room. The other occupant, Schmocker, had taken a strong sedative; I gave it him at half past eleven."

"But why did you keep quiet about it for so long?"

It was fear of dismissal that had sealed the nightwatchman's lips. His fear was understandable, even though it was groundless. As he explained in a whisper interrupted by the wheezing of his lungs, he had been working at the clinic for almost twenty-five years. As nightwatchman he was better off than the others because he was paid in lieu of board and that made 900 francs a year, which was not to be sneezed at. All the other staff, even those who were married, had to take their meals in the clinic. He didn't have any rent to pay, either, since he was also employed as caretaker at the school in Randlingen.

And yet . . .

Bohnenblust was one of those anxious types who have been on the breadline at some point in their lives – "I started off with sixteen francs a month, and we only got half a day off per week in those days. I once even heard my lad ask his mother who the man was who came to visit now and then" – and are scared the bad times might return. "Now that things are better and I've got something put away in the savings bank, 10,000 francs, Sergeant" – it was certainly more – "I wouldn't want to go back to the old days."

At the same time Bohnenblust was a man with a soft heart who found it impossible to refuse anyone – Pieterlen, for example – anything, all the while living in constant fear of a reprimand, for to him a reprimand spelt disaster. It showed in the way he suddenly started, then sat up, whispered, "I have to clock in," inserted a thin brass rod into the time clock, turned it round, once, twice, five times, shook the clock, held it to his ear to make sure it was going – and the fear, the flicker of fear in his eyes . . .

A man with a soft heart. It always happened when certain men were delegated to guard others. It was impossible to prevent purely human relationships developing between the guards and those they watched over, to stop them addressing each other with the familiar *du* as long as no superior was around, giving each other a helping hand, cigarettes, chocolate. It happened in Thorberg Prison, it happened in Witzwil Labour Camp, it happened in the police cells in Bern, too. And actually it was good that it happened, thought Studer, who had no great opinion of excessive discipline. He had no objection to buying a beer at the station buffet for a convicted criminal he was escorting to prison; one last pleasure, so to speak, before the long loneliness of the cell.

"So you let Pieterlen into the day room. What time was that?"

"Say half past twelve, a quarter to one . . ."

Studer went through the times. At half past twelve the Director had returned from his amorous walk and had gone to his office with Staff Nurse Jutzeler, while Irma Wasem waited in the courtyard. At a quarter past one the Director had come down from his apartment with a folder under his arm. So the folder had been in his apartment. What had it contained? It had disappeared, as had his wallet. That left the devastation in the office. Where did that fit in with everything?

Two women had seen the Director come out of the central block at a quarter past one. Two women and one man – the man was a patient, true, but in this respect certainly a reliable witness – had heard the cry, shortly before half past one.

Had the Director gone back to his office? Had some unknown person attacked and killed him, then dragged the body to the boiler room and thrown it down the ladder? *Chabis!* That couldn't be right. And yet, strangely enough, it was the devastation in the office that had caused Dr Laduner to request a police presence in the person of Sergeant Studer.

Pieterlen disappears at a quarter to one and the cry comes at half past ... time enough. But how had Pieterlen got out of the Observation Ward? The fact that he had been let into the day room explained nothing; there was the door into the corridor, and both the passkey and the triangular key were needed for that. And that still left the door from O Ward out into the courtyard ...

Bohnenblust gave a deep, wheezing sigh, then stood up and crept quietly round the dormitory. In one of the far corners a man was moaning as he dreamt. Studer watched Bohnenblust pick up the blanket that had fallen to the floor, cover the restless sleeper with it and whisper something to him. A man with a soft heart.

The dormitory had twenty-two beds. In each bed a man. The blue light from the ceiling etched patches of black on the stubbly faces. Twenty-two men ... Presumably most of them had families, a wife at home, children or a mother, a brother, sisters ... Their breathing was laboured, some were snoring, and the air was stuffy, rank with the pungency of human bodies. It made no difference that there was a window open, the window with the narrow bars that looked out onto D1.

Twenty-two men!

Suddenly Randlingen Clinic seemed to Studer like a huge spider stretching its web out over all the land around, and the inmates' nearest and dearest were caught in its threads, wriggling but unable to free themselves.

"Where's Father?" – "Father's ill." – "Where's Father ill?" – "In the hospital." And the whispering in the little villages when the wife went to do her shopping: "Her husband's a loony." It was almost worse than if they said, "Her husband's inside."

Twenty-two men! And they were just one small part.

"How many patients are there in the clinic?" Studer asked.

"Eight hundred," Bohnenblust replied. His head was resting against the wall again, on the large greasy mark that bore witness to the strenuous hours of the night shift.

Eight hundred patients! Doctors and nurses were mobilized to care for the sick ... The sick! Outside they weren't thought of as sick. If you were sick, you went into hospital. The lunatic asylum was for mad people. And in the eyes of the vast majority, to be mad was just as compromising as belonging to the Communist Party.

He was paying a visit to the subconscious, said Dr Laduner. He was in Matto's realm, said Schül ...

Studer stared into space, across the beds towards one of the large windows that broke up the wall on the long side of the dormitory. Sometimes a bright light went past outside, followed by another, then a short pause, another light, and another. Studer remembered that the main road must go past on that side. The flashes of light were the car headlights.

The flashing set off two lines of thought in Studer's mind. One was easily explained: it concerned the light he had seen from the window of his room. The light had approached across the courtyard: a man in a white apron carrying a stable lantern. He estimated it would have been at about a quarter to two.

Presumably the nightwatchman would also have done his rounds on the night the Director disappeared. It would certainly be advisable to have a word with him.

There was only a symbolic explanation for the second train of thought, but Studer did not let that worry him. It seemed like a ray of light in the surrounding darkness, and that was sufficient. It concerned the asthmatic nightwatchman. Bohnenblust's reaction when the sergeant suddenly appeared had been completely out of proportion to the trivial nature of his offence. Was there something else behind it? Studer decided to do some probing.

After a lot of questions, after much moaning and groaning, the following facts finally emerged: Bohnenblust had had two passkeys in his possession, one of which he had lost. And he couldn't remember where he had lost it. Nothing like that had ever happened to him in the twenty-five years he had worked at the clinic.

"But even if Pieterlen had found the passkey," Bohnenblust said, "it wouldn't have been any use to him. He'd have to have had the triangular key as well."

128

Studer knew that.

"And if a triangular key had been lost, it would have been reported."

"But you didn't report the loss of your passkey," Studer objected.

"Well, yes, but that's different. And it's just not possible that one of the young warders would have let him have a triangular key. Unless, that is, the warder was in cahoots with Pieterlen." (The fat nightwatchman said "warder" instead of "nurse"; he obviously belonged to the old school.)

"Which of the warders did Pieterlen get on well with?"

"Gilgen! The two of them were always together."

Gilgen! The red-haired nurse who had told the sergeant his troubles. "And you can't remember where you left your passkey?"

The nightwatchman spent so long tugging at his moustache anyone would have thought he was trying to straighten out each hair individually. Eventually he grunted that Schmocker might have something to do with it.

"Schmocker?"

Who was this Schmocker? Oh yes, the man who had threatened to murder a member of the Federal Council. The man who shared a room with Pieterlen.

"And why do you think Schmocker might have something to do with it?"

"You hear things," Bohnenblust said. "The pair of them used to spend half the night in the side room talking. At least, Schmocker did most of the talking. He told Pieterlen that the patients' poor condition was all the Director's fault, and got Pieterlen stirred up. He would have been freed ages ago, Schmocker said, if the Director hadn't been against it. In the end even

Dr Laduner couldn't do anything about it, Pieterlen was convinced the Director was his enemy. And the business with Irma Wasem didn't improve things one bit."

Studer's first attempt at psychotherapy

Studer stood up, squeezed his way out from behind the table and went across to the door to the side room. Seeing a light switch on the outside doorpost, he flicked it; the light went on inside.

He went in.

The would-be assassin's sparse hair was sticking out in all directions and his pink scalp shone through. There were heavy bags under his eyes that hung down almost to the corners of his mouth. They seemed to be filled with poison.

"Herr Schmocker," said Studer in a friendly voice, sitting down on the side of the bed, "could you tell me—"

That was as far as he got. In shrill tones the man screeched, "Get off my bed!"

Obediently Studer stood up. You shouldn't provoke a madman, he thought. Then he waited until the little man had calmed down. "I'd just like to know if it was you who found the nightwatchman's passkey, Herr Schmocker."

"One of those sneaky damn cops, that's what you are. See that you get out of my room, you've no business here. D'you hear?" As he delivered this tirade in his thick Swiss dialect he got up menacingly and stood there, supporting himself with the backs of his knees against the edge of the bed.

"Come now, Herr Schmocker," said Studer, still in friendly tones. The only disturbing thing about this was that he was starting to speak formal German; at least anyone who had ever encountered Studer would have found it a disturbing sign. "I just want to ask you a simple question."

But the would-be assassin continued his vituperation, waving his little clenched fist under Studer's nose, his whitish lips pouring a flood or, rather, a whole cesspit of foul language over the sergeant.

"Silence," commanded Studer.

The man had not the slightest intention of obeying the order. His bare hairy legs, sticking out underneath his nightshirt, were performing a veritable war dance and – yes! – he really was lifting up his right leg to kick Studer in the stomach!

That was going too far! What came next happened too quickly for Bohnenblust, who was standing in the doorway watching, to follow. There was a smack. And another. The modern William Tell was face down on the bed and Studer's hand came down two, three, four times, the smacking sound slightly muffled by the material of Schmocker's nightshirt.

"There we are. That's a good boy." Studer picked up the blanket that had fallen to the floor and tucked Schmocker in. "And now I want an answer. Was it you who took the key?"

The reply came in a whimper, as though from a defiant child. "Ye-e-es."

"Why?"

This time there were sobs of rage. "Because I didn't want to share the room with a murderer!"

"You must be out of your mind," said the astonished Studer, back with his native Swiss. Turning round he saw a smile beneath Bohnenblust's moustache. Then he remembered. Of course! He was in a lunatic asylum! And was surprised that one of the inmates was out of his mind! He had to smile too. Then he went to the door. As he closed it, he heard Schmocker still ranting. "I'm going to take this to the Federal Appeal Court."

"You do that," said Studer, reconciled.

Bohnenblust told him that while the harvest festival had been going on he had sat on Schmocker's bed; it was possible the key had slipped out of his pocket then. It had never happened to him before, but there was no other explanation he could think of.

Studer nodded. So that had been sorted out – though there still remained the question of the triangular key. If he found out where that had come from he would have established that Pieterlen could have left the ward without outside help – and that he would have been able to open the door to the heating plant.

Studer looked up in surprise. Bohnenblust was whispering to him. "We nurses are strictly forbidden to use physical violence on the patients."

Studer nodded reflectively. "I know," he said. And to show that he was au fait with the rules in the clinic, he added that he knew that Dr Laduner kept a sharp lookout for bruises.

In the dormitory the morning light was struggling against the blue gleam of the ceiling bulb. Studer went to the window. There were two lofty firs with pennants of delicate yellow floating out from their tops: scraps of mist aglow with the rays of the rising sun.

It was a quarter to six. Just as Studer was about to ask when the day shift started, Bohnenblust said softly that he was surprised how many deaths there had been again that night.

"Deaths? Deaths where?" the sergeant wanted to know.

"In the two wards for disturbed patients. There were

no deaths the previous two nights, as far as I know, but last week! At least two each night!"

"What did they die of?" Studer asked, at the same time recalling the coffin he had seen on his first morning.

"Well, there is talk of a new treatment Dr Laduner's trying out," said Bohnenblust. "But you never know if there's any truth in that kind of rumour. The staff nurse on D1, Schwertfeger's his name, is very discreet. But it's certainly true that many of the patients are bedridden. And word got round that the Director wasn't happy with the new treatment. He had an argument with Dr Laduner about it."

Just when you thought you'd managed to pin the murder on Pieterlen (the only thing that needed explaining was the male voice on the other end of the telephone), something else cropped up to throw a spanner in the works. It was like a cheap novel. Was he expected to believe some cock-and-bull story about Dr Laduner carrying out treatments that left the patients dead? What nonsense.

But he found he could not just put it out of his mind. After all, it was only the previous evening that he had heard a lecture about a sleep treatment, and he could still hear the doctor's strange remark: "I thought he was going to die on me."

"The day shift comes on at six?" Studer asked.

"Yes." Bohnenblust took his leave. He fetched a bucket, filled it with water, wrung out a cloth, groaning all the time, scrubbed the floor round the bathtubs with a brush, mopped up the water . . .

Then there was the screech of keys in the locks, the slamming of doors, the echo of heavy footsteps. The nursing staff were arriving.

134

The middle door of the dormitory opened, and a squeaky, up-and-down voice said in friendly tones, "Mornin' one and all."

It was the senior nurse, Weyrauch. With uncombed hair and no spectacles, he looked like an obese parrot.

"Ev'rythin' OK, Bohnenblust?" he asked, then, without waiting for an answer, went on, "Hey, it's Sergeant Studer. You up already too? A very good mornin' to you."

Studer mumbled something.

"Let's have the report book, Bohnenblust." With that the senior nurse waddled out of the door.

The scene in the awakening dormitory remained stuck in Studer's mind for a long time: men crawling out of their beds, traipsing over to the wash-basins against the long wall, passing a damp cloth over their faces, yawning as they peered at the windows because they simply could not understand that here was another day, time they had to kill, when they could just as well have lived it . . . At least that was how it seemed to the sergeant.

Following an impulse, Studer went to the dormitory kitchen to see Schül, the *grand blessé de guerre* with his *Légion d'honneur*, his *Médaille Militaire* and pension. He went quietly along the narrow corridor and stopped at the door to the blue-painted room.

Schül was opening a window. There was no bolt on it. Like the door into the corridor, it could only be opened with a triangular key. And Schül had just such a key in his hand, though it was definitely not an official key and in no way resembled the instrument Studer had in his pocket.

"Show me that, Schül," said Studer in a gentle voice.

Schül turned round. Making no objection, he said, "Good morning, Inspector," in a friendly tone, and

135

held out his key to the sergeant with a smile. It was a metal case that had been hammered into shape.

"Did you make a triangular key like that for Pieterlen?"

A look of astonished incredulity. "But of course. He needed one. I've even got a few more . . . er . . . old cartridge cases I found when I was out for a walk."

"Thank you for the poem, Schül. It was very beautiful. So you gave Pieterlen a triangular key? Would you give one to any of the other patients?"

"The others? No! The others are mad – *complètement fous*. But Pieterlen was my friend, so . . ."

"It's all right, I understand, Schül–"

But the friend of the spirit of madness refused to be interrupted. He pointed out of the window. "Over there," he said, "that's where Pieterlen's girlfriend was, and he often used to stand at the window. Sometimes she would come to the window, too, and wave, the woman over there, I mean. And when no nurse happened to be around, I would open the window, and then she would open the window over there."

Of course! "Over there" was the women's O Ward, where Irma Wasem was a nurse. There was a good hundred yards between the two windows, perhaps a bit more . . . An old folk-song came to mind:

> *There were two royal children,*
> *Their love was turned to grief.*
> *They could not come together*
> *The water was too deep.*

No, that wasn't quite right. They weren't two "royal children", for one thing, they were Pieterlen, the classic case, and Nurse Irma Wasem, and secondly there was no water, just a courtyard. Still . . .

"Tell me, Schül, what did Pieterlen look like?"

"Short, shorter than me, stocky, strong. The muscles he had on his arms! He was the only one who really understood me. The others laugh at me because of Matto and because of the murder in Doves' Gorge. But Pieterlen never laughed. *Mon pauvre vieux*, he used to say – he always spoke French to me – I know all about that, I've been in Matto's realm myself . . ."

Yes, that was true. Indeed, Pieterlen had spent a long time in that realm. Why did this all suddenly seem so sad, so hopeless to Studer? Why bring people back from a realm to which they had fled because they could no longer cope with the world as it really was? Why not leave them in peace? If Pieterlen had stayed ill – schizophrenic, to put it in scientific terms – he would never have fallen in love with Irma Wasem, would never have tried to escape, perhaps the Director would still be alive, even.

"Goodbye, Schül," said Studer. His voice was hoarse, he had a large lump in his throat.

"I have to get breakfast ready," said Schül earnestly. It was touching, coming from those scarred lips.

Studer met no one on the stairs. As he was crossing the courtyard in his thin-soled slippers, he caught up with a man with a time clock on a strap, like the one Bohnenblust had.

"Are you the nightwatchman who does the rounds?" Studer asked.

The man nodded eagerly. He was tall, broad and fat. The night shift seemed to be good for putting on fat.

"When you were doing your rounds the night before last, that is Wednesday night, did you notice anything in that corner over there? It would have been around half past one."

The man cleared his throat, gave Studer an odd look and hesitated. He had done his rounds a little later that night, he said eventually; it had been a few minutes after two o'clock when he had passed that corner. And he had seen something. Two men, in the corridor. One of them was Dr Laduner and he was running after the other, at least that was what it had looked like. But with the best will in the world, he couldn't say who the other man had been. There was a door in the basement leading directly outside and the second man had disappeared through it, with Dr Laduner hot on his heels.

Could he swear that it was Dr Laduner?

Could he swear? No. He hadn't been able to see his face, but the man had had his build, his gait. Did the sergeant believe Dr Laduner was guilty of the Director's death?

If there was one thing Studer hated, it was this kind of prying familiarity. Consequently he answered rather sharply, "I believe nothing. Right?" and strode off.

The sky had clouded over. The rays of sunlight on the tops of the pines and the delicate silk scraps of mist had been a delusion.

Studer was glad he managed to get back into Laduner's apartment unseen. It was quiet in the corridor. Everyone was still fast asleep, even the baby, for whose lungs crying was so healthy.

He slipped quietly into the bathroom, gently opened the taps and ran a bath. Then he locked the door, undressed and slid into the hot water.

But if he had hoped the bath would have a stimulating effect, he was sorely mistaken. It took urgent knocking on the door to wake him, and Laduner's concerned voice asking if there was anything wrong with the sergeant.

Studer replied in a husky voice that he had fallen asleep in the bath. Outside he heard Laduner laugh as he told his wife what had happened.

The wallet

The same brightly coloured woollen cosy was on the coffee pot. It was the same table with the same people sitting round it. Studer, at the head of the table, had his back to the window; to his left sat Laduner and to his right the doctor's wife, so that Studer was in a sense presiding over the meal, as he had the previous morning. There was just one difference: the mood. The sunshine was missing.

Outside the large window was a bank of cloud, like a huge concrete wall. The room was filled with grey light and the glow had gone from Frau Laduner's red dressing-gown.

"How did you like the dormitory in its blue, night-time lighting, Studer?" Laduner asked. He was reading the *Bund* and did not look up from his newspaper.

An excellent intelligence service Herr Dr Laduner had! Should he counter by asking him what he had been doing in the basement by the boiler room on the night of the harvest festival? Better not. Better confine himself to the simple remark that a dormitory like that made you think.

"As I looked at all those people locked in, Herr Doktor, I had this image of the clinic as a huge spider crouched there in the middle of the country, and the threads of its web reached even the most out-of-the-way villages. The patients' families are caught in the web and can't escape. The threads are the fates of men and

140

women spun by the spider – I mean the clinic – or Matto, if you prefer . . ."

Laduner looked up from his paper. "You're a poet, Studer, a closet poet. And that might perhaps be a disadvantage in the profession you happen to be engaged in. If you hadn't been a poet, you would have adapted to the real world and that business with Colonel Caplaun would never have happened. But that's the way you are, a poetical detective sergeant."

He'd often thought that himself, Studer said in his unpoetic Swiss dialect. But a poetic bent, now wasn't that connected with the imagination? And imagination wasn't something to be sneered at, was it? Had the Herr Doktor not advised him to try to get inside the minds of various people, to become those people, in a way, and he was doing his best. Now and then it worked. He had, for example, managed to get Schmocker, the would-be assassin, to confess to having stolen a key. It was his poetic bent that was responsible. He'd had this idea, a vague—

"Subconscious," Dr Laduner broke in.

. . . a subconscious feeling, if the Herr Doktor insisted, that the said Schmocker was a coward. He'd just patted him a few times and the man had come clean.

"Psychotherapy!" said Dr Laduner with a laugh. "Sergeant Studer as a psychotherapist! *We're* not allowed a few little 'pats'. *We* have to abide strictly by the rules. Even if our assistants, the nurses, get on our nerves, *we* have to keep calm. We train former butchers, carters, dairymen, cobblers, tailors, bricklayers, gardeners, clerks, we put on courses for them, drum the difference between schizophrenia and manic depression into them and then, once they've passed an exam, we give them a decoration, a white cross on a red background that they wear on the lapel of their coats. That's all we can do. And with the patients? That's where it gets even more difficult. We talk, we try to correct behaviour, we keep struggling with sick minds, we use persuasion. But the mind? It's difficult to grasp. You should see the look of relief on a junior doctor's face when a schizophrenic decides to have bronchitis or a simple angina. At last something they can use tried-and-tested medicines on, at last they can forget the mind for a while and look after the body. Bodies are much easier to treat: aspirin, gargles, cold compresses, the thermometer. But the mind! Sometimes we try to get at the mind through the body, we try treatments–"

"From which the patients sometimes die," Studer interjected, "sometimes two or three in the one night."

He stared at his empty cup, waiting for the comeback.

There was a rustle of newspaper and then the expected riposte came, as crisp and clear as one could wish: "As far as therapeutic measures are concerned, I am not accountable to any layman, but solely to my conscience as a doctor."

Neatly put. His conscience as a doctor. Fair enough. There was nothing you could say to that. Except, perhaps, what Studer said, in his politest, thickest Swiss: "I'd love another cup of coffee, Frau Doktor. An empty stomach gives you some funny ideas."

Frau Laduner laughed till the tears ran down her cheeks and even her husband gave a brief snort. Then he handed the newspaper to Studer, telling him to read that . . . yes, that paragraph there.

The distinguished psychiatrist Dr Ulrich Borstli, for many years the director of Randlingen Psychiatric Clinic, has died

142

as the result of a tragic accident. It is assumed that in the course of his rounds during the night he heard a noise in one of the heating plants and went to investigate. In the dark he must have missed his footing and fell ten feet into the boiler room. He was discovered the next day with a broken neck. Herr Direktor Ulrich Borstli, who never wavered in his zeal and devotion to duty, was . . .

Studer lowered the newspaper and stared into space. He saw the apartment on the floor below, the book open on the desk, the bottle of brandy and the photographs of the children and grandchildren, the large picture of Borstli's first wife.

Loneliness.

The journalists knew nothing of loneliness, all they knew was "zeal and devotion to duty".

Missed his footing in the dark and fell? But the light was on in the boiler room. The light was on! I switched it off myself, Studer thought.

Of course, Dr Laduner couldn't have known about the light being on, just as he knew nothing about the cosh on the landing.

Quietly the sergeant asked, "What did the autopsy show, actually?"

"Nothing special," Dr Laduner replied. "An accident, as I said in my report to the press."

"Then," said Studer, "there's no point in my staying here any longer. The mystery of the Director's disappearance has been solved – and the missing patient will doubtless be found without my help as well."

At these last words Studer raised his head and looked the doctor straight in the eye. Laduner had his smiling mask on again.

"There's no need to take it like that, Studer," he said.

It was meant to sound warm-hearted, but wasn't there an undertone there as well?

"From what has been reported to me," Laduner went on, "you've done an excellent job here. *You've* solved the question of how Pieterlen managed to escape, *you've* found the Director. But it will not have escaped your notice that some things still remain unexplained. I have learnt that a largish sum of money was paid out to the late Director on Wednesday morning. Where has it vanished to? As you will remember, the dead man's pockets were empty. Where did the money go? Did Pieterlen run into the Director? Did he push him down the ladder? That newspaper article, based on information from me, is just to calm things down, a blind. But what really happened? It's up to you to find that out, although it won't bring you any glory. Officially the Director will remain the victim of an unfortunate accident. But I think it wouldn't do any harm, if *we* discovered the truth ... The truth – you know what I'm getting at, Studer – would be of interest ... I mean, purely from a scientific point of view ..."

What Studer would have liked to have said was: "But, Doctor, what has happened to your witty remarks? You're getting in a tangle. You're unsure of yourself. What's the matter? I know, man! You're afraid."

But he kept silent, for he was looking into Dr Laduner's eyes and he saw the expression in them change. True, the mask, the smile was still there, but it was no longer a vague impression, it was there, visible, clear as daylight: Dr Laduner was afraid. Yes, afraid. But of what? It wasn't a question he could ask.

Detective Sergeant Studer was overcome by an odd feeling. In his long life it had never occurred to him to reflect on his emotions. He usually acted on instinct, or according to the principles of criminology established by his teachers in Lyon and Graz. But now he was trying to assess the feeling he had for this Dr Laduner. He concluded that it was pity. This clarity must be the result of staying in a psychiatric clinic. Didn't they spend all their time here dealing with feelings, emotions, the inner life? And didn't that rub off on you? Enough of that. What he felt was pity, but a special kind of pity. It was difficult to put into words.

It was a brotherly pity he felt for the strange person that was Dr Laduner, almost love; the closest comparison he could make was the feeling that an older brother, who has not got anywhere in life, has for the baby of the family, who is cleverer and has become famous, a great man – and for that very reason is surrounded by dangers that must be averted.

Above all, and that was what he had to bear in mind, Dr Laduner was afraid of a scandal, since a scandal would make his appointment as director impossible.

Studer smiled and said in reassuring tones, "Right, then, Herr Doktor, I seek out the truth . . . the truth for *us*."

He stressed the "us".

There was a knock at the door. A young girl announced that nurse Gilgen was asking if he could speak to the doctor. She'd put him in the study.

"Fine," said Dr Laduner, "I'll be right there."

Then for a while he just stared at his empty cup, as if he were trying to read the future in the grounds, like a clairvoyant. Finally he raised his eyes again. Their expression was calm, and there was a softness round his lips, as there had been the previous evening when he had talked about Pieterlen, the classic case.

"You're a funny fellow, Studer," he said. "And you seem not to have forgotten that I offered you bread and salt."

"Perhaps," Studer replied and looked away. He hated an excess of emotion. That was why he immediately started to talk about Gilgen, who had asked him to put in a good word for him with the doctor, since he was going to be dismissed.

"There's no question of that," said Laduner with a look of astonishment. "Has the man gone mad? Along with Jutzeler, Gilgen's my best nurse. I'd even go so far as to say he's the better of the two. He didn't get very good marks in the exam, but what does that mean? He knows how to deal with people, he knows more with his instinct than we do with all our medical science – I'll happily admit that. You should have seen the way little Gilgen once calmed down an overexcited catatonic who was two heads taller than him. All by himself. I just happened to turn up . . . You must have seen stockmen who know how to deal with a recalcitrant beast. The bull lowers its horns, it's about to charge, and they go 'Whisht, whisht.' Little Gilgen went 'Whisht, whisht' to the catatonic, too . . . and he calmed down, let himself be led away to the bath – and Gilgen stayed with him by himself, even though the man was extremely disturbed; that didn't bother Gilgen. There are people like that who sense what is going on inside sick people. No, we're keeping Gilgen . . . I did hear hints that he was supposed to have taken underwear belonging to patients, the Director was furious last week and Jutzeler stood up for his colleague – though solidarity among the staff here is problematic, to say the least . . . It's a pity Gilgen's got problems . . . I'll go and have a word with him now."

Studer stayed at the table, letting Frau Laduner pile his plate high, though his mind was elsewhere and he was only half listening to what she was saying. The funeral had been set for the next day, she told him, then things would quieten down and that would be good for her husband, he was so overworked—

She broke off. Studer must be tired, she said. She'd had to laugh that morning when he'd fallen asleep in the bath, it had happened twice to her husband – shouldn't he go and have a lie down? She'd have a quick look to see if the girl had done his room yet, in the meantime he could go and sit in the study, her husband had probably gone to hear reports by now.

She got up and opened the door to the neighbouring room, telling Studer to go in and sit himself down in a comfortable chair, there were plenty of books – and his room would be ready in no time at all. Soon the apartment was filled with the monotonous hum of a vacuum cleaner.

So Studer stood there in the study, regarding the couch on which Herbert Caplaun had cried – the tears running down his cheeks – with a certain awe. He thought of Pieterlen and the previous evening's session. Today everything was different. Like Frau Laduner's dressing-gown, the flowers on the parchment lampshade had lost their glow.

He walked up and down, stopped beside the bookcase, took out a book whose spine projected a little, leafed through it, read an underlined passage: . . . *the psychogenic-reactive symptoms, which partly determine the primary symptoms, for example of the paraesthesias* . . . then skipped a few words: . . . *catatonic behaviours, stereotypes, hallucinations, dissociations* . . .

It was all Greek to Studer. He leafed through some more and found another passage that was underlined. Studer started to read, his attention was caught, he sat down, holding the book up close to his eyes. He read the passage once, read it again, checked the title of the book then read the underlined passage a third time, this time muttering the words to himself, like a boy in his first year at school who still has difficulty grasping the meaning of the printed characters.

The psychotherapist is emotionally involved in what happens to his patient; that can lead to the danger of too intense a reciprocal emotional bond with the patient, in the doctor–patient relationship shifting to the level of a friendship. If that should happen, the doctor might as well throw in the towel. One must never forget that every course of psychiatric treatment takes the form of a battle, a battle between the doctor and the illness. If this battle is to end in victory, the doctor must not be a friend supporting the patient, he must be, and continue to be, the leader. And that is only possible if a certain distance is maintained . . .

Studer closed the book with a snap.

Distance!

That meant keeping the patient at arm's length. How did you manage that? You want to help, but you have to keep a close eye on yourself, make sure you go by the book and don't get too friendly. Studer snorted.

The things we human beings invented! There were marriage-guidance counsellors, official psychologists, psychotherapists, social workers; we build clinics for alcoholics, convalescent homes and reformatories, all of them administered with bureaucratic zeal. But greater zeal, though less bureaucracy, was lavished on chemical bombs, aeroplanes, battle cruisers, machine guns . . . All for the purpose of mutual destruction. Progress certainly had its disadvantages. We belonged to the human race, but all we seemed to want to do was to wipe it off the face of the earth as quickly as possible . . .

Chabis! The ideas you got when you had a case in a

psychiatric clinic, when you were in the realm where Matto ruled!

Distance!

Had Dr Laduner always kept his distance? Apparently not, otherwise why would he have underlined the passage? As these thoughts were going through his mind, the sergeant tried to replace the book. But it wouldn't go in. He put his right hand behind the books – and felt a soft leather object, gave a start, then pulled it out.

Serve him right! . . . A wallet . . . a 1,000-franc note . . . two 100s . . . a passport:

Name: Borstli. First name: Ulrich. Profession: Doctor. Born: . . .

But what was the point of reading on? It was clear, crystal clear. Though what was not in the least clear was how the late Director's wallet came to be hidden behind the books of Dr Ernst Laduner, of all people.

Since there was no answer to the question, Sergeant Studer decided to give himself time. He stowed the wallet in his pocket, went to the telephone and got Dreyer, the porter, to put him through to the chief of police. The Deputy Director's number was red and therefore had an outside line.

No problem! was the reply. Studer should stay in Randlingen for as long as he thought it necessary. He was no use in the office anyway . . . Yes, he'd heard Director Borstli was dead . . . It was Studer who had found him, was it? A blind hen sometimes found a grain of corn . . . The description of Pieterlen? Yes, he'd received it. It had already been phoned through, it would be going out over the radio at midday . . . Bye.

Two little tests

That morning his decision to give himself time was subjected to two tests. The third test did not come until the afternoon.

Once the vacuum cleaner had fallen silent, Frau Laduner came to fetch the sergeant. He could go to his room and have a lie down, she said, no one would disturb him.

When Studer went to get the sandbag out of his suitcase to examine it again – he'd decided to spend part of the morning at the microscope – he discovered it was missing. It hadn't got mixed up with his underwear, it was simply gone, vanished.

These things happened. Making the best of a bad job, Studer carefully placed all the items in his case on the table. On the bottom of the suitcase he found some grit, which could only have come from the cosh, collected it in an envelope and labelled it.

Then he went to the window and looked out into the courtyard.

The rowan tree with its yellow leaves . . . otherwise the courtyard was empty.

And then came the second test.

At the far end of the courtyard he saw two men in white aprons carrying a stretcher with a coffin on it. He waited as they approached and went into D1. After a while they came out with a second coffin. Keeping in step, though swaying a little, they headed towards a building at the other end of the courtyard, close to the tall chimney, half concealed by the kitchen.

One dead two nights ago, two last night – Bohnenblust was right. But wasn't that a matter for the conscience of the doctor alone? After all, not every operation was successful, so why shouldn't it sometimes be a matter of life and death in mental illness as well? Dr Laduner was right, what business was it of a layman?

The best thing would be to lie down and think it over ... Should he perhaps go and see how Gilgen was? Give him some reassurance? ...

Studer shot up ...

The girl was doing the dining room.

"Hey, lassie," Studer called out quietly to her, "did you take Nurse Gilgen straight into the study this morning?"

"No. He said he'd left something in your room yesterday, Sergeant, so I took him there. Is something missing?"

"No, no, that's fine."

Studer lay back down on his bed and wondered what to do next. Grill the red-haired nurse? Not a pleasant task! Still, Gilgen had been in the study – and the Director's wallet had been hidden behind the books in the study. And Gilgen had been in the sergeant's room – from which the sandbag had disappeared ... and it was pure chance that the first envelope, the one with the sand from Borstli's hair, had been left untouched.

Gilgen, who went out for walks with Pieterlen every Sunday ... What had the two of them talked about on their walks? ... But Gilgen had problems, Gilgen had a wife with TB in Heiligenschwendi ...

Funny how un-keen on your work the atmosphere of a psychiatric clinic made you ...

Perhaps he should do some work with the microscope after all . . . Later. Perhaps he should go and visit the late Director's friend, Fehlbaum he was called, the butcher and landlord of the Bear, who had eased the old man's loneliness with a carafe of wine every evening . . . Later, later.

The junior doctor, Neuville, was rather surprised when, at around eleven o'clock, Sergeant Studer appeared at the door of the room that served as a pharmacy and politely enquired if he might use a microscope.

"But of course you may, *naturellement*. Please . . . *Entrez*."

And when the doctor with the black hair and weasel's face realized that Sergeant Studer could speak French as well as any of his colleagues from Geneva, he was delighted with his new acquaintance. He cleaned the eyepiece with a soft leather cloth, got some slides ready and watched in astonishment as Studer took two envelopes out of his pocket and prepared a specimen. The sergeant seemed pleased with the result. He whistled four bars of the folk song about the farmer from Brienz, went through the elaborate process of lighting a Brissago and asked Neuville whether he fancied a stroll down to the village. An apéritif wouldn't go amiss.

Dr Neuville was delighted and talked all the way there. His steady flow of words sounded just like the incessant sameness of the Pisse-vache waterfall, though that famous waterfall was in the Valais, while Dr Neuville definitely came from Geneva.

What Neuville had to say wasn't of particular interest for his investigation. He told Studer about having – as the youngest of the junior doctors – to do the rounds of the wards with the Director one Sunday. All the way from the central block to D1 and across the courtyard . . . But no, it could really only be put in Neuville's French: "*Il a, comment vous dire, il a . . . oui . . . il a . . . eh bien, il a pété tout le temps . . . Figurez-vous ça?*"

Well, it did add an amusing, if rather pungent touch to the picture of the old man, but that was all.

That was all? Not quite. He also recounted a few bits of scandal. The youngest junior doctor seemed to be well informed about all the romantic and not-so-romantic entanglements in the clinic. With whom this male nurse was "going" (and when he said "going", well . . .), that such a female nurse was *facile*, while with another there was *rien à faire* . . .

According to Neuville, Irma Wasem had originally been one of the *faciles*, but since her acquaintance with the Director she had moved over to the second category . . . Which was understandable. One thing was clear from Neuville's chatter: underneath the surface all sorts of things were going on that were better left out of official speeches, those speeches, given on ceremonial occasions, which would certainly only concentrate on "the selfless devotion to duty of our nursing staff in the service of suffering humanity . . ." That kind of speech wasn't difficult to make up. On similar occasions the police were told they were "the guardians of law and order who protect the state and society from the encroachments of lawlessness and anarchy . . ." An hour later the speaker was back to cursing the bloody cops. It was the way of the world. Anyway, didn't all sorts of things go on in police circles that the public would never imagine in their wildest dreams? It was better if the public didn't imagine anything; it was pointless and counterproductive . . .

Idle thoughts, Studer told himself. That was what

153

you got when a distinguished psychiatrist told you, gently and with much beating about the bush, that you had only joined the police in order to work off – to "abreact" – your criminal urgcs. If he insisted. But then why had Dr Laduner become a psychiatrist? To serve suffering humanity or to abreact his own urges? Eh?

It was a relief when they finally arrived at the Bear, with its butcher landlord, and could drink a vermouth, comfortably installed at a well-scrubbed table in the bar panelled in light wood.

Fehlbaum wasn't actually as fat as, by rights, a man who was both a butcher and a landlord ought to have been. It turned out that he really was a pillar of the Agrarian Party, and had put a spoke in the wheel of the Young Agrarians – "those troublemakers" – at the most recent local elections.

Nor did he have a good word to say about Dr Laduner, because he used to be a member of the Party. The way he pronounced the word "Party"! Perhaps he still was, the landlord went on. But whether he was or not, he had tried to organize the nurses in the clinic – against the will of the Director. Not that he had succeeded, mind. Most had joined the Association of State Employees, which, as they would be aware, united – yes, united – priests and teachers, that is to say reliable elements of society, whereas Jutzeler, who like Laduner was a member of the Party, had tried to get the employees organized – or-gan-ized! – in a union. But most of the nurses were religious people and had rejected the idea. Class warfare! In a state institution! Why not a nurses' soviet? Eh?

Oh yes, Herr Fehlbaum could speak all right. His voice filled the bar, but it was pleasant to listen to, reassuring, soporific. Studer was sure the butcher/

landlord's speeches would be a great success in the local council.

Just recently, that is two days ago, Fehlbaum continued, the Director had complained that Jutzeler had tried to get the warders to go on strike. It was a murky business. One of the warders had stolen various items and the Director had been going to sack him, but Dr Laduner took a different view ... There must have been more to it than met the eye! The death of the Director had been very convenient for some people. Dr Laduner would have got his knuckles rapped over that business with the strike, oh yes! It wasn't for nothing that Herr Fehlbaum's friend, the late Director, had made his brother-in-law the hospital mechanic. He had pushed through the affiliation to the Association of State Employees. Yes, despite Jutzeler. Now Herr Fehlbaum leant forward and whispered conspiratorially that he had heard the police were already in the clinic to start their investigation. Did Dr Neuville have any news about that?

But Dr Neuville just yawned. He wasn't interested in politics. In fact, he didn't seem to be interested in much, apart from a bit of gossip. Presumably that was why he had omitted to introduce the sergeant. Now, though, he had to laugh when Studer said who he was. The landlord immediately drew back and abandoned his familiar tone. When, however, he was further informed that the officer in charge of the investigation – the death of the Director, by the way, was a genuine accident, Studer added – was staying with Dr Laduner, that pillar of the Agrarian Party withdrew in pique behind his beer pumps.

Then Studer and Dr Neuville set off back so as not to miss lunch. The vermouth had been worthwhile, Studer concluded to himself.

There were more people round the table than at breakfast. Kasperli was sitting next to Frau Laduner and telling some long story from school that sounded rather tangled but must have been very amusing since he waved his soup spoon in the air and laughed out loud. It's all right for you, Studer thought, and set about his food.

Opposite him was the maid, the girl who had been making the noise with the vacuum cleaner in the morning. Yes, she had her meal at the table, eating with the family, not in the kitchen, the sergeant noted with surprise. And there was something else that struck him. Two or three times during the meal Dr Laduner spoke to the girl. "Anna" he called her, and the way he spoke the word was no different from the way he said "Studer", for example, or "Blumenstein", or "my dear girl". To stress that people are equal by the way you said their names, there was something rather fine about that, Studer thought.

But lunch did not pass without disturbance. While they were all occupied with their dessert, there was a ring at the door. Anna got up and came back to say that Colonel Caplaun wished to see Dr Laduner urgently.

Studer went pale, the plum tart suddenly lost its flavour. Dr Laduner's reaction, however, was to fling his napkin down on the table, growl something ill-tempered and storm out into the neighbouring room.

After Kasperli had left the room, and the maid had gone too, Studer enquired in a husky voice what the purpose of the visit was. "You must excuse me if I appear inquisitive, Frau Doktor," he said, "but I feel involved . . ."

As he spoke, the thought that kept going through his mind was, the enemy's in the apartment! For all that, he scarcely knew Colonel Caplaun. In the business about the bank all those years ago everything had been done behind closed doors, Colonel Caplaun had never shown himself.

"No need for excuses," said Frau Laduner. "It's an awkward matter my husband's let himself be landed with. He's much too kind. He wants to help wherever he can." She was silent for a moment. "You've seen the son, Herbert Caplaun?"

Studer nodded silently. He was listening to the murmur of voices from the neighbouring room. A deep bass boomed on and on, almost without interruption; Dr Laduner's voice was hardly heard at all.

Frau Laduner played with her pince-nez and stared morosely at the tablecloth.

"My husband accepted Herbert for analysis because Staff Nurse Jutzeler asked him to. His wife is distantly related to the Colonel's late wife. Herbert's a musician, but he drank too much. At one point his father was going to have him put away, and my husband had great difficulty persuading him his son needed treatment. My husband is doing it for free, partly as practice ... You do see? This kind of analysis is complicated, usually the parents get extremely worked up about it. You see, the patient recounts all his childhood experiences and the parents usually have a bad conscience if all their mistakes in bringing the child up come out ..."

Analysis? Childhood experiences? It wasn't quite what Studer had imagined was involved from what he'd read in the book he'd borrowed from his lawyer friend, Münch. And Colonel Caplaun? What had he been doing recently, the man the chief of police would most like to see in Thorberg Prison? There had been talk of deals involving the export of cattle, the Volksbank. But no one had ever been able to pin the

Colonel down. And now he was in the next room, his bass voice getting louder and louder. Some words could even be understood: " ... irresponsible behaviour ... police ..." Then the door was flung open.

A moral dilemma

A white patriarchal beard, skin unhealthily pale and, right in the middle of his face, a nose like a red pepper with lots of lumps and bumps. A mouth, hidden in the tangle of beard, opened and bawled, "You there . . . yes, I mean you . . . You're a representative of the police, or so I've been told. I need your support. This gentleman's behaviour is absolutely unacceptable. Come with me."

Studer had nothing against people addressing him, as Caplaun had just done, in formal German; or they could be as coarse as they liked – he just shrugged his shoulders; the Chief of Police could swear and curse at him – Studer said nothing, just grinned a little grin to himself maybe. But if there was one thing that got his back up and really made him angry, furious, it was someone addressing him as "You there . . . yes, I mean you." Then he could become a dangerous customer.

He stood up and placed his hands on the tablecloth. No one would have taken him for a simple detective sergeant as, politely, in a quiet voice, and speaking formal German, he asked, "With whom do I have the pleasure ?"

The Colonel with the patriarch's beard was clearly no fool. He immediately realized he had adopted the wrong tone and switched to a sonorous, soothing bass.

"But, Sergeant – what was your name? – Studer, that's right, Studer. Well, Sergeant Studer, I'm an old friend of your boss, the chief of police, and he's always

159

praising you. 'That Studer,' he says, 'he's one of my best detectives.'"

Strangely, Studer didn't even smile. So Herr Caplaun had completely forgotten the chief inspector of the Bern city police whose career he had destroyed. Of course, the Colonel had other, more important things to think about. What was a little policeman when you were dealing with financial restructurings, the cheesemakers' consortium etc, etc.

" ' . . . one of my best detectives.' And you're in charge of the investigation here, so the porter tells me. Then I'm sure you won't refuse me. My son, Sergeant, my son has disappeared."

"That can't be true," said Studer, genuinely surprised. Only yesterday afternoon Herbert Caplaun had been lying on the couch, the tears rolling down his cheeks. And today he was supposed to have disappeared?

"Can't we discuss the matter quietly?" boomed the deep bass. "Come along with me, Sergeant, we'll go down to the village together, I have to get the train pretty soon . . ." – the typical gesture of the busy man taking his watch out of his waistcoat pocket – "but I still have some time. We can decide what steps are to be taken. I will be reassured if I can count on your support. A father's heart, you know . . . Ah, good afternoon, Frau Doktor."

Only now did Caplaun seem to register the presence of Frau Laduner. He bowed, a stiff bow. Frau Laduner said nothing, just nodded.

"Well then, as I said, Sergeant, will you come with me?"

A pause.

Studer looked at Frau Laduner, who had put on her pince-nez and was herself looking at the sergeant. She had screwed up her eyes slightly, creasing the skin round the bridge of her nose.

Plaisir d'amour ne dure qu'un moment . . .

She had a nice alto voice, Frau Laduner, and she stuck by her husband . . .

"Well?" the Colonel asked.

"I think it would be appropriate," Studer said, "if the doctor treating the patient were present at our discussion. If he should deem it desirable that your son's whereabouts should remain concealed from you for the moment, then . . ." Studer completed the sentence with a gesture as if to say "I can do nothing about it."

"Appropriate? What insolence!" the bass voice exclaimed in deepest outrage. Frau Laduner smiled, and the smile suited her so well that Studer would have liked to take her hand and pat it – just to soothe her nerves, of course. He did nothing of the kind, however. Instead he said in a matter-of-fact voice, "If you would . . ." gesturing towards the open door to the study. Colonel Caplaun shrugged and went in. Studer followed him. Dr Laduner was sitting on the edge of the desk, his silhouette slim against the bright white of the window.

He stood up, waved them to two armchairs and sat down on the couch.

Studer's eyes went back and forward from one man to the other.

What a contrast!

One, in his light-coloured flannel suit, had crossed his left leg over his clasped hands, which were resting on his right thigh. The loosely knotted tie between the points of his unstarched collar was cornflower blue. The other was leaning back in his armchair, his hairy hands resting on the arms and his head turned towards Studer, allowing him a view of the stiff detachable collar with a small black bow tie. He was wearing a dark cutaway and dark trousers with no crease and no turn-ups above his black lace-up shoes. The similarity to the late Director was unmistakable.

The Colonel addressed his remarks exclusively to the sergeant.

"When, like me, one can look back on a life spent in the service of the common good, when, like me, one can say with a clear conscience that one has spared no sacrifice, however great, to lead one's only son onto the right path, when, like me, one has grown old with one's reputation untarnished, only to have to look on as the name one bears is dragged through the mud by a son who has gone to the bad, then one cannot protest too strongly when a doctor, a psychiatrist, sides with that son against his father . . ."

Studer made a face as if he had toothache. Dr Laduner leant forward to say something, then changed his mind, took his hands out from between his crossed legs and lit a cigarette. Colonel Caplaun took out a leather case; the lighting of the cigar was a solemn ritual. Studer lit one of his Brissagos. The temperature in the room seemed close to freezing.

"I agreed to allow my son," said Colonel Caplaun, "who has given me nothing but trouble, whose thoughtless behaviour sent his mother to an early grave, whose depravity has caused me nothing but worry for twenty-five years –"

"To understand all this properly, Studer, there are two things you need to know: Herbert's mother died when he was six, that's one. The other is that Herbert is now twenty-nine. For twenty-five years, the Colonel says . . ."

162

"I will not tolerate ironical remarks," the Colonel barked angrily.

Laduner said nothing.

"It was Dr Laduner who came to me and begged me to let him treat my son – to *analyse* him, as he put it." Caplaun pronounced "analyse" as if it had six pairs of quotation marks round it. "He promised to take full responsibility for my son and thus relieve me of a burden. Initially a brief stay in the clinic was necessary. I would have wished it to be longer, but since Herr Doktor Laduner was willing to assume responsibility, I raised no objection. But how did he administer that responsibility? My son is an alcoholic, Sergeant, though it pains me as his father to have to say so; he does not take after anyone else in the family, at home he always had a shining example before his eyes . . ."

Studer's eyes were so obviously fixed on the burgeoning red pepper of a nose that the Colonel could not very well ignore it. He cleared his throat and said, in a noticeably less declamatory tone, apologetically, in fact, pointing at his nose, "It's a skin disease."

"Sure-ly," Dr Laduner said, a deadly earnest expression on his face.

"Hm-hmm," said the Colonel, pulling on his cigar. He grimaced, as if the smoke was bitter. "What I was going to say was that my son Herbert gave his word that for the duration of the 'analysis' he would work in a market garden here in Randlingen, keep off alcohol and be conscientious in his attendance at the . . . errm . . . analysis. He promised me on his honour, even though he has often abused my trust . . . very often . . . And what do I hear when I come to Randlingen to visit my son? That he gave up his room a week ago and only appears at work occasionally. Nobody knows where he is living and Dr Laduner refuses to reveal his

163

whereabouts. And when I turned to him in my distress, such as only a loving father can know, what does Herr Doktor Laduner say? What does he have the insolence to—"

"That it is unnecessary to get worked up, since it is I who bear the responsibility."

"Is that an answer, Herr Studer, is that an answer? At the same time you must remember that some odd things have been going on in Randlingen Clinic. The Director – an old friend of mine, who at one point confided in me his doubts, arising from his many years of experience, about Dr Laduner's modern methods of treatment – the Director is dead. What was the cause of death? That is a mystery you are better qualified to clear up than I, but my assumption was that this new situation would mean that Dr Laduner would no longer have the time he would like to devote to my son. I therefore came to offer to take a share of the responsibility, to hold out an olive branch ... And what is the answer I get from Herr Doktor Laduner?"

Poor Herbert Caplaun, thought Studer; with a father like *that*, it wasn't surprising he couldn't cope with life. He was seized with pity for the wretched lad.

"And what is the answer I get from Herr Doktor Laduner? Would I please not come charging in, disrupting the course of treatment that was going so well. I ask you, what does this treatment consist of, this 'analysis'? My reprobate of a son telling outrageous lies about his father – you can believe me, I've made enquiries, of the experts – pretending to be a martyr ... And all this with the specific permission of his psychiatrist!"

"Might I point out, Colonel, that I am acting director here and my time is limited." This with a glance at his watch.

164

"Oh yes, I will come to the point. I have just one question for Sergeant Studer. Is it his intention to carry out a conscientious investigation into the circumstances surrounding the mysterious death of the longstanding director of this clinic, my friend Ulrich Borstli, or is he going to allow himself to be so influenced by Herr Doktor Laduner, the *acting director*" – those two words in a particularly venomous tone – "that his investigation will amount to little more than a cover-up? Or is he determined to report the truth, to the best of his knowledge and belief . . ."

A pause. Something seemed just to have occurred to the Colonel. He leant forward and scrutinized Studer with his large, red-rimmed eyes – the iris was an unpleasant blue, like a Siamese cat's – then nodded, as if something had been confirmed, and went on in a soft voice, keeping his eyes fixed on the sergeant.

"I remember you now, Sergeant Studer. You suffered a grave injustice. But there were such important interests at stake that I could not act in any other way . . . Can we come to an agreement? I see to it that you're given leave and you look for my son, whose whereabouts a certain psychiatrist refuses to divulge. Do that and you will bring comfort to the heart of a grieving father. I will get someone else to take over the investigation here – is it proper, by the way, for you to be staying with a doctor who is involved in the case? – someone impartial. If you succeed in finding my son, I will do my utmost to make your future as smooth as possible. I am not without influence, as you well know" – his right hand grasped his beard around his chin and let it gently slide through his fingers – "so you can rest assured . . . Well?"

Silence. An expectant silence. Dr Laduner stared fixedly at his knees. Studer sighed. The answer wasn't that simple. This lunatic-asylum case was a tricky business, wouldn't it be better to keep well away from it? Feelings! You got nowhere with feelings, even if they did have their attractions, such as being the elder brother trying to protect the baby of the family. Once his feelings had cost him dear because he had got on the wrong side of the Colonel. Start from scratch again? At fifty? It needed thinking over at the very least. Studer took a deep pull on his Brissago and kept the smoke in his mouth a long time, only letting it out when he was forced to.

On the one hand, he could abandon the investigation, hand over the wallet (pity he no longer had the cosh) together with what he had learnt about Pieterlen and Dr Laduner's night-time excursion in the basement of P Ward to the man who took over, and concentrate on finding Herbert Caplaun. In that case he would be covered – yes, *covered*. Then in five years at most he could retire with the rank of inspector. All very nice, and his wife would be pleased. No one would ever get the Colonel sent to Thorberg Prison, despite the pious hopes of the chief of police. On the other hand, he could help Dr Laduner. He would get nothing out of it, indeed, he could end up in one hell of a mess, since he would have the Colonel out for his blood.

"Well?" Caplaun repeated his question.

Inspector . . . pension . . . ex gratia payment – an ex gratia payment! The Colonel was rich.

But then there was the way he had been addressed. "You there . . . yes, I mean you." And the business with the bank. And there was a song that began "*Plaisir d'amour*", and another that had been sung by the same voice: "*Si le roi m'avait donné Paris sa grand' ville*". Why was it the two songs that tipped the balance? Or the woman who had sung them? There was never a logical explanation for a decision.

"Enough!" Studer suddenly said and, turning to Dr Laduner, "Do you know where Herbert is?"

Laduner nodded silently.

"In that case," said Studer, standing up and stretching, "in that case I must unfortunately decline the Colonel's kind offer."

"You must? . . . Well, then . . . I see . . . In that case I know what I must do."

Studer would most of all have liked to tell the Colonel to go and take a running jump. But that wouldn't do, so he just bowed. Dr Laduner stood up and opened the door.

What a small man the Colonel was! He had short legs, which were slightly bowed. Outside he put on a panama with a red hatband, hung his umbrella over his arm and went out without a word of farewell. The panama hat and the umbrella! thought Studer. They put the finishing touch to his image of the man.

"Has he gone?" asked Frau Laduner. She was pale. And was the sergeant going to stay? she added. It looked as if she had been listening.

"Studer's staying with us," said Laduner curtly, staring into a corner of the room. "I'll send him back up for tea. You can sing him a song, Greti, he's earned it."

Studer stared at him open mouthed. Was it coincidence or could the psychiatrist read thoughts?

Laduner took off his jacket and went out to get his white coat. "Come with me, Studer, I've got something to show you."

As they were crossing the courtyard, Studer suddenly felt Laduner put his hand on his upper arm and give it a squeeze. Then the pressure slackened, though the hand remained. Thus Studer was gently led back to the door of D1. He no longer felt a shiver of fear at the insect eyes, nor did he bow his head as he passed beneath the window at which, according to Schül, Matto darted out and in. Studer was content. After all, thanks do not always have to be expressed in words. There are other means of communication.

Kind and good

"So this is where I murder my patients," said Dr Laduner as he opened the door to D1. "But it's not my victims I want to show you. There's something else . . ."

A bare room. Wooden tables, old, rough, greasy. Low benches with no backrests. A door leading into the garden. They were in the basement.

Sitting at the tables were men plucking at matted horsehair. Their eyes were empty of expression. At times one would leap up, as if trying to catch a fly, jump high in the air, squeal and fall down. Another crept round Studer, came close, with a fixed stare, and started to whisper in the most matter-of-fact tone such incredible obscenities that Studer automatically drew back. Some jabbered. A minor brawl was calmed down by a man in a white apron.

"Schwertfeger!" Dr Laduner called. The man in the white apron came over. He was short, with well-developed biceps. He looked like a dairyman.

Laduner introduced them. "This is the staff nurse in charge of D1. And you'll already have heard about Sergeant Studer, won't you, Schwertfeger? Bring Leibundgut to me."

He drew Studer to the door into the garden and went out.

"That's going to be changed," he said, pointing back into the room. "Fresh paint, brightly coloured benches, pictures on the wall. But you can't get every-thing done at once . . . Anyway, I'm going to introduce

169

you to Leibundgut, but it's just to help make the Caplaun case clear. You'll understand. I trust you, Studer . . . Leibundgut – in dialect it comes out as *lieb und gut*, kind and good . . ."

They walked round a trampled patch of lawn until they came to a spluttering fountain. The leaves on the maples were drooping and the sun, when it appeared between the clouds, was very hot . . .

Schwertfeger came back with a man with a twisted mouth. There was such a terrible expression of fear in his eyes, it sent a shiver down Studer's spine.

"Hi, Leibundgut," said Laduner in a friendly voice. "How's things?" You could see the man was making an effort to answer. His eyelids fluttered up and down, his lips moved, but all that came out was a hoarse stammer.

He took Laduner's hand, then let go of it again. Suddenly he bent down and put his hands flat on the gravel. In that posture, on all fours, he spoke, directing his words at the ground.

"Much better, thank you, Doctor," he said. His voice was hoarse but clear. "Can I go home soon?" He pushed off the ground with his hands and straightened up, looking at Dr Laduner expectantly.

"Aren't you better off here than at home with your brothers?" Laduner asked.

The man thought, went back down on all fours and in that posture said, in the same hoarse voice, that he wanted to be freed, he had to go and work in the cowshed.

"You'll have to be patient for a little while longer, Leibundgut," said Laduner. "First of all you have to get well again and be able to speak like other people."

A sad shake of the head. Then the answer, again on

170

all fours, directed at the ground. "I'll never be able to do that."

"Go back to your work," said Laduner in a friendly voice. And the man went, head bowed.

Laduner looked sad. He took Studer by the arm again and drew him to a bench.

"Fritz Leibundgut, from Gerzenstein, twenty-three years old. Runs a middle-sized family farm together with his three brothers. He's the weakest, not very bright. But good-natured. The parents are dead, the four men are still bachelors. Fritz had to work. He's not lazy, but he's so good-natured he never asked for money, never went to the inn, always stayed at home. I'm sure he never had a girlfriend. The brothers are odd. They didn't actually torment him, but they bullied him. He accepted everything. One winter's night seven months ago the three came home, somewhat the worse for drink. Fritz hadn't cleaned the cowshed properly, so they dragged him out of his bed, thrashed him, threw him in the trough, pulled him out, beat him up again and left him lying there. Later on, when he tried to crawl back into the house, the door was locked. He spent the whole night outside. As he was robust, he didn't get ill, but since that day he has been unable to speak to anyone if he's standing upright, on two feet. He can only speak when he gets down on all fours. There are no other signs of mental illness, it's just that he cannot speak if he's standing up. It's obvious what the man is trying to say with his simple image: you treated me like a dog, so I'll stay a dog . . . I'll only talk when I'm on all fours. Obvious, don't you think? And the remarkable thing is that we are going to discharge the man in the next few days. Without having cured him, of course. His brothers refuse to go on paying for him. The eldest said he couldn't care less if

Fritz couldn't speak standing up, as long as he did his work. And Fritz Leibundgut is hard-working. He has no objection to going back to his brothers. Being free is more important to him than a nice bed and decent treatment. His brothers, you see, are human beings, not lunatics. And human beings, well, you know what human beings are like" – and Laduner repeated his pun on their name – "human beings are kind and good."

Silence. Laduner twirled a yellow maple leaf between his thumb and index finger. He stared at the wooden fence round the D1 garden.

"It's not only the body that can get deformed, the mind can too. I'm supposed to twist Herbert Caplaun back into shape as well. He can only think, feel, decide, act on all fours. One punishment in the old days was to lock people up bent. In his childhood, Herbert Caplaun's mind was locked up bent. I can't say any more, but you've seen the Colonel . . . After that the rest isn't difficult to understand. I'm taking pains with Herbert Caplaun because I genuinely believe I can put something right. By taking an objective approach. I can't change Leibundgut. The danger is to try to make too many changes. Lots of the minds that are sent to us are like crumpled clothes. I've often thought of the clinic," said Laduner with a weak attempt at a joke, "as a huge steam laundry. We moisten the minds with steam, then iron them out . . ."

Silence. The fountain gave a loud splutter.

"Herbert Caplaun," said Laduner in concerned tones.

Studer felt as if a book lay open on his knees. He had no trouble reading it: . . . *emotionally involved in what happens to his patient; that can lead to the danger of too intense a reciprocal emotional bond with the patient . . .*

Put in scientific terms. It sounded convincing.

But how did it work in practice?

A reciprocal emotional bond! A fine phrase! . . .

But how could you rule feeling out?

Studer did not ask, instead he stared at the gravelly path in the sunlight. Yet there were many things he would have liked to ask: What were you doing in the corridor in P Ward on Wednesday night? What do you know of the whereabouts of Pieterlen, your classic case? And where have you hidden Herbert Caplaun?

But the sergeant remained silent. He felt like a bank manager who, with a heavy heart and only out of pity, has granted a close friend a large overdraft and now can't sleep at night because he doesn't know whether his friend is solvent or about to declare himself bankrupt.

A break-in

Later Studer would think that there is nothing more confusing than becoming personally involved in a case. Had he not, during his discussion with Colonel Caplaun, spent the whole time thinking about the decision he would have to make, then there was one thing that would have struck him. The Colonel had mentioned it in passing, but it was so obviously the key to the whole business that Studer must have been really blind not to see that it was a passkey he could use.

So Studer spent a sleepless night. He had decided to give himself time, but his thoughts would not leave him in peace. Thoughts! Rather they were images that passed before his eyes, confused and without any obvious connection, like one of those modern French films. What tormented him most, however, was the accordion playing. It started, in muted tones, at around eleven o'clock, and he could not tell where it came from. One minute it was playing, quietly and almost without any bass, "The Roses Are Blooming in Sans Souci", an old tango, and then "Somewhere in the world there's a little happiness, somewhere, some when, somehow" . . . a sentimental ballad. Then sometimes Studer was convinced the invisible musician must be playing above his room. He decided to get up to go and see, but in the end he stayed in bed. He kept feeling that nothing could be achieved with normal detective methods in this case, that he just had to sit still and wait for chance to do the work for him.

So Studer listened to the mysterious accordion playing – what with the sleepless night and all the strange new experiences, he was overtired – and it was inevitable that eventually Pieterlen should come to mind; Pieterlen, who had played at the harvest festival and then disappeared, together with his instrument.

And there was another thing that bothered Studer. He had gone to see Gilgen in the afternoon, but it had been the nurse's day off.

Finally morning came, an early autumn morning with drizzle, grey and misty, cold and damp. Studer could not bring himself to leave the Laduners' apartment. It was the day of the Director's funeral and the central block was alive with people, though that probably wasn't the appropriate word. When Studer did eventually attempt to go down the stairs, he stopped on the landing above the first floor. There were women in black veils standing in the open doorway of the apartment in which an old man had dwelt with his loneliness, men in black frock coats were bustling to and fro, there was the flowery smell of wreaths. Studer beat a retreat. When he met Frau Laduner in the corridor, she looked as if she had been crying. Had she taken the death of the Director that much to heart? Studer didn't have the courage to ask ... He stayed in his room, looking out over the grey courtyard and cursing his own pigheadedness, which had prevented him from accepting the Colonel's offer ...

In the study in the afternoon he still hadn't found the courage to ask Frau Laduner why she had been crying that morning. Dr Laduner had gone to the funeral and it was roughly a quarter to three; ten minutes earlier the funeral procession had gathered outside the entrance. A lot of cars had driven up.

Then the hearse had set off. The mourners formed a long, black line, which wound its way beneath a clouded sky as dazzling as molten iron. After the mourners on foot came the cars, crawling along like huge, exhausted bugs.

Frau Laduner had a large basket of mending in front of her and was busy darning a hole in the heel of a man's sock. "The Board of Governors has turned up, too," she said, a smile glinting in her eyes behind her pince-nez.

The Board of Governors. Studer should have had a look at them, she said. There was a clergyman on it whose face consisted of little more than a mouth, an enormous mouth, making him look like a red frog. Sometimes he stood in for the prison chaplain on Sundays, and he had a nickname. Reverend Veronal, they called him, after the well-known sedative, because two thirds of the congregation always fell asleep during his sermons. Little Gilgen, she went on, had once said they should experiment with using the priest for their sleep treatment. Since they were trying to economize on everything, they could replace expensive medicines with sermons, they'd be cheaper. Then there was a retired schoolteacher who supervised released prisoners and discharged patients. He was hard of hearing, but probably only because he had such thick tufts of hair growing out of his ears, she added. And there was the wife of a member of parliament, too, a friendly, intelligent woman who kept embarrassing the others by asking, every time they were taken round the clinic, what was the point of having a Board of Governors? So that the gentlemen could pocket their expenses? Everything was running so well without the Board. When she did that, the former teacher turned probation officer would pretend to be even more hard of hearing than usual and ask two or three times, "What was that you said?"

The telephone rang.

"Could you answer that, Herr Studer," Frau Laduner said. "I feel so lazy."

Studer stood up, lifted the receiver and said in a friendly voice, "Yes?"

It was Dreyer, the porter. "Who's that on the line?"

"Studer."

"You must come at once, the administration office's been broken into."

"What?" Studer asked in astonishment. "In broad daylight?"

"Yes. You must come down at once, it's urgent."

"Hardly," said Studer, then replaced the receiver and told Frau Laduner he had to nip down to the ground floor, the porter had something he wanted to ask him. Things were all at sixes and sevens down there. He walked slowly to the door, followed by suspicious looks from Frau Laduner.

He closed the apartment door behind him and ran down, taking the stairs three at a time. He was somewhat out of breath by the time he reached the ground floor.

Dreyer, pale and agitated – his left hand was still bandaged – was waiting for him at the bottom, and grasped his arm.

On the right, along the corridor leading to the female wards, a door stood open. Dreyer pushed the sergeant into the room. An oldish woman, hair dishevelled, was going in circles round and round the double desk. She reminded Studer of a cat that has had valerian drops sprinkled on its nose.

"In there," said the porter.

In the neighbouring, smaller room (obviously the private office of the clinic manager) the safe was open. There were files in it. Studer went over.

The woman gave up her circuits, joined him and began to moan. "My God, this is terrible. The manager's gone to the funeral and something like this has to happen while he's away. I only left the office for five minutes at the most, I just dashed out to wash my hands . . ."

She broke off, raised her eyes to heaven, clasped her hands, unclasped them. "Six thousand francs! Six thousand francs! Three bundles of twenty hundreds! Just vanished! And the manager? What will the manager say?"

She went back into the other room and started going round and round again, mumbling to herself.

In a low voice Dreyer explained that Fräulein Hänni had taken the death of the Director so much to heart because she was his sister-in-law, the sister of his second wife.

"Fräulein Hänni," Studer asked, "was the safe locked?"

"No, it wasn't." The manager, she said, had been in a terrible hurry, he'd had a lot of work on, the quarterly accounts, and it wasn't until the last moment that he'd been able to go up to his apartment to change – forgetting to lock the safe.

The tears were rolling down her cheeks. Studer shrugged his shoulders. An old spinster, got worked up easily . . . But why did she keep on trotting round the table, like a cat that . . .

Studer muttered a goodbye. Was there any point in looking for fingerprints on such an invitingly open safe? Outside he asked the porter who he'd seen in the central block after the funeral procession had left.

Dreyer thought, scratched his bandage. "No one . . ." he said finally, if a little hesitantly.

"And where were you?"

"In the porter's lodge, of course."

"And no one came to collect or buy anything, or to ask a question? Think, man!"

"Oh yes! About ten minutes ago Nurse Gilgen of O Ward came to buy a packet of cigars and a little later Nurse Wasem came for some chocolate."

Aha! So Irma didn't go to the funeral. Why did she need chocolate if there was nothing wrong with her? And what did Gilgen think he was doing, leaving his ward in the middle of the afternoon to buy cigars? The copper-haired nurse who had passed with a run of four to the acc of spades – and had been in Laduner's apartment yesterday morning, after which a sandbag . . .

It was all happening at once, just like in a bad film in which, out of laziness, they didn't bother with the transitions between scenes. Studer left the porter standing there and hurried off, down the steps, out into the courtyard and on past the rowan tree with its withered leaves. He went up more steps, crossed a corridor, unlocked the door to O dormitory and stopped, breathing heavily, at the foot of one of the twenty-two beds. They were all empty, the whole ward seemed deserted, there was not a sound . . . Although noise was coming from the garden below.

Studer went over to the window. In the middle of a round patch of lawn two men in white aprons were engaged in a bout of Swiss belt-wrestling. One was Staff Nurse Jutzeler, the other a man Studer didn't know. He cast an expert eye over the contest. The two men weren't bad at all. A *Brienz* lock – the other countered with a *Schlungg*, well done! – the first man formed a bridge . . . A draw. It was as if he could hear the puffing and grunting of the two wrestlers up in the dormitory.

Where was Gilgen? Gilgen because of whom a strike had almost been called in Randlingen Clinic? He wasn't in the garden. The patients were running about down there, one was going round and round the patch of lawn. Others were lying on the damp grass under the trees.

Not a sound broke the silence.

Suddenly Studer thought he could hear a sound. But not there in the dormitory . . . In the day room?

Quietly he went to the door, his passkey turned in the lock, just as quietly as it had on the night when he had surprised Bohnenblust . . . He flung the door open.

At the table where Studer – it seemed an age ago now – had once played *jass*, Gilgen was sitting, slumped, staring at the table. His shirtsleeves were rolled up; his arms were covered in freckles.

A slow-motion film: on the screen you see racehorses taking a jump. You expect their back legs to spring off the ground, but no, they stretch, and slowly, very slowly detach themselves from the grass. That was the speed at which Studer crossed the threshold.

Gilgen did not start at the noise. There was an odd expression on his face, as if he was completely at a loss what to do.

"What's wrong, Gilgen?" Studer asked. The nurse straightened up and the bib of his apron sagged, as if something was hidden behind it.

"What have you got there?" Studer asked, pointing to the bulge. Gilgen shrugged wearily. His blue shirt had lots of patches, some of different-coloured cloth.

180

He shrugged his shoulders, as if to say, Why do you ask such a stupid question?

His hand disappeared under the bib, pulled something out and threw it on the table.

Two bundles of banknotes. Studer picked them up and flicked through them. Twenty . . . forty. Four thousand francs.

"Where's the rest?"

Gilgen looked up in astonishment. He said nothing.

Studer slipped the bundles into his jacket pocket. Then he started to pace up and down.

The case with the wrong notes – and not just the banknotes.

There was always something that wasn't quite right. Within an incredibly short time he'd managed to clear up a theft and recover the money – but then of course some was still missing . . . And Gilgen was supposed to be the thief . . .

Grumpily Studer told Gilgen he'd have to search his belongings. Where was his room?

Gilgen pointed to a door opposite the door to the dormitory. That was where he slept, he said, when he had to spend the night in the clinic.

Pieterlen had escaped via the day room. The question of the key had been solved, but still . . . Gilgen slept in a room, the door of which opened off the day room.

The little copper-haired nurse stood up wearily and preceded Studer into the room.

The window looked out onto the kitchen and was wide open.

Two built-in wardrobes, painted light blue. Gilgen went over to one, opened the door with a key from his keyring, then sat down on the bed. It had a red counterpane with white fringes that reached down to the floor.

It was quiet in the room.

Three shirts, one apron, a cardboard box with a razor, shaving brush, soap, leather strop. One old patched coat. A white coat, neatly pressed; on the lapel the white cross on a red background, the badge of the qualified nurse.

Poor little Gilgen, thought Studer. What kind of a mess had he got himself into? He presumably only wore the nurse's coat on special occasions. When the Board of Governors was going round the wards, for example. The Board of Governors with Reverend Veronal, whom Gilgen loved to mock . . .

"You didn't take just two bundles of banknotes, Gilgen," said Studer. He continued to search the wardrobe, though he really had no idea what he was expecting to find. "Where's the rest?"

Silence.

"Did you take something from my room yesterday?"

Silence. You couldn't call it either defiant or obstinate. More sad, despairing. It would be a terrible blow for his sick wife, up there in Heiligenschwendi, when she heard her husband was in prison. Studer would have liked to help Gilgen, but how could it be done? He sat down on the edge of the bed, patted Gilgen on the shoulder and spoke the sentences that were traditional in that kind of situation.

"You'll only make things worse for yourself, Gilgen, if you don't tell me where the other two thousand francs are. You'll feel better for it . . ."

Silence.

"Then at least tell me why you stole the money. Unburden your conscience."

As he said this, the sergeant had an uncomfortable feeling again – he seemed to feel that way all the time in this clinic. He had a vague sense that behind the

182

apparently clear facts of the case lay something disturbing, something he couldn't quite grasp.

"Debts." Gilgen suddenly spoke quietly, then fell silent again. Although the expression on his face was like that of an anxious mouse, it was also remarkably determined.

Still silence in O block. Presumably all those who were not in the garden had gone to the funeral. At that moment one of the Board of Governors was probably giving a speech at the open grave. God, they had to have something to do.

"Debts?"

Gilgen nodded and Studer didn't probe further. He knew the story of the house and the mortgage.

Gilgen recounted what had happened in a monotone.

"During my hour – you must know that when we're on duty until nine o'clock we have the right to one free hour in the day – so during my free hour, I went to Dreyer to buy a packet of cigars. Then I thought that as I was there I might as well go to the admin office and ask when the next wage-cut was due – you never know, nowadays they can come overnight. I get on well with Fräulein Hänni, I thought I'd ask her. The manager had gone to the funeral and you hear all sorts of things in the admin office. The door was open, so I went in. I saw the safe open in the other room and . . ."

"How many bundles did you take?"

"Two . . ."

"Two? Where were they? On the top shelf? On the bottom shelf?"

"On . . . on . . . on the bottom shelf, I think?"

"Not on the middle one?"

"Oh yes, on the middle one?"

"How many shelves are there in the safe?"

183

"Three . . ."

Studer looked at Gilgen.

The safe was divided in two by one shelf halfway up. Studer had seen that.

Therefore . . .

Gilgen's expression was like that of a whipped dog. Studer looked away. His eye fell on the open wardrobe. There was something grey right at the bottom, behind the shoes. Studer got up, bent down – the sandbag! The cosh in the shape of a huge salami.

"And this?" asked Studer. "Are you finally going to come clean?"

But Gilgen maintained his silence again. He passed the flat of his hand across his bald head once – his fingers were trembling visibly – then shrugged his shoulders. The shrug of his shoulders could have meant anything.

"Where were you on Wednesday night?"

"Here in the clinic." The answer was accompanied by a wave of the hand, as if to say there's no point to all this.

"You sleep alone in this room?"

A nod.

"Did you talk to Pieterlen when he was having a smoke in the day room?"

Studer placed his powerful, broad-shouldered figure in front of the little man.

Gilgen looked up fearfully. "Don't bully me, Sergeant," he said softly.

"Then I'll have to take you in," said Studer, "so you'd better think it over first. The charge might not be just theft, it might be murder."

A look of horrified amazement.

"But the Director's death was an accident."

"That hasn't been established yet. Stand up."

184

Studer went up to the man, patted him all over, took his purse out of one pocket, his keyring out of the other, all the while wondering how to carry out the arrest without attracting too much attention. He could telephone the local policeman from the porter's lodge. Yes, that would be best.

"Apron off! Coat on!" ordered Studer. The rest would sort itself out.

Obediently Gilgen went to the wardrobe and put on his coat, without rolling his shirtsleeves down. It was a pretty wretched coat; it must have been his wife who mended it, before she fell ill . . .

"In the bedside table," said Gilgen shyly, "there are the photos of my wife and the two children. Can I take them with me?"

Studer nodded. The table was jammed in between the window and the bed. Gilgen went round the bed, took a wallet out of the drawer, pulled out a picture and looked at it for a long time before handing it across the bed to the sergeant.

"Have a look, Studer," he said. The sergeant took the photo and turned away to get a better light on the picture. The woman in it had a thin face with a good-natured smile. She was holding a child with each hand. As Studer looked at the picture, he suddenly felt that something in the room had changed. He looked round. Gilgen had vanished.

The open window! Studer pushed the bed aside and leant out as far as he could.

Down below, Gilgen lay on the ground in almost the same position as the Director at the bottom of the ladder. But his fringe of copper-coloured hair shone in the sun. The courtyard was empty. Studer slowly went out of the room, through the glass door, down the stairs and out into the courtyard. There he gently picked up Gilgen's body – he hardly weighed anything – and carried it back up the stairs to the first floor with slow, heavy steps.

Back in the room, he covered the body with the red counterpane and stood there looking at it. His head seethed with unfocused fury.

Then he suddenly started. In the day room a schmaltzy voice began to sing:

> *Somewhere in the world the road to heaven starts,*
> *Somewhere, some when, somehow . . .*

Who was trying to make a fool of him?

What Studer could not know was that at that moment the porter, Dreyer, had switched on the clinic receiver because it was four o'clock and it was one of his duties to provide all the wards with radio music. He had been a little late, which was why it had started in the middle of a song. Thus it was that the loudspeaker on the wall of O Ward day room quite innocently sang a grotesque dirge for little Gilgen.

Studer, though, had no idea where the song was coming from. He just flew into a rage. He went into the day room and glared round furiously, looking for the voice that seemed to be mocking him. Eventually he found the loudspeaker up on the wall. It was just a huge mouth covered in cloth and was a good ten feet from the floor. Studer grabbed one of the chairs by the backrest, swung it in the air and scored such a direct hit on the speaker that the voice just sang one more "Some—" before it disintegrated in a crash of splintering wood.

Having recovered his calm, Studer went back into the small room. He closed Gilgen's eyes. As he was doing so, his eye was caught by something in the drawer of the bedside table which was still open. A photograph.

An amateur snapshot showing Dr Laduner in his white doctor's coat and smiling mask standing beside his wife. Behind him the entrance to the clinic could be seen.

On the back was written: *A memento for Nurse Gilgen, Dr Laduner*

How did the doctor come to be giving a photograph with a personal dedication to a nurse? Studer stood there studying it. Finally he decided to go and look for Staff Nurse Jutzeler. He was desperate for some expert advice.

Colleagues

It was clear that the appearance of Sergeant Studer was unwelcome to Jutzeler, the staff nurse with the brown doe-eyes. He was standing in the garden, still flushed from the wrestling, but he had put his white coat back on, the nurse's badge a red glow on the lapel.

"Can you come with me for a minute?" Studer asked, fixing him with such an earnest, urgent expression that Jutzeler nodded.

"Has something happened?" he asked.

"Gilgen threw himself out of the window. His body's upstairs," Studer told him in a matter-of-fact voice and asked how they could avoid attracting too much attention.

"Gilgen." Jutzeler nodded. "Dead!" Then he shook his head.

They went to the room off the day room. For a brief while Jutzeler stood silently by the dead man, then he drew up a chair and gestured to it. Studer sat down. Jutzeler set his slim frame down on the edge of the bed, beside the body, and said it was perhaps better it had happened this way.

One thing seemed certain: people at Randlingen Clinic were fatalistic . . .

"Why?" Studer asked.

Jutzeler sighed. "You don't know what things are like in a place like this, Sergeant."

He seemed to be wondering whether to say more when Studer interrupted him. He'd long meant to ask

Jutzeler, he said, why he'd had an argument with the Director on Wednesday evening.

Jutzeler asked who had told him that.

That didn't matter, Studer replied, and, anyway, he knew the argument was Gilgen's fault.

Jutzeler had leant back and folded his hands. He subjected the sergeant to a long look of assessment and Studer did not lower his eyes. He knew what the result of the assessment would be.

How often had this sort of thing happened to him! At first people only saw him as the detective, the policemen they had to beware of. Their mistrust was understandable; after all, who had a completely clear conscience nowadays? But when Studer managed to get a person to himself, face to face, the mistrust generally vanished as the other came to feel that here was a man, a middle-aged man, who radiated a rare sense of security, of peace. And sometimes, when Studer was not unhappy with himself, he got delusions of grandeur: he began to imagine he was a strong personality. Perhaps he wasn't even entirely wrong.

Finally Jutzeler seemed to have made up his mind, for he started to speak. It was a long story he had to tell, sitting beside the body of little Gilgen. Several times he was called, his name echoing through the corridors of O Ward, but he didn't stir from the bed, he went on talking, in a slightly monotonous voice, his hands clasped round his knees . . . And although his story touched only briefly on the events of the last few days, it explained quite a lot . . .

It started with the founding of the Randlingen brass band. The nurses who played brass instruments had decided to get together. They looked for and found a conductor, a certain Knuchel, a nurse in T Ward. With a broad chin and thick lips, he was a man who knew his

Bible, a member of one of the sects in the village. They held a meeting and Knuchel made a number of demands: they could only play hymns and serious folk songs, no marches, no dances. At the start of every rehearsal there would have to be prayers and a chapter of the Bible read out, the same at the end. Little Gilgen played the trombone. He was also the leader of the opposition.

The "opposition" consisted of the more worldly among them. They refused to have anything to do with that kind of circus, as they put it. Gilgen saw a band as a first step towards getting the staff organized in a union. He wanted a clear decision: no religious circus, solidarity instead ... He was outvoted. The 'unbelievers' withdrew at the very first meeting and set up their own group, which was to play marches and waltzes and provide dance music at "events". But they lacked a conductor. Although he had more than enough troubles of his own, Gilgen rehearsed them. They played once, at New Year ... They were awful: out of tune, no rhythm ... Even the patients laughed, there were whistles and catcalls, and the Director was furious because there were a few guests present and he felt he'd been made to look a fool. The "profane brass" disbanded and the few instrumentalists who were keen to play donned sackcloth and ashes and went to join the Bible-thumpers. As a conductor Knuchel was good. Two weeks later they played on a Sunday morning, a serenade for the Director, who congratulated them; they were given a grant from the clinic's entertainment fund. Knuchel made his conditions. He was happy to play at events with his musicians, but there must be no dancing during the music. The brass band played funeral marches – so dancing was out of the question anyway – hymns and, at most, the Song of the Beresina.

Studer might think this was all irrelevant, Jutzeler went on. On the contrary, it showed up the tensions among the nursing staff. If the sergeant had no objections, he'd tell him a little about himself.

Jutzeler spoke very calmly. It sounded as if he were giving a report on some boring topic to a meeting of the Board of Governors, though there was an emotional undertone buried somewhere beneath the unmoved exterior.

"As a boy I was put into service with a farmer. In the Bernese Oberland. You'll know what that means, Sergeant: hunger, beatings, never a friendly word. No point in wasting my breath on it, the facts are well enough known, too well known perhaps. I had a piece of luck. I came to the notice of the village priest because once, in a high Alpine meadow, I put a tourist's broken leg in splints. The doctor was amazed. The result was that I managed to get accepted into a nursing school at eighteen. It was a very religious place, but I'll spare you the details of what went on underneath the pious surface, Sergeant. Nothing very pleasant, I can assure you. After I'd passed the examinations I worked in various hospitals as a nurse. Then one day, while I was travelling about on holiday, I had a look round Randlingen. I found it interesting – also the pay was better in the psychiatric clinics than in the hospitals. I was thinking of getting married. The Director happened to be away on holiday; Dr Laduner was acting director and took me on. At that time the clinic was–"

"I know," said Studer. "Dr Laduner's wife told me."

Fine. Jutzeler was telling him things he knew already: the use of narcosis, the dogged struggle for the mind of Pieterlen (perhaps the only odd thing was that Jutzeler used Dr Laduner's expression, "the classic case"), his attempt to establish a degree of unanimity among the nursing staff, an attempt that had been discussed with Dr Laduner.

"It's just like it was at nursing school. All the nurses do is hassle each other. No solidarity. They're always complaining about the long hours we have to put in – from six in the morning to eight in the evening – but no one does anything to try and get it changed. In the other clinics the nursing staff got organized, we always lagged behind. They threatened to go on strike if conditions weren't improved, in Randlingen we knuckled under. The Director had appointed the brother of his second wife as chief mechanic and he sabotaged everything he could. I've not given up, I've read a lot about tactics, the workers' struggle. I've read other books, too; one in particular stuck out. In it the author said, 'Proletarian, your worst enemy is your fellow proletarian.' I've seen that here in the clinic. If Dr Laduner hadn't always shielded me, I'd have been kicked out long ago. I've had to take over one ward. I'm responsible for everything that happens in P because Weyrauch, the senior nurse –"

"Takes nudist magazines."

"Exactly, Sergeant." Jutzeler gave a faint smile.

"I did manage to get a few nurses together and we tried to get in contact with the nurses who have organized themselves into unions in other hospitals and clinics. But the religious fanatics and the mechanic . . . What you must realize, Sergeant, is that in a clinic like this it's not just two large groups – the religious ones and those who want to form a union – the great majority drift between the two. Have you studied the French Revolution?'

"Not much . . ."

"Between the two extreme groups," Jutzeler explained, now speaking formal German, though his

Oberland origins were still audible in the lilting accent, "between the right wing and the extreme left, the 'mountain', lay the centre, the swamp they called it, *le marais*. Those were the people who just wanted to live, earn money, have a good life again. They were the ones who tipped the balance. We have our own 'swamp', the people who are happy for others to get them a rise in wages, who have money saved up in the bank, who are worried about losing their jobs–"

"Bohnenblust," said Studer quietly.

"Among others. They tipped the balance. We joined the Association of State Employees, and the pious Christians went into the Protestant Workers' Party. The Director was happy, of course. When I went to see Dr Laduner after the meeting, he just shrugged his shoulders and said there was nothing you could do. When times were hard ... The others have never openly attacked me, but the whole campaign against Gilgen was really directed at me."

Jutzeler looked at the dead body. Gilgen seemed to be smiling.

"Dr Laduner liked Gilgen. And the others knew that. I have good people on the ward here, almost all of them young nurses, but I have to keep on at them all the time.

"Gilgen was the oldest. I made him my deputy, and that was a big mistake. Gilgen was a good nurse, but he had no idea how to maintain discipline. And when all's said and done, you have to have order in a ward. Things are different now, especially since Dr Laduner introduced occupational therapy. We have to take time with the patients, keep them occupied, even in their free time, get them reading, playing games, stop them sinking back into lethargy. We want to be able to discharge them."

Studer was amazed. This Jutzeler was a simple man, had started out as a farmer's boy, yet he spoke in a calm and considered manner, he knew what he wanted.

"I had to tick Gilgen off. I have one free day every fortnight and a half day in between. Plus fourteen days holiday a year. Whenever I came back, everything was at sixes and sevens. Gilgen was hopeless at giving orders. Like all shy people, he was either too hard or too soft. The others started to hate him.

"There's a lot of gossip in a clinic like this. I've never joined in, but you can imagine, Sergeant, you're in a similar kind of organization. And you can never quite tell exactly where Matto's realm stops – as Schül would say. The young nurses would go to Knuchel in T Ward, the conductor of the brass band, to complain about Gilgen. Perhaps" – Jutzeler patted the red counterpane over the dead body – "perhaps he had done something not quite according to the rules. Knuchel advised them to keep an eye on Gilgen. It was generally known – it's like living in a glasshouse here – that Gilgen was having a difficult time of it. Once, when he was out working in the fields, he was caught wearing a pair of boots with a patient's name written inside them. One of the young nurses told Knuchel, Knuchel went to the staff nurse on T, another of the religious crowd, an Anabaptist or a Sabbatarian or one of the Evangelical Brethren, I'm not really very well up on all these sects, and the staff nurse went running off to the Director. I knew nothing at all about the matter. The Director took statements from the staff nurse on T, from Knuchel, from the young nurse on my ward, all behind my back, behind Gilgen's back. After that the other nurses were interviewed, then they searched Gilgen's locker. They found a pair of underpants there that also had a patient's name in them. Now Gilgen was summoned to the Director and given the third degree ... You knew Gilgen. He told me yesterday evening he'd spoken to you the afternoon before ... He was confused ... I'm convinced he didn't take the boots, nor the underpants. The underpants could easily have got mixed up in the wash. The boots? I've always suspected they were planted, and in the morning, when you're going off to work in the fields, you're in a hurry, you don't look too carefully ... But Gilgen was no good at defending himself. He just stayed silent."

"Yes," sighed Studer, "he was good at that."

"And you have to remember: his wife ill, debts, worries, his children boarded out ... People can be pretty mean ... Little Gilgen never harmed a soul. You couldn't hold it against him that he didn't like the way the brass band was run. But they did. They informed on him. The statements were taken by the Director three days before the harvest festival. He was going to send them to the Board of Governors with the demand that Gilgen be dismissed.

"If the other party has its spies, I have mine, too. I heard about the business that evening. Around six o'clock. I'm allowed to sleep at home, but that night I stayed in the clinic. I went from one ward to another, from half past six to eleven o'clock. I talked to them. We have to stick together, I said, the same thing could happen to any of us, just think, it's our freedom that's at stake here. They all turned a deaf ear, found excuses. The next day I tried again, only I took a stronger line. If Gilgen's dismissed, I said, we'll call a strike ... You could say that was stupid ... The 'swamp' didn't go along with it. The frogs in the swamp are timid little things; somebody just has to walk past on the bank and they immediately hide in the mud. It's only when it's all quiet again that they start croaking. Now that the Director's dead the frogs are croaking very loud. They know there'll be big changes under Dr Laduner . . .

"The day of the harvest festival arrived. I heard that the Director knew of my plan for a strike. It could cost me my job, but I wasn't afraid. I'll always be able to find work, at the hospital they were unhappy to see me leave. With Gilgen it was different . . .

"That evening I answered the telephone and fetched the Director."

Studer was leaning forward, his forearms on his thighs. Now he raised his head. "One question, Jutzeler. Didn't you recognize the voice on the telephone?"

A pause. A long pause. Jutzeler frowned. Then he went on, just as if the sergeant had not asked his question.

"I stopped the Director when he came back from the telephone and told him I had to speak to him that evening. He gave me a mocking look and said, 'Urgent all of a sudden, is it?' I stayed calm and just said, 'Yes.' In that case, he said, I should wait for him outside his office at half past twelve. Then he walked off.

"He kept me waiting, but not for long. He came and we went into his office. I demanded to see the statements, but he just laughed. So then I told him what I thought of the whole business and made some threats. I told him I'd get the newspapers onto him. It was disgusting the way he treated the nursing staff, I said. I upbraided him for his little love affairs and at that he started to bawl at me. He'd put a stop to my games, he'd have me blacklisted, he said, I was dismissed on the spot and he'd see to it I never worked again. I kept on about the statements. After all, I pointed out, the business with Gilgen had happened in O Ward. I was the staff nurse there and that gave me the right to ask to see the statements. It was all an attempt to get at me, I went on, but I knew that Dr Laduner was on my side . . . I shouldn't have said that . . . He picked up on it straight away and told me he had a score to settle with Dr Laduner as well. Did I know, he asked me, how many patients had died in D1 over the last few days? He'd had a list drawn up and he was going to submit it to the Board of Governors to show them the kind of havoc a doctor could wreak, who . . . While he had been Director, he said, mortality had always been very low in the clinic, it was only since they'd introduced all these fancy modern methods that there'd been so many deaths. He'd checked Dr Blumenstein's autopsy reports; there were discrepancies, he claimed. He'd carried out a second autopsy on two bodies himself, he said, and sent blood samples to forensics. He was just waiting for the results, then he'd start proceedings against Dr Laduner. That gentleman had been getting on his nerves for long enough; he'd turned all the other doctors against him, but he, Ulrich Borstli, was still Director of Randlingen Clinic and Dr Laduner, for all his cleverness, for all his influence and diplomacy, could do nothing about that . . . There were the autopsy reports, he said, tapping his desk, and there were the statements about Gilgen – and I was to get the hell out of the office.

"We left together. I stood in a dark corner of the corridor; the Director went up to his apartment and came back down with his loden cape on. He switched the corridor light off before he went out into the courtyard . . .

"Then I did something stupid, Sergeant. I wanted to

see the statements regarding Gilgen, but, even more, I wanted to see those autopsy reports . . . I felt it was my duty to take them to Dr Laduner to give him a chance to defend himself. So I went back into the office. I switched the light on and went through all the drawers, but I couldn't find anything.

"Then I heard steps outside and I quickly turned the light out. I didn't want to be caught in the Director's office like a thief.

"The door opened. A hand went towards the light switch and I grabbed it. We wrestled silently in the office for a while. The typewriter fell on the floor, a window-pane was broken. Finally I got the man on the floor and made off. I went to see Gilgen. He was still up, he was on duty that night, but he hadn't gone to the harvest festival. He was sitting here on the edge of his bed. I told him not to lose heart, we knew now what was going on. I intended to speak to Dr Laduner the next morning, but all sorts of things happened before then."

"Did you meet anyone on your way back to O, Jutzeler?"

Jutzeler avoided the question. He said, "It was striking two when I went across the courtyard."

"You didn't hear a cry?"

"No . . ."

"Fine," said Studer. "And that's all you have to tell me?"

Jutzeler thought for a while, scratched his head, then shook it, smiled and said, "If you want to learn more about us warders – as they used to say, nurses they call us nowadays – I could go on for ages. About the long days with time dragging by because you've almost nothing to do. You stand around, hands in the bib of your apron, and supervise the patients, serve their meals, supervise them again, 'tend' them in the garden, come back up here . . . And eat. Food is very important, not only for the patients, for us nurses, too. We know the menu for weeks ahead: the sweetcorn on Mondays, the rice on Wednesdays, the macaroni on Fridays and the Saturday sausage. We know when we'll get *rösti* in the morning, when we'll get butter. We've developed a special walk for going across the court-yard, slowly, slowly, to use up time. We get married so that we've got a home somewhere, at least during the night. We feel it when there's a change coming in the weather – the patients in our care are irritable, and so are we . . . We get paid, but not much . . . Some build themselves a house and have a mortgage to pay off. It's as if they feel they need worries just to fill the empty days . . . We stand around waiting for the day to end. They give us courses, but we're not allowed any responsibility. Every aspirin, every bath we give, we have to ask first. Why do they give us courses when we're not allowed to make use of the things they teach us? Courses! My colleagues who took their diploma two years ago, what do they remember from it? Nothing. I'm a bit better off: I read, and then Dr Laduner explains to me things I don't know. But it's all so point-less. What use is it that I can make a better diagnosis than an assistant doctor who's just started? I have to stand and watch a junior doctor, Neuville for example, doing stupid things, making silly jokes with a patient under stress, say, and I'm the one who has to deal with the patient when he goes and smashes a few windows. If only they were all like Dr Laduner."

Silence. The dead man on the bed had a smile on his face. Outside the twilight was red . . .

"I have to go now," said Studer. "*Merci*, Jutzeler. What will you do with . . . with Gilgen?"

199

"I'll wait until it's dark, then take him to M with Schwertfeger. There were three of us who stuck together, Schwertfeger from D1" – in his mind's eye Studer saw the man with the muscular arms who looked like a dairyman – "Gilgen and me. We stuck together. Now there's only two of us. Though now it's Dr Laduner who's in charge."

Passing the porter's lodge, Studer went in and enquired politely whether Dreyer sold Brissagos as well. Receiving an affirmative reply, Studer took a packet, then pointed to Dreyer's bandaged hand and asked, in a quiet voice, "Why didn't you tell me you broke the window in the Director's office? Was that how you cut yourself?"

Dreyer gave a slightly foolish smile. He thought for a moment, then took a deep breath and said, "Yes, I heard footsteps in the office and went to see what was up. I was attacked and cut my hand. Why didn't I say anything? Simple. By that time the Director had disappeared and I was afraid I'd get involved. How did you find out I'd been in the office?"

"Deduction," said Studer, and had the satisfaction of seeing a glint of admiration in the porter's eyes.

It might be true, it might not. Dreyer could have had reasons of his own for looking round the office. Though what those reasons were would be difficult to establish. He'd have to wait again ... But he wasn't going to go and have dinner with Dr Laduner. He needed to be alone. There was the clock in the clinic tower just striking six with its usual sharp clang. Studer went down the steps of the main entrance, heading along the avenue of apple trees for the village of Randlingen.

He saw a couple walking in front of him. Dr

Laduner, with his wife on his arm. They were walking in step with each other, slowly, through the twilight, which was cool and strawberry coloured. An orange cloud was hanging over the snowy mountains.

They weren't talking. The couple did not have the look of lovers, Studer thought, but one thing was obvious: they belonged together, they would stick together. Studer was comforted by the feeling that, whatever happened, at least Dr Laduner would not be alone. For, to be honest, the situation looked a lot less rosy than the evening sky . . .

When he reached the inn, Studer ordered a portion of ham and a carafe of blanc de Vaud. He ate a few mouthfuls, took a sip of his wine, then got up and asked where the telephone was.

It was Frau Laduner who answered. Studer made his excuses and said he wouldn't be coming to dinner, something important had cropped up.

"Yes," said Frau Laduner in her warm, deep voice which sounded pleasant even on the telephone, "but you must be back by half past eight. You must meet the Board of Governors."

Studer promised he'd be on time.

Matto appears

It was as a doctor that Studer most admired Laduner. He had the ability to be at the centre of things while at the same time giving whoever was speaking the feeling they were the sole focus of attention . . . Diplomatic skills.

He got Reverend Veronal, the priest with the big mouth, to talk about the attitude of the Swiss church to the Oxford Movement, listening with an expression of interest to his long-winded explanations, before interrupting him with a polite, "You'll excuse me, Reverend?" and turning to the wife of the member of parliament with a few words in praise of the Welfare Board, which responded positively to all suggestions from the clinic. The wife of the member of parliament beamed with delight: one of her brothers was an official at the Welfare Board. Studer happened to know the man; Laduner wasn't exaggerating, he thought. The doctor then turned to the deaf probation officer and asked him about a certain Schreier, who had been in Randlingen for assessment and then been sent to the labour camp at Witzwil for a year. How was the man? he asked. Was he behaving himself? He was sure, he went on, that the probation officer would find him a good job when he was released. No, no, the prognosis was very promising. He refused to let the constant "What was that you said?" disturb his composure, repeating things three times if necessary. While all this was going on, Frau Laduner chatted with the wife of the member of parliament as she poured tea. Reverend Veronal took it with plenty of rum. Studer too.

The sergeant had been introduced to the Board. Now he was sitting, silent, in a corner by the window, observing the proceedings.

The Board took their leave at nine. Studer stayed in his chair as Dr Laduner offered to drive the members to the station. The offer was accepted with thanks.

Studer waited in his corner for the doctor to return. Frau Laduner asked him why he was so silent, but the only answer she received was an ungracious mutter. So she fell silent too and went across to the window in the corner opposite Studer, where there was a shiny box on a little table. She turned a knob . . . A band was playing a march. Studer didn't mind. A march was better than "Somewhere in the world . . ."

So they both waited in silence for Laduner to return. When he came in he sent his wife off to bed – in a voice that was full of warmth and concern – then asked, "You'll sit up with me for a while, Studer?"

The sergeant muttered something that could, at a pinch, be taken for assent.

At first Laduner was silent. Then he said, "Pity about Gilgen . . ." He seemed to be waiting for an answer, but when none came, he went on. "Has it ever occurred to you, Studer, that no one can spend a long time dealing with mad people and not be affected by it? That contact with them is contagious? Actually, I've sometimes wondered whether it isn't the other way round and only people who are already a bit round the bend, to use a popular expression, go to work in psychiatric clinics, either as nurses or as doctors. The one difference is that people who feel the urge to enter Matto's realm know there's something wrong with them.

Subconsciously, if you like, but they know. It's an escape. Other people out there are sometimes even further round the bend, but they're not aware of it, not even subconsciously. Once, you know, I was going past the town hall at lunchtime, when the people who work there came pouring out, and I stopped and observed them. Gait, posture ... It was instructive. One had his thumb stuck in his waistcoat and was strolling along, legs swinging, a fixed expression on his face, which was red, with a vacuous smile on it. 'Look at that,' I told myself, 'incipient catatonia,' and tried to work out when the next phase might start. Another had a fixed stare. He kept looking round, then he looked down at the ground for a while, carefully balancing on the kerb ... Neurotic, perhaps schizoid, I thought. Another had one of those smiles people usually call sunny. Head in the air, he was swinging his walking stick, saying hello to everyone. 'Aha,' I said to myself, 'manic depression, like my would-be political assassin, Schmocker.'"

The radio in the corner was still quietly playing its marches. It made a pleasant accompaniment to Dr Laduner's thoughts.

You've talked to Schül, or so I heard. Did he present you with his poem? You must admit it's not stupid; it's full of symbolic meaning. Sometimes I envy him his Matto. Matto, who rules the world. Matto, who plays with red balls, flings them in the air and Revolution flares up. The coloured streamers flutter and War blazes ... There's a lot to be said for it. We'll never be able to draw a line between mental illness and normality. All we can say is whether a person can adapt to society, and the better he can adapt to society, the more he tries to understand his fellow human beings, the more normal he is. That's why I always tell our nurses to get organized in a union, to stick together and try to get on with each other. Being organized is the first step towards fruitful communal life. First of all a community of interest, then comradeship. The one comes from the other – or at least it ought to . . . Responsibility assumed voluntarily . . . 'All for one and one for all' – wouldn't that be marvellous?"

Another quiet march. It was a military band that was playing.

"If only we didn't hear it so often prostituted by certain folksy public speakers . . . What do we actually do, we much-maligned psychiatrists? We try to create a degree of order, we try to convince people it makes sense to behave more or less rationally, not to give way to every impulse that comes from the darkness of the subconscious, which can only lead to disorder. There's one thing people haven't yet cottoned on to, namely that suffering can be enjoyable. Do you see what I'm getting at? If a nation has it too good, then they get cocky and long for suffering. Being satisfied with what you have is probably the most difficult thing to achieve."

Laduner fell silent. He seemed to have been talking more for himself. Studer suddenly had the feeling he'd misjudged everything the doctor had said the previous evening about Pieterlen.

What was it that was at the bottom of every human being? Loneliness.

Perhaps Dr Laduner was lonely too? He had his wife, true, but there are certain things you can't discuss with your wife. He had colleagues, but what can you talk about with your colleagues? Shop! And with the doctors here? They regarded him as their teacher. Then one day a simple detective sergeant turns up in Dr Laduner's apartment. Dr Laduner seizes the opportunity and talks on and on at the said detective sergeant. And why not?

"He flings his paper streamers and War flares up . . ." Laduner repeated, then fell silent. The military march faded out and a foreign voice filled the room. It was an urgent voice, but its urgency was unpleasant.

It said:

"Two hundred thousand men and women are gathered here to cheer me. Two hundred thousand men and women have come as representatives of the whole nation, which is behind me. Foreign states dare to accuse me of breaking a treaty. When I seized power this land lay desolate, ravaged, sick . . . I have made it great, I have made others respect it . . . Two hundred thousand men and women are listening to my words, and with them the whole nation is listening . . ."

Laduner slowly got up and went over to the shiny box from which the words were coming. A click, the voice fell silent.

"Where does Matto's realm end, Studer?" the doctor asked quietly. "At the fence round Randlingen Clinic? You once talked about a spider sitting in the middle of its web. The threads reach out, they spread over the whole world. Matto flings his balls and his paper streamers . . . You'll be thinking I'm a poetic psychiatrist. That wouldn't be a bad thing. It's not much we want, just to bring a little reason to the world. Not the reason of the French Enlightenment, a different kind of reason, the reason of our times. Reason that can light up the darkness inside us, like a lantern, and bring us some clarity . . . Get rid of some of the lies, clear away the grand words: Duty, Truth, Honesty . . . make people more modest. We're all of us murderers, thieves and adulterers . . . Matto is lurking in the darkness. The devil's been dead for ages, but Matto's still

206

alive, Schül's quite right about that, and if he wouldn't keep bothering the police with his murder in Dove's Gorge I'd let him go. It's a pity Schül's never written a history of Matto, as I asked him to. I can't get any newspaper to publish a short poem in prose."

He stopped. Studer gave a quiet yawn, but Laduner didn't notice. "Two hundred thousand men and women . . . the whole nation," he went on. "And Bonhöffer, the psychiatrist, our teacher, with all his knowledge he collapsed like a house of cards. You remember the trial about the fire, Studer? The man who was talking just now was lucky. Had he had a psychiatric examination at the beginning of his career, perhaps the world might look a little different today. As I said before, contact with the mentally ill is contagious. And there are people who are particularly susceptible – whole nations can be susceptible. I once said something in a lecture to which people objected. Certain socalled revolutions, I said, are basically nothing more than the vengeance of psychopaths – at which a few colleagues left the room demonstratively. But it's true."

Laduner looked tired. He put his hand over his eyes. "We're fighting a losing battle, but we must keep going. No one's going to help us, but perhaps it's not entirely pointless. Perhaps others will come after us – in a hundred, two hundred years? – and take over where we left off."

A sigh. All was quiet in the apartment.

"You'll have a glass of Benedictine?" Laduner asked. He went out and took a surprisingly long time to return with two glasses on a tray.

"*Prost,*" he said, clinking his glass with Studer's. "Down in one." Studer emptied his glass. The liqueur had a strangely bitter aftertaste. The sergeant looked at Laduner, but he turned away.

"Good night, Studer. And have a good sleep," he said, He was wearing his smiling mask.

You're lying in bed and you've no idea whether you're asleep or awake. Sleep's like a black blanket; you're lying underneath it and you can't get out of the folds. You're dreaming you're awake . . . perhaps you really are awake?

And the room's brightly lit. The only thing you can't understand is why the light is green, when the bedside lamp has a yellow shade. And in the green light you can see someone sitting at the table. He's leaning back in his chair with an accordion on his knees, and he's playing . . . playing: "Somewhere in the world, the road to heaven starts . . ."

The only odd thing is that the man – is it a man? – the man sitting at the table keeps changing his shape. One moment he's tiny, only the nails on his fingers are long and the colour of green glass . . . then he's bigger and fat, very fat. He looks like Schmocker, the would-be assassin, and he's making a speech while he's playing the accordion: "Two hundred thousand men and women . . ." He's singing it to the tune of "The Roses Are Blooming in Sans Souci". Then the little fat man suddenly has a second pair of arms growing out of his shoulders, they're long and thin and the hands are playing with balls and paper streamers. The balls fly out of the window and the streamers decorate the walls . . . Of course, you're in the casino, sitting at the table with the VIPs, glasses of white wine in front of everyone. But sitting on a corner of the stage, his legs dangling, is the four-armed man. He's playing the accordion and juggling with rubber balls. There are couples dancing in the open space below the stage and the four-armed man jumps down. He mingles with the dancers, he walks among them like the leader of a gypsy band, bowing to every couple, his music ingratiating.

"Reason!" Dr Laduner says it out loud and the casino disappears. There are tenements in a dreary landscape. A star appears in the sky, falls down and becomes a glowing factory with innumerable buildings. There's a stench of gas; it makes your eyes water. The four-armed man is playing "Fridericus Rex, Our King and Lord".

There they are, like a mute regiment standing to attention: bomb after bomb, tall, slim, elegant. "My invention," says the man with four arms. A bomb explodes, yellow gas pours out, everything goes dark, the music stops and Dr Laduner's voice can be heard, loud and clear, "In two hundred years we'll carry on . . ."

Then the yellow curtain of gas disperses and there are corpses scattered over a wide plain. They look strangely distorted, like the Director or little Gilgen. Yes, that's right, one of them is Gilgen. He's standing up and saying, "Somewhere in the world the road to heaven starts . . ." And he starts laughing, and the laughing wakes you up . . . With a muzzy head . . . The room is dark and out of the window you can see that the courtyard is dark as well . . .

Christ Almighty! Why had Dr Laduner put a sedative in your Benedictine?

A noise in the corridor. Studer sat up. A click as the corridor door closed. With one leap Studer was out of bed. Where was Dr Laduner creeping off to?

Had the lecture on Matto's realm been nothing more than a diversionary tactic, like the lecture on Pieterlen?

His leather slippers. A quick glance at the time: two

o'clock. A quick glance out into the courtyard: a figure was cautiously crossing, heading for the corner between T Ward and P.

What was it Dr Laduner had said? Contact with people who were mentally ill was contagious . . .

There was no accordion music trickling down through the ceiling this time. Where could Pieterlen be? He really ought to have had a look at that attic by now, the one with the window from which, according to Schül, Matto's head darted out and in, out and in. Perhaps Schül really had seen something, perhaps he'd just dressed up what he'd seen as an image? The chief of police, whom he had rung up immediately after his conversation with Frau Laduner, had told him there was still no trace of Pieterlen.

Studer slipped across the silent courtyard and went down to the basement of P Ward. The door to the heating plant was open, the light on.

At the foot of the ladder, in the same place as Studer had found the Director, lay Dr Laduner. The furnace door was wide open.

Dr Laduner was not dead, just unconscious. For the moment Studer left him where he was. He shone his pocket torch inside the furnace. A leather briefcase, beside it half-burnt papers. Carefully Studer pulled them out.

On the unburnt part of one of the documents he read: *Nurse Knuchel claims he was told by Nurse Blaser that Gilgen had a pair of underpants in his cupboard . . .*

The rest was missing.

On another sheet was:

Schäfer, Arnold † 25. 8. Embolism. D1.
Vuillemin, Maurice † 26. 8. Exanthematic typhus. D1.
Mosimann, Fritz † 26. 8. General debility, heart failure. U1.

The list of patients who had died that the Director had had drawn up. And there was another sheet, scarcely singed:

Dear Colonel,

In response to your letter of 28 August, I have the pleasure to inform you that I have carried out the enquiries you requested. Recently your son has been indulging in alcohol again; I myself encountered him twice on licensed premises in a state of semi-inebriation. It is my opinion that the course of treatment undertaken by Dr Laduner has been ineffective and I therefore humbly suggest you take the necessary steps to have the aforementioned course of treatment terminated . . .

"Thank you," said a voice beside Studer. The sergeant turned round. Dr Laduner was standing beside him, a smile on his face. He took the documents out of Studer's hand and put them back in the furnace. Then he lit a match. The papers flared up. Dr Laduner fetched a bundle of firewood and put it, thinnest pieces first, on the papers. Finally he placed the leather briefcase on top.

"Let's burn the past," he said.

For a moment Studer imagined he was still dreaming, but then he saw the colour drain from Laduner's usually bronzed face. The doctor started to sway. Studer caught him. The man was heavy.

"Who knocked you down, Doctor?"

Laduner closed his eyes. He was refusing to answer.

"And," Studer went on, "it wasn't right to put a sedative in my liqueur. Why did you do that? After all, I'm supposed to be here to protect you. I can't do that if you put me to sleep."

Laduner opened his eyes. "You'll come to understand everything, eventually. Perhaps I should have trusted you more, but it just wasn't possible."

Dr Laduner had a lump on the back of his head, visible under the strand of hair that stuck up like a heron's crest. Blood was trickling down.

"I need to sit down for a bit," said Dr Laduner in a weary voice. "A little water – if you would be so good," he added with a smile, parodying the senior nurse, Weyrauch.

Studer left the boiler room and went over to O, the only ward he was familiar with. There he broke into the ground-floor kitchen, found a large milk jug, filled it with water and set off back. On the way, in the basement, he met a man creeping along in the darkness. The man stopped. He was short and muscular, perhaps a nurse returning from an assignation.

What was wrong? the stocky man wanted to know.

Nothing to do with him, Studer replied grumpily.

Had something happened to Dr Laduner?

No, he'd just had a bit of a dizzy spell, that was all.

The man breathed what sounded like a sigh of relief, but when Studer tried to grab him, in order to question him, he vanished down a dark side corridor. No steps could be heard – he must have been wearing slippers too.

Studer washed Dr Laduner's wound and bandaged it with his clean handkerchief. Then he carefully led him across the courtyard and up the stairs.

It was a good job the nightwatchman had already done his rounds.

In the bell turret of the clinic the hammer struck four times, then came three more strokes, hardly any sweeter. The last had a tinny echo.

"Oh, Ernst!" Frau Laduner exclaimed reproachfully. She was wearing her red dressing-gown. Studer helped her put Laduner to bed. Then he said goodnight and left. Frau Laduner gave him a look of gratitude, which pleased him.

Back in his room, he was suddenly reminded of the scene in Eichhorn's reformatory in Oberhollabrunn. Letting resentment play itself out was sometimes not without its dangers, he thought. And hazily he saw for the first time something that was like the end of a thread, a symbolic thread you have to pull to unravel a tangle. But he couldn't quite grasp it . . . He could see the colour, that was all. Perhaps the reason he couldn't grasp it was that his head was dizzy with sleep.

Sunday shadows

It was good that Dr Laduner was not on duty that Sunday. It meant he could stay in bed and rest his sore head. Studer's head was throbbing too, but the suspense, his interest in what was happening in Randlingen, was stronger than his headache. Thursday, Friday, Saturday – three days. He would have to get this finished, or he'd be ending up in Matto's realm himself.

As he was wandering round the wards at about ten o'clock that morning, he thought about his dream the previous night. The doctor's rounds were over, he was told. The lady from the Baltic had sprinted round the wards. Studer had seen her coming back, galloping across the courtyard, alone, white coat fluttering, and into the central block.

Now he was in T, the ward for those whose bodies were ill as well as their minds. He was looking for Knuchel, the conductor of the Randlingen brass band, who ought to be on duty in T Ward. He had no idea why he was looking for him, why he wanted to see him, but he sensed that he needed to speak to the man as a way of sharing the guilt he felt at the death of the little red-haired nurse.

The patients in the beds were mostly very quiet, staring blankly at the ceiling with large eyes. There was just one, in a corner, who kept repeating the same words over and over again. "Two hundred thousand cows, two hundred thousand sheep, two hundred thousand horses, two hundred thousand francs . . ."

That number: two hundred thousand.

Studer heard a voice saying, "Two hundred thousand men and women . . ." It made him feel uncomfortable.

Just as the sergeant was about to go over to Knuchel (he remembered now that he had seen him when he had accompanied Laduner on his rounds; he was the nurse the doctor had given a ticking off), there was a noise and shuffling of feet out in the corridor. Throats were cleared, then women's voices started to sing a hymn.

Studer went out into the corridor. There were three old women with a fourth, who was younger and carrying a guitar on which she played a simple accompaniment.

In slow, dragging voices they sang of the kingdom of heaven and its glory, where sinners would know bliss. Nurse Knuchel, with his broad chin, was standing in the doorway, a vacuous smile on his thick lips. Or perhaps it was a pious smile. The younger woman tuned her guitar, played a few chords and they burst into a cheerful melody, which sounded very strange coming from those withered lips: "The cause is thine, Lord Jesus Christ . . ."

After they had finished, one of the old women turned to Studer and said, "The poor patients, they're ill and we must do something to cheer them up. Otherwise there's nothing for them."

The patient in the corner at the end of the ward was still counting his herds of cows, sheep and horses. He hadn't been listening to the singing. And the others were staring at the ceiling, slobbering on their sheets. The women transferred their attentions to the next ward, to refresh other souls.

"That is practical Christianity," said Nurse Knuchel.

You could see the brass top of the stud holding his collar together. "Doctors and their science!" he said scornfully. "Nothing for the soul, nothing for the spirit . . . Occupational therapy! I once tried to start regular Bible study in the evenings, but I got short shrift from Dr Laduner. He'd nothing against religion, he said, but here in the clinic it was important for the patients to learn to face up to reality without fear."

Knuchel spoke like a revivalist preacher. Studer had once gone to one of their meetings – for professional reasons: a swindler, who was wanted in five cantons for fraud and theft, had wormed his way into their confidence. Studer knew the words of the hymn, he knew the tune. They were harmless, the people who went to these meetings, proud of what they called their Christianity, and it allowed them to look down self-righteously on others.

"But what about Gilgen?" said Studer. "You didn't behave very well towards him, not even like a good Christian."

The expression on Knuchel's face froze. "Worldliness must be rooted out, wherever it appears," he replied. "I came not to bring peace, but a sword." Studer wondered if you could really call tale-telling a sword.

Again the expression on Knuchel's face changed. A sugary smile, presumably intended as kindly, appeared on his lips. "Those who have not ears to hear, must be made to hear," he said. "Only through religion can the world be made whole again. I preach reconciliation, but," he went on with a frown, "if they mock my Saviour, then they must be chastised with a rod of iron."

Poor little Gilgen with his sick wife and his debts and his sad life. A man who had believed in something, who had given comfort to the patients, who had told stories to an overexcited catatonic, stories the patient didn't understand, but which calmed him down ... Now don't start getting sentimental, he told himself. But there was no way round the fact that he had liked little Gilgen, who passed with a run of four to the ace, from the very start, and that he was partly to blame for his death.

That made him think. Why did he throw himself out of the window? Because of the theft? *Chabis*! There was no proof that Gilgen had stolen anything from the manager's office. There was something else behind it ... Why did he have this vague feeling Gilgen was trying to shield someone else, that he was afraid he'd betray someone and that was the reason he'd jumped out of the window? It looked like his suicide was a heroic gesture. Perhaps there was fear behind it, fear of giving something away under cross-examination. People generally went in fear and trembling of the investigating magistrate. And they were right to, they were right!

Who had he been trying to shield? Pieterlen? That was the most obvious answer. He had gone out for walks with Pieterlen every Sunday, they'd chatted together. Gilgen had talked about his debts, Pieterlen about his monstrous crime. Though after what Dr Laduner had told him, it was difficult to regard the murder of his child as monstrous ... Still ... Pieterlen had disappeared at a critical moment, his escape coinciding with the death of the Director, although he had proof that the sandbag had played no part in the Director's death. The slides he had prepared with Neuville's help confirmed that. But someone had pushed Borstli down the ladder.

Jutzeler? There was much that spoke against him as

a suspect. His calm, his detachment, for example. But his job had been at risk. Being blacklisted was no joke for anyone, including those who worked in hospitals. It could mean the end, even for the most competent of men. Things hadn't got to the point where professional competence was more important than political convictions. It would be a long time before they did.

But Jutzeler couldn't have made that telephone call. Who in the clinic had telephoned, and why? Everything he had turned up in the course of his investigation pointed so clearly to the fact that it was the telephone call that had taken the Director to the corner of the clinic, from which a cry had been heard at half past one, that it would be a waste of time looking for another solution. But who was it who had cried out? The Director? His attacker? . . . Attacker? . . . . The word came almost automatically, but who could say it was an "attacker"?

Pieterlen had played the accordion at the harvest festival. Pieterlen, who had disappeared, together with his accordion. Pieterlen had had good reason to waylay the Director, given that he believed the machinations of the Director had prevented his release. Against that was the fact that Dr Laduner had also been hit on the head in the boiler room . . . And that Dr Laduner had known that the briefcase and its contents had been hidden in the furnace . . .

And what about the wallet he had found behind the books in Dr Laduner's apartment shortly after Gilgen had been there?

The accordion! . . . Studer remembered the tunes that had trickled down through the ceiling of his room, remembered Matto darting out and in of the window above his room.

And while Nurse Knuchel, conductor of the

Randlingen brass band (remember, no dancing while they were playing!), taking Studer's silence for approval and hoping for a conversion, went on about the Kingdom of God and redemption, Studer was racking his brains so furiously that the skin on his forehead wrinkled – which Knuchel took as another sign of pensive introspection.

He was all the more surprised, therefore, when Studer bade him a curt farewell and trotted off at the double. His shoulders were hunched . . .

The corridor above Dr Laduner's apartment smelt of dust and nothing else; the smell of medicaments and floor polish was completely absent. On the left was a series of rooms. Servants' quarters. Some doors were locked, the last was ajar.

The first thing Studer saw when he opened it was an accordion. Then, lying on old suitcases and chests, greasy paper and scraps of bread . . . Someone must have been staying in the room for quite some time. When had he left? He felt the pieces of bread . . . They weren't very stale. Yesterday?

And once more he recalled the attempted break-in at the administration office, after which Gilgen had committed suicide because he was afraid he would not be able to stay silent.

But there was another person apart from Gilgen who had gone to buy something from the porter. Not cigars, not tobacco . . . chocolate.

Irma Wasem. She had been in the central block during those critical five minutes. He must ask her if she'd seen anything.

But when the sergeant dialled the number of the female O Ward from Laduner's study and asked for Nurse Wasem, he was told it was her Sunday off and that she was unlikely to be back before evening. When the voice at the other end asked who was calling, Studer simply hung up. A nice life these girls had, nothing but days off.

The afternoon dragged on . . . Dr Laduner had got out of bed. He was sitting on the couch in his study drinking gallons of coffee – because of his sore head, he explained. He had a large bandage round his forehead and the back of his head.

But his answer to all Studer's questions about who had hit him or what he was doing in the boiler room was silence. A stony silence. He had even lost his smiling mask. He looked tired and disheartened.

The afternoon dragged on and on. A real Sunday afternoon, with accordion music – this time clearly coming from the wards – yawns, boredom . . .

It was time he wrapped up this case . . .

Around half past six Studer said he was going out and told Frau Laduner not to wait for him before starting their evening meal, he really couldn't say when he'd be back. At the porter's lodge he went in and asked Dreyer where Gilgen's house was. A little outside the village, he was told, quite near to the river that was about a mile away from Randlingen.

The avenue with the sour green apples again. The twilight was grey. It must have been some instinct that was taking Studer to Gilgen's mortgaged house. It was the last of a row of similar detached houses with steep roofs. They all appeared to be empty; only one had grey smoke rising up into the twilight. Studer examined the names on the letter boxes. Finally: *Gilgen-Furrer, Nurse.*

He walked round it, tried the handles on all the doors. Locked. There were asters in the garden, the endives were still small. It was a tidy garden, no weeds . . .

Studer decided to wait. He could have gone back to the clinic to ask after Nurse Wasem again, but he didn't. Sure-ly, as Dr Laduner would say, the house seemed to be unoccupied. . . . Seemed to be. What was it that gave him the feeling there was someone in there. A curtain moving slightly?

He went out of the garden and a little way back down the road that ran alongside the estate. There was a bush, big enough for him to hide behind. A look round, then Studer slipped behind it. He sat down . . . he might be in for a long wait . . .

The twilight thickened and night started to fall. In a sky of bottle-green, like Matto's fingernails, one star appeared, shining as blue as the lamp in the dormitory of O Ward. Then came darkness. Black. There was no moon.

Steps. A sharp tap-tap, like high-heeled shoes. Carefully Studer peeped out from behind his bush. A woman was coming along the road, turning round frequently, as if she was afraid she might be being followed. Outside Gilgen's house she stopped, looked to the left, looked to the right, then went into the garden. She knocked at the door, waited. Slowly the door opened. In the quiet of the night Studer could hear the woman's voice clearly.

"I think you can come out and walk with me for a while. It's better talking outside. I've brought you something to eat."

A man's voice replied. "If you think so."

The couple came out of the garden and went down the road towards the river. Studer let them get a little way ahead, then followed them cautiously. His caution was unnecessary; the night was very dark. He could only see the others because the woman was wearing a white dress. The river whispered as it flowed. The moon rose over the horizon. It looked like a huge slice of orange. Its light was very soft.

Matto's puppet theatre

"Did everything go all right?" the woman asked

And the man answered, "The cop didn't catch me."

Studer smiled in the dark. The leaves of the alders and willows were a shimmer of grey in the colourful moonlight. The river flowed sluggishly, murmuring dark words no one could understand.

"What happened yesterday?" the woman asked. "Weren't you being a bit careless, Pierre?"

"I ran into the cop when I went to see Dr Laduner. Pity Gilgen's dead, he was a good man."

Silence. The woman was leaning against the man. In front of them was a small area of sand, which glittered in the light of the moon coming through the branches.

"Didn't you ever feel jealous, Pierre?" the woman asked. How a voice could change! Studer had heard it when it was moist with tears. Now it sounded energetic. And at the same time warm and tender.

"Jealous?" It sounded astonished. "Why jealous? I trusted you. You told me you were only going out with the Director so as to get him to change his mind about me. I'm not so stupid as to believe everything people tell me, you know, but why should I not have believed you?"

"You were right, Pierre . . . D'you know what that cop thought? He thought I wanted to become Frau Direktor. Oh, these cops. Just a load of big-mouths, that's all."

"No," said Pieterlen, the classic case, "he's actually

quite a decent bloke. He's stuck by Laduner. If he'd wanted he could have caused him all sorts of problems by now."

"Do you like Laduner better than me?" Irma Wasem asked. It was the kind of question women like to ask. Studer listened sympathetically. There was something about the whole business he found heartening, though he couldn't have said why. He recalled what Dr Laduner had said: "And why shouldn't we have an idyll within these red walls, once in a while?" In a case like this it was nice to be proved wrong. Even Dr Laduner, the great psychiatrist, had been mistaken. The lassie was all right. She stuck by her boyfriend. Though, of course, women were odd sometimes, you couldn't always believe what they told you. But in this case Irma Wasem seemed to be being honest, and he'd been well wide of the mark when he'd seen her as a calculating young miss with an eye to becoming the Director's wife. The one who'd been taken for a ride was Herr Direktor Ulrich Borstli, but since he was dead and buried it presumably didn't matter much to him.

"You know what?" said Irma Wasem. "I think it would be best if you didn't stay in Gilgen's house any longer. I went to see my brother today. He's the same age as you and he's OK. I've brought his certificate of domicile for you. Go to Basel with it and register under his name. In a week you can get a passport and go to France. I've a sister-in-law who lives in Provence, you can go and stay with her. I'll write to you then. After all, it's only the clinic that's looking for you, I don't think Laduner will have said you're a danger to the public, so the police won't exert themselves too much trying to find you."

"I wouldn't have been able to stay in Gilgen's house any longer anyway. That other bloke's making a racket

223

the whole time. I don't think I was ever as mad as him. He's got a gun as well and he keeps threatening to shoot himself. And thank you. Y'know what? I'll walk all night and get a train in Burgdorf in the morning."

"Have you any money?"

"No . . . Can you let me have some? I'll send it back if I can earn any."

Irma Wasem told him not to talk rubbish. She even used Studer's favourite word, *Chabis*. Studer heard the rustle of banknotes.

"I'll come and see you in Basel, if I can manage it," said Irma. Then it was quiet for a long time, apart from the murmur of the river. A light breeze was playing with the alder leaves.

"Bye," said Pieterlen, the classic case.

"Take care," said Irma Wasem.

And with that the two shadows disappeared into the darkness.

It was the best solution: Pieterlen, the classic case, disappears. He deserved it. Nine years! Locked up nine years for killing his child. And what had he been through in those nine years? Making coffins in his cell, then sewing buttonholes until he went mad because he couldn't stand it any longer. Smashing windowpanes, being force-fed, narcosis. Then waking up, coming back from another realm, fleeing the land where Matto ruled . . . But didn't Matto rule the whole world over?

There was that dream he'd had of the elegant bombs, standing there like soldiers on parade, and there was the voice on the radio, "Two hundred thousand men and women . . . " and the voice had sounded no different from the voice of the patient in the corner, counting his imaginary herds and his imaginary fortune . . .

224

He should wish this Pierre Pieterlen luck. He was going back to face the world, and all the dangers that entailed. But perhaps Irma Wasem might succeed in getting the classic case to understand that even a labourer with philosophical pretensions has the right to bring children into the world and be happy with them. Happy! That was another of those words. Contented, perhaps.

To France. Good. Studer liked France. There was a lot of disorder over there, and their politics were sometimes – God help us! But still, the Germans did say it was God's favourite country. Let's assume they're right and wish Pierre Pieterlen the best of luck. If Irma Wasem ever handed in her resignation, he'd know what was up. Perhaps a little card with his congratulations would be in order.

Anyway, it shouldn't be difficult to persuade Dr Laduner that this was the best solution. Dr Laduner had a lot to thank Studer for; Dr Laduner who was so free with the bread and salt.

What had Pieterlen been? A bundle of files. And Dr Laduner had brought the bundle of files to life.

But why was it on the evening of the harvest festival that Pieterlen had run off? That would be explained too. It was always the same in these cases: you groped around in the dark, you did your utmost and then at last you got hold of the end of the thread. And that was that. One pull and the case untangled itself.

Arrest Pieterlen? Why? It was well known in Bern that Studer could be cussed once he'd made up his mind. He had been asked to cover Dr Laduner. Had he not done that? Pieterlen's description had been circulated. Were his colleagues in Basel stupid enough to let a classic case like that slip through their fingers? And what if they were? He couldn't be everywhere at once.

Pierre Pieterlen, schizoid psychopath, you've been deprived of your freedom long enough, try and make a go of it. If you succeed, all the better. We're all poor sinners. What did someone once say? Let he who is without sin cast the first stone.

Studer went back along the road, deep in thought. When he came in sight of Gilgen's house he slipped quickly behind the bush he had used as cover before . . . The door was wide open and light was flooding out onto the garden path. The shutters on one window downstairs were open.

But it was not the unexpected light that had sent Studer scurrying behind his bush. There was a man walking up the garden path. Studer recognized Dreyer, the porter.

The sergeant crept up to the house and looked in through the lighted window. There were three people in the room. In one corner was the fair-haired young man who had been crying on the couch in Laduner's study. He had a Browning in his hand. Opposite him, in a frozen posture, sat Staff Nurse Jutzeler. Then the door was quietly opened. Dreyer entered the room, pulled a chair over by the backrest and sat down beside Herbert Caplaun.

Studer went in . . .

A Chinese proverb

On Monday morning, towards nine o'clock, Studer came out of the guest room. He was carrying his battered pigskin suitcase. In the corridor he met Frau Laduner.

Was the sergeant leaving? she wanted to know. Studer took his watch out of his waistcoat pocket, nodded and said as far as he knew there was a train to Bern at eleven, which was the one he intended to take. Could he have a word with the doctor first?

Frau Laduner said her husband wasn't well, he was still in bed. Still, if it was important she would go and call him. There was an anxious look in her eyes. Wouldn't the sergeant like to have breakfast first? she asked.

Studer thought for a while, then he nodded deliberately. "If I might have a cup of coffee," he said. "But after that would you be so kind as to let Dr Laduner know I'll be waiting for him in his study. I've something to tell him and it will take about an hour. And you can say I'll be happy to tell him the truth, if the doctor wants to hear the truth. Would you mind using those exact words?"

"Yes, yes, I'll do that," she replied. "But in the meantime why don't you get some breakfast. The coffee's on the table."

Studer kept his suitcase in his hand when he went into the dining room. A pale sun, that only just managed to penetrate the mist, was shining. Studer drank and ate. Then he took hold of his case, which he had put down beside him, stood up, went into the study, sat down in an armchair and waited. He kept the case on his knees.

Dr Laduner was wearing a grey dressing-gown over his pyjamas. He had leather slippers on his bare feet.

"You want to speak to me, Studer?" he asked. The white bandage round his head made his skin seem even browner. He sat down, a weary expression on his face, then put his hand over his eyes. He remained silent.

Studer opened his suitcase and placed various objects on the round table, which once, on an evening that seemed long ago, had had a lamp on it with a glowing floral shade. Beside the lamp had been the files on Pieterlen, the classic case.

Dr Laduner took his hand away from his eyes and looked at the table. Neatly laid out on it were the following objects: an old wallet, a sandbag that looked like a huge grey salami, a piece of coarse grey cloth, two envelopes, a piece of paper with writing on it and a wad of hundred-franc notes.

"Very nice," said Laduner. "Are you going to present these objects to a police museum, Studer?"

Before Studer could answer, the telephone on the table rang. Dr Laduner got up. At the other end of the line was an agitated voice. Laduner covered the mouthpiece with his hand and asked Studer, "Do you know where Dreyer, the porter, is?"

"If the Randlingen gendarme has carried out my orders, then Dreyer's probably at the police station in Bern by now."

Laduner still had his hand over the mouthpiece. His smiling mask reappeared.

"Accused of?" he asked.

"Theft and murder," Studer replied in a matter-of-fact tone.

"Murder? The murder of the Director?"

"No. Of Herbert Caplaun." Studer's voice was so calm that Laduner stared at him for a moment in amazement. Then he took his hand away from the mouthpiece and said, "I'll come down myself later. Just now I have an important meeting . . . No!" he suddenly shouted, his voice cracking. "I haven't got time at the moment," and slammed the receiver back on the rest.

He sat down again, leaning back and closing his eyes for a moment, then he bent forward and picked up the objects on the table one after the other while Studer gave his explanations in a low voice.

"That," he said when Laduner picked up the sandbag, "I found on the platform at the top of the ladder to the furnace. And that," indicating the piece of cloth, "was hidden under the mattress of Pieterlen's bed. The wallet was behind those books there; I found it by chance. It caused me a bit of a headache because I found it immediately after Gilgen had been to see you, Herr Doktor."

"And the envelopes?"

Studer smiled.

"One has to show," he said, "that one has been trained in detective work." He lifted up one of the envelopes. "Sand!" he said. Then the other. "Dust from the hair of the body." He paused. "However, the Director wasn't knocked down with the sandbag. He simply . . . But you can read it yourself, Herr Doktor." Studer picked up the handwritten sheet, unfolded it, then hesitated for a moment. "Maybe it's better if I read it out myself," he said, cleared his throat and started to read.

I, the undersigned, Herbert Caplaun, hereby declare that I was responsible for the death of Dr Ulrich Borstli, Director of Randlingen Clinic. On 1 September, at 10 pm, I rang Dr Borstli, who was attending a party for the patients, and, under the pretext that I had important information for him, arranged to meet him in a corner of the courtyard at two o'clock. At the same time I had asked him to bring the documents referring to the deaths in D1. That, however, was only a pretext. I had learnt that the Director had contacted my father in order to have me committed to a penal institution for a period. I had obtained a sandbag and had decided to kill the Director and hide the body in the heating plant. However, things turned out differently. An argument arose and the Director tried to hit me. I called out for help. In order to avoid arousing attention, the Director ordered me to go into the heating plant with him. I followed him. He switched on the light, then opened his file and showed me the copy of a letter to my father. When I had read it, I became furious and raised the sandbag. The Director stepped back, lost his footing and fell down. I locked the door to the heating plant, but forgot to switch off the light. During the days following I hid in Nurse Gilgen's house.

Randlingen, 5 September 19. Signed: Herbert Caplaun.

Witnesses to the signature:

Jakob Studer, sergeant in the Bern police force

Max Jutzeler, nurse.

Studer stopped. He was waiting. The silence lasted for a long time.

Finally Studer said, "You will have noticed, Herr Doktor, that your name is not mentioned in this document. You requested my presence in order to be covered by the police. I have tried to carry out my assignment."

"And Caplaun's dead?" Dr Laduner asked. Studer

230

did not look up, he was afraid of the smile that was sure to be on the doctor's lips.

"It was an accident," said Studer, embarrassed.

"You mentioned a murder."

"Actually it was both. But it's a long story. And it's one I'm not very keen to tell, because actually I'm to blame for Herbert Caplaun's death myself."

"If I understand you correctly, Studer, your clumsiness has caused the death of two people: Nurse Gilgen and Herbert Caplaun."

Studer said nothing. He pressed his lips together. His face gradually went red.

The mocking voice continued. "You've been trying to identify with me, Studer."

"Identify?"

"Yes, you wanted to take my place, play the psychiatrist, slip into my persona . . ."

"Persona?" There was another of those words.

Dr Laduner stood up. He took one object after another from the table – ignoring only the wad of banknotes – went over to a cupboard in the corner, placed them inside, locked it, put the key in his dressing-gown pocket and then came and stood over Studer.

"The forced confession," he said, and his voice was harsh, "will certainly be very useful. But you've made a botched job of it, Studer, you've tried to do my job for me. D'you understand? . . . I took you in, I hoped you would help me. And what did you do instead? Acted on your own initiative! Without asking my advice. I haven't asked how Herbert Caplaun came to die – it's irrelevant anyway. But there's no point in going on if you have problems understanding these foreign words."

Studer's thin face grew even redder. He clenched his fists; he knew that if he looked up and saw the doctor's

231

smiling face, the face with the smile that was like a mask, he would not be able to restrain himself. He'd wipe the smile off his face! . . . Who did the man think he was? Studer had protected him, had done everything possible to avoid a public scandal – and this was all the thanks he got?

"There are a few more things I'd like to point out, Studer. Do you think I really was so stupid that I didn't know from the start what had happened? Can you really only understand things that are explained in words of one syllable? We got to know each other in Vienna. You were less ponderous then. Is it old age that makes you so slow on the uptake? You learnt from the nightwatchman that I had met Herbert Caplaun just after two o'clock in the corridor of the heating plant. Why did you not question me about it? Why did you not tell me you'd found the sandbag – and the wallet? Why did you insist on pursuing the investigation under your own steam? I'll tell you why. You saw it as a trial of strength. You wanted to show the psychiatrist that a simple detective sergeant can have a talent for psychology too. But you have to be careful when you're dealing with minds, minds are fragile things. And you haven't found out anything about Pieterlen either? So you're a failure as a detective, too, aren't you? You're a bungler, Sergeant Studer, a bungler and nothing more."

Studer leapt up. That was too much!

He stood facing Dr Laduner in the classic boxer's stance with only one thought in his mind: to smash his fist into that smile. He drew his right arm back. Dr Laduner had his hands stuck in the pockets of his dressing-gown, he didn't move. Very quietly he said, without the smile disappearing from his lips, "Sergeant Studer, there is a Chinese proverb which is well worth taking to heart: 'An angry fist cannot hit a smiling face.' Just think about it, Sergeant."

Studer sat down. He was very pale. It was true, this case was just like flying over the Alps. And now it was over, over in a way that was humiliating. He felt so immensely weary. Most of all he would have liked to go to bed and not get up for four days. Four days? And never get up again, more like it!

What was it Dr Laduner had said? An angry fist cannot hit a smiling face . . .

Two men dead.

Studer pressed his fists into his eyes, as if he could erase the scene that was haunting him: the riverbank – one man pushing the other into the water. I could have intervened, thought Studer, why didn't I? Why didn't Jutzeler intervene? Has this Dr Laduner got us all under a spell? Little Gilgen, who kept the signed photo in the drawer of his bedside table, Schwertfeger, Pieterlen, the classic case, and Caplaun, the neurotic? Should I tell Laduner why Caplaun pushed the Director down the iron ladder? Or does our psychiatrist know that too? I'm a bungler. OK. Not everyone can handle other people's feelings like a chemist does his reagents. Should I point that out to Herr Doktor Laduner? It wouldn't get me anywhere. The man's bound to have an answer to that kind of objection that would take the wind out of my sails. It's hopeless . . .

"Do you know what you need, Studer?" Laduner asked. The sergeant looked at him in surprise. The doctor went to the door. "Greti," he shouted, "bring our sergeant a kirsch, he's not feeling too good."

He came back, went over to the window and said, "Perhaps alcohol should be counted as a psychotherapeutic medicine. At least that's what my celebrated colleague used to maintain and I wouldn't want to say he was entirely wrong. Drink up Studer, then you can tell us what you know. You stay and listen too, Greti."

Frau Laduner sat down on the couch. She clasped her hands. Studer poured himself a glass of schnapps, emptied it, filled it again and kept the drink in his mouth for a while before swallowing it and clearing his throat. Then he began.

Seven minutes

"Little Gilgen committed suicide," said Studer, "out of fear – but fear of what I couldn't work out. You're about to arrest someone for stealing money and he throws himself out of the window ... The question was, what happened in the seven minutes during which the money disappeared from the administration office.

"Gilgen had no idea what the safe in admin was like. He had *two* bundles of hundred-franc notes in his possession, but had no idea about the third. Therefore, someone else had stolen them. Gilgen kept his mouth shut. But he was afraid of being arrested. Why? Presumably because the examining magistrate would have forced him to come clean. Logical conclusion: Gilgen was shielding someone.

"Who was in the corridor at that time? The porter was in his lodge. Later Irma Wasem came to buy some chocolate. I think we can assume Gilgen wouldn't have kept silent to shield Dreyer. Who, apart from those two, did he meet in the lodge?

"Pieterlen?

"We can discount Pieterlen. He had played the accordion in the room with the window from which, according to Schül, Matto kept darting out and in. But Pieterlen wasn't in that room any more. I'd seen him in the corridor by the boiler room, when you were knocked out, Herr Doktor. It wasn't Pieterlen who knocked you out – there was someone else creeping round the corridors of the clinic. Who was this other person?

"It would have been easier to find the solution if I had listened more carefully to what Colonel Caplaun said, but I was preoccupied with a moral dilemma of my own."

Studer gave a shy smile, put his hand on Laduner's arm and said, without looking up, "Why did you not tell me Herbert Caplaun spent three months in O Ward?"

The doctor stayed silent. Frau Laduner cleared her throat. Studer continued.

"I suppose everyone in O Ward knew Herbert Caplaun was going to be your private patient. I presume he told them. I still don't know all that much about the clinic, but there's one thing I can well imagine: in all the long, empty days the patients will chat, chat a lot, tell each other about their lives, their hopes . . ."

Pause.

"Two warders in O . . . two warders who have stuck by you, Herr Doktor. The 'young guard' if you like: Max Jutzeler and little Gilgen. You gave Gilgen your photo. I found it in the drawer of his bedside table. Do you think it was difficult to guess who Gilgen met in the porter's lodge, who he was trying to shield? . . . Herbert Caplaun described how he came in by the main gate and went into the porter's lodge . . . Dreyer had three bundles of hundred-franc notes in his hand. What followed I've had to reconstruct since the two of them refused to say anything. I imagine the porter had put the fear of God into Herbert by threatening to reveal how the Director had died. That was the point when Gilgen came in. Caplaun probably had the bundles of notes in his hand."

The third wad of banknotes was on the round table. Studer picked it up and tapped the edge of the table with it.

"Herbert knew Gilgen had debts. He knew the porter was a thief. He handed Gilgen four thousand francs, and Gilgen went back to his ward."

Frau Laduner sighed.

"Then a certain Sergeant Studer was wanted on the telephone. Then this sergeant was informed by the porter that there had been a break-in at the admin office. And Sergeant Studer was taken in by the porter. He didn't see who the guilty party was, even though he spoke to him. He believed him, too, and went off after Gilgen. Did you know your husband called me a bungler, Frau Doktor, and he was right."

Studer sighed.

"Little Gilgen ... You must have put your spell on him, too, Herr Doktor. I can just imagine what the man was thinking. He had looked after Caplaun on the ward and met him again later when he took Pieterlen out for walks on a Sunday. All this would have been easier for me, Herr Doktor, if you'd told me just a little more. They became friends, the neurotic and the schizoid psychopath – you see I have made some progress in psychiatry. I can assure you, Herr Doktor, I understand little Gilgen very well now. Two of your problem children had been put in his care. One of them goes off, comes back and hands him four thousand francs. Little Gilgen doesn't understand what's going on. Then along comes a detective sergeant who's a bungler. So what does little Gilgen do? He wants to cover Dr Laduner. Actually, Dr Laduner is supposed to be being covered by the police, but Gilgen knows nothing about that. Little Gilgen had just one thought in his simple mind: if I tell the cop I found

Herbert Caplaun with the money in his hand, then the cop will go and arrest Herbert. And that would be a black mark for Dr Laduner, who is supposed to be making Herbert well again . . . But such a complicated matter was too much for a simple mind. He knows he must hold his tongue, but he also knows how weak he is and that he will be forced to talk when he's brought before the examining magistrate. It's the last straw for him. I can imagine how he felt. Debts on his house, his wife ill, his colleagues have told on him, the Board of Governors knows about the thefts, the thefts he didn't commit – it all became too much for him. He gave me the photo of his wife and his two children, and while I was looking at it, he jumped out of the window."

Dr Laduner muttered, "I always said you were a poetic detective, Studer."

Studer nodded. After a pause, he said, "The wallet. Did you know that I found the wallet behind those books there?"

"Behind those books?" Frau Laduner asked in astonishment.

Studer nodded.

"Yes, on the morning that Gilgen came here. I knew the Director had received 1,200 francs, but we were both there when we established that his pockets were empty. Then the wallet suddenly turned up behind your books. Who had put it there? Gilgen? Naturally I considered Gilgen. He went into my room that morning and took the sandbag I'd hidden in my suitcase. And where did I find the sandbag on Saturday afternoon? Behind a pair of old shoes in Gilgen's wardrobe. You, Herr Doktor, think like a psychiatrist, you know how minds work . . . What do I know? Well, I do know my job, and part of my job is to follow up clues and

238

arrest the people they point to. Did not all the clues point to Gilgen? I'm a bungler, you said, but any other detective would have done the same. You have to admit that the atmosphere here in your clinic is unfamiliar to me. Perhaps I know a little more about it than my colleagues, but still. I'm told about this Matto, and you spend a whole evening explaining to me that murdering a child is an understandable crime, that murdering a child, in other words, is an act of humanity. You confused me instead of giving me information. You wanted cover, and yet I sensed very clearly that you were afraid.

"For a long time I thought you were afraid of Pieterlen. And then, gradually, I realized Pieterlen was quite harmless, that he was trying to cover for you. And every time your two problem children met on their Sunday walks (did Herbert tell you about those during analysis, too?) there was just one topic of conversation: how they could help you become Director. And Gilgen listened. He probably expressed his opinion as well, he probably agreed it was unfair; you did all the work and the Director got all the glory . . ."

Laduner broke in, saying in a quiet voice, "There's another Chinese proverb, Studer: 'Men get glory, pigs get fat.'" He gave a brief snort.

"You've always got a neat answer, Herr Doktor, and a witty one, too. But I don't find the affair that funny. You said that by staying silent I was to blame for the death of two people. I'll tell you how Herbert Caplaun died, but first you must answer me one question: do you know why Caplaun pushed the Director down the ladder?"

"Pushed him down?" Dr Laduner asked. "Let's stick to the facts. In his confession he said the Director lost his footing."

Studer gave a faint smile. "Do you really believe that, Herr Doktor?"

"What I believe is neither here nor there, Studer. I stick to facts. What Caplaun actually did is nothing to do with me."

"I thought you wanted to know the truth, Herr Doktor. I was supposed to seek out the truth – *for us.*"

"You've got a good memory, Studer. And you seem to know a bit about psychology, as well. But I can tell you one thing: you're in danger of oversimplifying psychological mechanisms. In your opinion Herbert Caplaun had good reason to want the Director dead. Sure-ly. But what is my role in all this? Won't you reveal your psychological insight to me?"

Studer looked up. His elbows were resting on his thighs, his chin in his hands. "Herbert Caplaun committed the murder out of gratitude. He was of the bizarre opinion that he should be grateful to you . . . Grateful for treating him, grateful for protecting him from his father . . . Gratitude! A strange motive for a murder."

Silence.

It was broken by Frau Laduner's Swiss dialect. "You're sure, Sergeant?"

"I think so, Frau Doktor."

"My dear Studer, if you'll forgive me using one of your favourite expressions, what you have just said is *Chabis*, nonsense. I'm not denying that it is possible to see gratitude as one element in the motivation. However, everything I know about Herbert Caplaun forces me to the conclusion that the hatred he projected onto the Director had a different determinant. His fear of his father is important here. Not, however" – Dr Laduner raised his hand, index finger outstretched, and continued, like a professor giving a lecture – "the

240

fear of being put away. He knew that, if necessary, I would have taken every step possible to prevent such a measure. The root causes lie deeper. You will know that images we absorb during childhood live a life of their own inside us; that the image of the father, as it has been branded on the mind of the child, continues to be active in the subconscious of the adult. For Herbert Caplaun the Director was nothing other than an image of his father. I know from analysis that the wish to kill his father was very much alive in Herbert Caplaun. But his inhibitions about fulfilling that wish by killing his own father were so strong they were transferred to a person who could substitute for his father, i.e. the Director. That what you call gratitude did perhaps play some part" – Dr Laduner drawled the words – "I will allow, to a certain degree. But–"

Studer interrupted him. "Then I'd better tell you about the death of Herbert Caplaun."

Forty-five minutes

"The house that plunged Gilgen into debt – everything revolves around that house. And here you'll have to admit that if I hadn't turned up at the right moment there would have been another dead body.

"On Sunday I went looking for Staff Nurse Jutzeler, but I couldn't find him. I kept Gilgen's house under surveillance, then I eavesdropped on a conversation – but that conversation is none of your business. When I went back to the house after that, a window was open. I looked in, and what I saw was . . .

"When I went into the room, Herbert Caplaun was sitting in one corner and on a chair opposite, rigid, was Staff Nurse Jutzeler. Herbert had a small Browning in his hand and was about to shoot Jutzeler. There was another man in the room and he seemed very happy with the idea of Jutzeler being shot.

"You walked past the porter every morning and I don't know how many times during the day. He put your telephone calls through, he sat there behind his grille, selling cigars, cigarettes, in the morning he swept the corridor, polished the offices . . . A useful man! . . . He knew about things in the clinic . . . Do you know why I found him slightly sinister from the very beginning? He had a similar smile to you, Herr Doktor. But the deciding factor was the cut on his hand.

"You'll remember the Director's office and the window . . . Dreyer had a bandage on his left hand. Later I found out he'd had a fight with Staff Nurse Jutzeler in the office. But the reason the porter gave as to why he had gone creeping into the Director's office at one o'clock in the morning just didn't make sense to me. And the more I thought about it, the more I kept asking myself: who knew about the money from the insurance company? Dreyer, the porter, he knew.

"In the room he was sitting next to Herbert Caplaun, and it looked as if he was trying to get that young man to pull the trigger. Why was Jutzeler to be shot? Most probably because he knew something.

"That is the moment when I, Sergeant Studer, entered the room. I'm not easily scared, Herr Doktor. I'm not even frightened of a loaded gun. If you'd been there you'd have had to laugh. I just went up to Herbert and said, 'Give me the gun.' Dreyer tried to intervene, so I gave him a little tap on the chin. He fell down."

Studer regarded his fist thoughtfully, looked up and saw that Frau Laduner was smiling. The smile did the sergeant good.

"Jutzeler didn't get worked up, either. He just said, '*Merci*, Sergeant.' Then we turned our attention to Herbert and made him tell us all about it. Did he never tell you about the porter, Herr Doktor?"

"Analysis does not concern itself with such irrelevancies," said Dr Laduner in an irritated tone. "Usually they are just evasions . . ."

"It might have been a good idea if you had concerned yourself with that particular evasion," said Studer. "An irrelevancy for your analysis, perhaps . . ."

"It could be interpreted as such," said Laduner, placated.

" . . . but I don't find the part Dreyer played in all this the least bit irrelevant. It was the porter Colonel Caplaun had to thank for the fact that he was so well informed about his son, about conditions in the clinic – and about you, Herr Doktor . . . Did you know that the man had worked as a porter in large hotels in Paris and in England? Did you know that he had become involved in gambling there . . . that he had lost a lot of money? He hadn't got out of the habit. A telephone call was all that was necessary for me to learn all about your porter. He needed money. It wasn't difficult to work out what he was looking for in the office: the money from the insurance company.

"Jutzeler and I asked Herbert where he had phoned the Director from on the evening of the harvest festival . . . He'd slipped back into the clinic, through the door in the basement of P Ward. Have you never lost a passkey, Herr Doktor?"

Studer waited for an answer. He waited a long time, then wearily shrugged his shoulders and continued.

"It looks as if I have completely forfeited your trust, Herr Doktor. Well, here is the passkey; Herbert Caplaun had it on him. I took it – as a little memento for you."

Studer gently pushed the dully gleaming key across the table, but Dr Laduner just dug his hands deeper in his dressing-gown pockets, then stared at the window, as if there was a draught coming from it.

"We can do without the sentimental gesture, Studer," he said surlily.

"Sentimental?" Studer queried. "Why sentimental? We're talking about a man who wanted to show you his gratitude and is now dead. A week ago yesterday Pieterlen and Herbert Caplaun met. Pieterlen had brought the sandbag, they'd both decided to get rid of the Director, both out of gratitude. Gilgen was there, too, and he thought it was a crazy plan. He tried to talk them out of it, but Herbert Caplaun just wouldn't listen. Herbert told me he had been out of his mind that Sunday, and the previous Sunday too. He'd managed to convince Pieterlen. But Pieterlen refused to leave all the glory to Caplaun, he wanted to show his gratitude too. He decided to run away. He also had reason enough to hate the Director. Hadn't your would-be assassin drummed it into him that it was the Director's fault that he – Pieterlen – couldn't be released?

"I'm willing to admit that you're right when you say it wasn't gratitude alone that was the motivation for the murder plan. Each of them had his own, personal reasons ... Little Gilgen was a weak man, and weak people are dangerous when they're in a rage ... I'm sure it was well known throughout the clinic that you got on badly with the Director, that he would have liked to destroy you ... Wasn't it? ... It seems to me you were in a similar position to Chief Inspector Studer when he started his campaign against Colonel Caplaun. Perhaps that's why you remembered Sergeant Studer and asked for *him* when you needed cover ... Was that it?"

Silence. Then Dr Laduner said slowly, "It seems to me your mind must be going, Studer. To be perfectly honest, the few reports of yours I've seen were considerably more coherent than this story you've come up with. You keep hopping from one thing to another, you don't express yourself clearly. Might I, in all politeness, ask you to put things more plainly? At least to finish one story before going on to the next? For example, who was it who hid the wallet with the Director's passport and money behind my books?"

"I'll come back to that," said Studer, unmoved. "You must let me tell my story as well as I can, Herr Doktor. It's not a simple case, not like the kind we get outside, among normal people. There I have so-called circumstantial evidence, which I can interpret in one way or another. Here every piece of circumstantial evidence comes with a whole skein of psychological complications – if you'll allow the expression – attached . . .

"Right then. You want a story with a beginning and an end. Let me tell you the story of yesterday evening. It lasted forty-five minutes, no longer.

"Try and picture the sitting room in little Gilgen's house. There's a lamp hanging down from the ceiling with a green silk shade fringed with glass beads. In the middle there's a table, a solid table. A few pictures on the walls – and postcards. You know the kind of post-card: a young lad with beautifully combed hair and a coloured handkerchief in his breast pocket is kissing a rosy-cheeked lassie. And a little verse, in silver writing, underneath: 'When lips are sealed with a kiss,/ The music whispers this:/ I'll love you for ever, my . . . ' There were postcards like that fixed to the walls with drawing pins. Dreyer was stretched out on the floor. And Herbert Caplaun was sitting between me and Jutzeler.

"I asked Jutzeler why he'd come here. Initially he refused to answer, just shrugged his shoulders. Finally he said he'd come to look for Pieterlen. He was convinced Pieterlen had hidden in the clinic at first, but then it must have got too dangerous. So he'd asked himself where Pieterlen could have gone to hide, and he'd thought of Gilgen's house. He'd come in; the room had been dark, then suddenly the light went on and Herbert Caplaun was standing in front of him, threatening him with a gun . . .

"'Why were you going to shoot Jutzeler?' I asked Herbert.

"'Because he's been spying on me ... Because he was going to tell on me to my father ... Because he told on me to Dr Laduner!'

"'But, Herr Caplaun,' Jutzeler said, 'I haven't done anything of the kind. Who told you that?'

"At that Herbert flew into a rage. He yelled at Jutzeler, 'You told the doctor I was in the heating plant. How else could he have appeared at the door to spy on me immediately after I'd pushed the Director down. But I was quicker, I gave him the slip, he couldn't catch me ... But I still couldn't get away from him, from Dr Laduner. I went to his apartment the next morning. He gave me a frosty reception, he was so cold. He kept saying, "I don't want to hear anything, Caplaun. Anything you have to say to me, you have to say during analysis. I can't see you outside analysis." That's what he told me that morning. And in the afternoon I was on the couch and he didn't ask me anything and I couldn't speak, all I could do was cry. I only did it to show him my gratitude, but I couldn't tell him that, he wouldn't have believed me ... Things are always different when you're lying there and the other person is invisible and just smokes and doesn't say anything, doesn't say anything at all ... I cried, but I couldn't speak ... I kept thinking of the briefcase and the list of deaths and the report on Gilgen's thefts ... I'd hidden the briefcase well, in the furnace ... But I didn't tell the doctor where I'd hidden it. I didn't say anything about the Director, either. I knew you'd found the body already and Dr Laduner knew everything ... But the doctor didn't say anything, and I lay on the couch and cried ... You don't know what it's like, Sergeant, analysis. I'd rather have pneumonia three times over. It's supposed to be for my own good, it's supposed to make me a different person ... But to have to tell everything! You can't tell everything – especially not a murder. He was my father confessor, was Dr Laduner. If I'd told him I'd pushed the Director down the ladder, what could he have done? Have me arrested? He couldn't do that ... No more than a Catholic priest can get someone arrested who's just admitted to a murder during confession ... '

"There you are, Herr Doktor, that's what Caplaun told us, the two of us beside him, Jutzeler and me. And Dreyer was still on the floor, still unconscious."

Studer fell silent, exhausted. He had worked himself up into a fever as he spoke, but he did not dare to raise his eyes.

"And you believed all that, Sergeant Studer?"

Studer looked up, giving the doctor a look of disbelief. Dr Laduner had no intention of lowering his gaze. His eyes were sad.

At last Studer said angrily, "Herr Doktor, you wouldn't be trying to teach an old detective when a confession's true and when it's false, would you?"

"Sure-ly not," said Laduner calmly. "Carry on with your story, I'll make the necessary deductions."

Studer scratched the back of his neck, unsure of himself. Again he felt uncomfortable. He was like an eel, was this Dr Laduner, always slipping out of your grasp. What else did he know? Was there something to this analysis after all? Had he really been taken in by a false confession? But Herbert Caplaun's story had sounded so genuine.

Better just get on with it, for God's sake, the next bit was difficult enough to tell anyway.

"But you wanted to be covered, Herr Doktor," said Studer reproachfully, "and I hadn't forgotten that you'd offered me bread and salt, that you showed me

Leibundgut in order to explain Caplaun's case, that you took me in like a friend – and Frau Doktor Laduner, too, she's been very kind, she's even sung songs for me . . . So I thought the best thing would be for Caplaun to write down his confession and the two of us, Jutzeler and me, that is, to sign it. I took great care to see your name wasn't mentioned. I'd have to arrest Caplaun, of course, but first of all I wanted to bring him here and discuss with you how to proceed. Lord in heaven, Doctor," said Studer with a heartfelt sigh, "believe me, I wasn't trying to do your job for you. I'm a simple man, Herr Doktor, I wanted to do what I could to save you trouble—"

"Studer, Studer," Dr Laduner broke in reproachfully. "Those are all excuses. You protest too much! You went on to do something you have difficulty justifying. Just tell me what it was, as calmly, as objectively as you can, then we'll see what's to be done."

Studer gave another sigh . . . One more little effort and everything would be over . . . Then he could leave Matto's realm.

"Ernst," Frau Laduner suddenly said, "don't torment our sergeant like that."

"*Merci*, Frau Doktor," said Studer in relief. Then he went on.

"While all this was going on, Dreyer had been lying motionless on the floor, his eyes still closed. But I could clearly see his eyelids twitching. He'd come to a long time ago. I left him there; however, I still had a couple of questions I wanted to ask. I was supposed to be seeking out the truth, Herr Doktor, the truth *for us*. So I asked Caplaun, 'And the wallet? Why did you hide the wallet behind Dr Laduner's books?' At that Caplaun blushed. Eventually he mumbled that he'd expected that you, Herr Doktor, would thank him for what he'd done for you. He'd heard about the investigation that the Director had set in motion concerning the deaths in D1 and he thought you were in terrible danger. That was the reason why he'd pushed the Director down the ladder. But you didn't show the least gratitude . . . And that made him furious, so he'd decided to get his own back on you. If there was an investigation, he thought, and the wallet was found in your apartment, suspicion would fall on you and then he, Herbert, would be able to come forward and confess, so that the whole world would see how noble such a depraved character could be. Those were his own words, more or less . . . I accepted his explanation, but then I wanted to know why Gilgen had stolen the sandbag out of my suitcase.

"It was then that I learnt I'd been kept under observation by – however unlikely it sounds – Pieterlen. Pieterlen had hidden in the empty attic above my room; he'd felt that was the safest place for him. He felt so safe he even risked playing the accordion there. That's why Gilgen got such a shock when he was in my room and I asked him who was playing. There was a hole in the attic floor, so Pieterlen could observe everything that went on in my room. He saw me hide the sandbag and the piece of grey cloth in my suitcase. During the night he slipped into Gilgen's room on the ward and told him. But coming into your apartment was too dangerous for him, which was why Gilgen had to do it. Fear of getting the sack was just a pretext, he knew he had nothing to be afraid of now you were director."

Studer paused for a while, then went on.

"Caplaun calmed down . . . his hatred of Jutzeler seemed to have evaporated too . I went over to Dreyer, prodded him and told him to stop pretending. He gave me a venomous look . . . I really should have kept a closer eye on him. But you can't think of everything all the time.

"We, that is Jutzeler and I, had the pair of them between us. Caplaun was walking beside me, then came Dreyer and right over on the left was Jutzeler. We were going along the road and Jutzeler said taking the path along the river would mean a considerable short cut . . ."

"Are you sure, Sergeant" Dr Laduner broke in, "that it was *Jutzeler* who suggested it?"

Studer gave him a look of astonishment. "Yes, Herr Doktor, quite sure."

"Aha," was all Dr Laduner said. Then he took his hands out of the pockets of his dressing-gown and folded his arms across his chest.

Studer became unsure of himself. "I don't know," he said hesitantly, "if you know the place where the bank is steep and close to the path? The river's deep there."

Laduner nodded silently.

"The path along there is so narrow we had to walk in single file. I was in front, Dreyer came next, then Herbert, and Jutzeler at the back. I looked round from time to time, but Dreyer kept his head bowed. It was dark. On the left the bank dropped away to the river, on the right was a steep slope with thick bushes growing up it. Suddenly I heard noises behind me, heavy breathing, scuffling. I turned round. Caplaun and the porter were grappling, each trying to push the other into the river. I called out to Jutzeler to separate them, since I was in a precarious position myself, right on the edge of the path, with the ground crumbling away under my feet. Jutzeler didn't move. He just stood there, arms folded, like you, Herr Doktor, and watched the struggle. Then everything happened very quickly. I

251

had just managed to get a firm footing when I saw Dreyer free his right arm, take a swing and hit Caplaun on the chin. He toppled backwards into the water . . . Believe it or not, Herr Doktor, at that moment the image of the Director falling backwards down into the boiler room came to my mind. It seemed to me like . . . well, yes, like poetic justice. I might have been able to grab hold of Caplaun, but then I would have certainly fallen in the river with him. It's incredible how quickly you think in moments like that, Herr Doktor. I didn't move – I'm a poor swimmer, you see. Caplaun sank straight away . . . he didn't even cry out. The blow had stunned him. The two of us, Jutzeler and I, seized Dreyer and took him to Randlingen. I gave instructions for him to be sent to Bern this morning."

Silence, a silence that was suddenly broken by the shrill ring of the telephone on the table. Dr Laduner stood up, gave his name, then handed the receiver to Studer. "It's for you, Studer. I think it's the head of the police unit at Bern railway station."

Studer listened in silence, then said, "Right," carefully replaced the receiver and turned round. His face was pale.

"What's happened, Studer?" asked Dr Laduner.

"Dreyer tried to escape and ran straight into a lorry. He was run over . . . dead . . ."

Dr Laduner seemed still to be listening, even though the word "dead" had died away a long time ago.

Then the smiling mask appeared on his lips again. He held up his right hand, fingers spread out, and placed his left index finger on the thumb. "First the Director," he said, then the finger moved on to the tip of his right index finger, "then Gilgen, that makes two." Now it was the turn of the middle finger: "Three, Herbert Caplaun," then the ring finger: "and four,

Dreyer, the porter. I think you'd better give up this case, or I won't have enough fingers, even with both hands. But perhaps it's best like that." He paused, felt for the bandage round his head, straightened it out and said, "I was almost the fifth."

"Ernst!" exclaimed Frau Laduner, aghast, and grasped her husband's hand

The Song of Loneliness

"That's enough of that, Greti." said Laduner calmly as he stood up and started to walk up and down the room. Finally he stopped in front of Studer and folded his arms over his chest again.

"You still haven't asked me about the deaths in D1, Sergeant. What conclusion have you come to? Am I a doctor who puts the lives of the patients in his care at risk by carrying out dangerous experiments on them, or not?"

Studer pulled himself together. He tried to look the doctor straight in the eye, but found he couldn't, so he addressed his reply to the floor. "I presume that is a matter for your conscience as a doctor and is no business of mine as a layman."

"Well answered, Studer." Laduner gave an appreciative nod. "But I still owe you an explanation. In this clinic typhus is endemic – that is, we have never managed to eradicate it completely. Despite all our precautions individual cases keep cropping up from time to time. Then it disappears, only to flare up again weeks or months later. Now, I observed that some hopeless cases – mental defectives, catatonics – showed a sudden improvement after recovering from typhus. Two cases who'd been in the clinic for ten years, classified as incurable, we could even discharge after they recovered from typhus. That gave me the idea of deliberately infecting patients. I only tried it out on patients who had been in hospital for at least ten years, whose condition had remained the same and for whom there was not the slightest hope of improvement.

"I did it openly, my colleagues knew about it, it was discussed at the staff meeting a year ago. It was no more dangerous than narcosis, for example. In those we reckon with a mortality rate of five per cent. It was never higher in the typhus experiments.

"As I said, the matter was discussed at a staff meeting; the late Director had given his approval. To explain the behaviour of the Director during the last few months, I would have to give you a course on arteriosclerosis – hardening of the arteries, that is – and a mental illness we call senile dementia – mental decay in old age. It is difficult to diagnose in the early stages; it starts insidiously. It was impossible for me to draw up a medical report on Ulrich Borstli, MD, Director of Randlingen Clinic. We couldn't have the man put away. We did try to persuade him to take his pension and retire, but he wouldn't. Obstinacy, a refusal to see reason, is one of the standard symptoms of senile dementia – but you do also sometimes get a persecution mania. The director felt he was being persecuted by me. Earlier on our relationship had been excellent. He was glad I took so much work off him, he agreed when I suggested innovations. But recently he had started to think I was trying compromise him, to oust him, to have him put away. That's why he hated me so much.

"What should I do? It was just at the time when the signs of mental illness in the Director were becoming clearer that I made the acquaintance of Herbert Caplaun. Jutzeler, who helped you yesterday, was distantly related to him through his wife. Jutzeler asked me to take Herbert on. I wanted to think about it, but I told Jutzeler he could bring the man round so I could see him. Herbert was a musician. He'd composed songs. On that first visit he brought a song with him; verses by a German writer he'd set to music. We liked it, didn't we, Greti?"

Frau Laduner gave a weary nod.

"He was like Leibundgut, the man I showed you, Studer. Herbert drank. I kept him on O Ward for three months, as you discovered. You found out about his friendship with Pieterlen, his friendship with Gilgen. He was a nice lad, Herbert Caplaun. Then I took him on as a private patient. I couldn't help him hearing about the tension between the Director and me. You believe Caplaun tried to pay his debt of gratitude to me by murdering the Director, and all the indications are against him: the sandbag Pieterlen got for him, the telephone conversation on the evening of the harvest festival . . . But, Studer, doesn't something strike you? Do you really believe the Director, given his distrustful nature – and his illness had made him even more distrustful – do you believe the Director would have agreed to go and meet someone just like that? Given how distrustful he was? Do you really believe that, Studer?"

Silence. Frau Laduner's eyes were wide, she was staring anxiously at her husband.

"Someone helped. Who? Three men come into consideration, three men who could have talked to the Director between the telephone conversation and him going to the heating plant . . . Three men – and one woman. No, we can rule the woman out. That leaves: 1: me – no, don't protest, I had an interest – 2: Jutzeler and 3: Dreyer, the porter.

"My wife can confirm that during the night of the first of September I left the apartment at a quarter to one and only returned at about half past two. Which was still early enough for me to be called out to O when it was discovered Pieterlen had disappeared. What was I doing during all that time? A nightwatchman saw me at the door to the heating plant. I was chasing someone – Caplaun, obviously. You really ought to have made me your prime suspect after the nightwatchman told you that, but you refused to entertain the idea . . . OK.

"The second possibility is Jutzeler. He'd had an argument with the Director – about Gilgen. Jutzeler could have been the one who said whatever it was that lured the Director to the heating plant. But we can eliminate him because . . ."

Dr Laduner paused for effect. He slowly lit a cigarette.

"Because after I had abandoned my unsuccessful pursuit of my problem child, I came across a man in the basement corridor who was locking the door to the heating plant. Do you know who?"

Studer nodded. Suddenly everything was clear. He felt ashamed. He had understood nothing . . .

"Dreyer, the porter," Laduner said softly. "I'm convinced it was Dreyer who persuaded the Director to meet Herbert, though we can only guess at the arguments he employed. However, I didn't know what had happened in the boiler room, so I didn't stop him. I followed him quietly. He didn't see me. When, then, the news came that the Director had disappeared and his office looked as if a struggle had taken place there, I considered what would be the best thing to do. I knew Caplaun was involved in some way or other . . . That was when I remembered a man I'd met some years ago, a man I knew was interested in psychological puzzles, so I said to myself, I'll get them to send that man, then I can go on treating my patient with an easy mind. Herbert Caplaun's worth taking trouble over and there'll never be a better time to let his resentment play itself out. If there should be complications, I'll have a certain detective sergeant to hand who will help me.

"Caplaun lied to you from beginning to end, Sergeant. His confession was false, his claim that he said nothing during analysis untrue. You don't know what terrible pressure silence can exert – my silence, for example, when I'm sitting at the patient's head and he can't see me. During that session on the second of September, when you came barging in and saw Caplaun crying, he'd already confessed everything: that he'd pushed the Director down the ladder, that he'd done it to help me. I said nothing ... I knew better. I knew Caplaun was incapable of such a deed, I knew his inhibitions were too strong. It was possible that he had met the Director in the heating plant, but he'd neither hit him over the head (at that point I knew nothing about the sandbag) nor given him a push. I'd seen Dreyer coming out of the boiler room. I knew what had happened.

"All the time you assumed he was pushed, Studer. I knew when I saw the body, when I examined the position it was in more closely, that the Director had been *pulled* down. Remember his spectacles. On the ground beside him! If he had fallen down backwards, they would never have come off. Didn't you notice the abrasions on his nose? His face hit the edge of the platform, his spectacles were knocked off *and only then* did he fall down backwards and break his neck.

"One foot steps over the edge. A man hidden under the platform grabs the foot. A little tug ...

"But that's all detective work. I'm a doctor, Studer, as

I've told you before . . . I try to heal minds . . . Can you imagine the power that is given me? You don't understand what I'm talking about, do you? A man comes to me, his mind broken, twisted, and I'm supposed to straighten it out, to heal it. This man imagines he's a murderer, he admits it to me because he knows I can't betray him. I'm his father confessor. Now I *could* reassure him with one word, I *could* prove to him that he's not a murderer. Why don't I? Because the idea that he's a murderer can accelerate the healing process. It gives me a lever: his mind is like a door with bent hinges and I can use the lever to straighten out the hinges.

"I thought you'd understood that, I thought you remembered Eichhorn, the scene with the knife . . .

"Dreyer wasn't going anywhere, I could leave him until you found him.

"You even believed Caplaun when he told you *he*'d hidden the wallet in my room.

"I hid it myself . . . I found it in a drawer of the desk in the Director's office, in the morning, before I set off to pick you up in Bern. Dreyer looked for it, but he didn't find it. I wanted to have the wallet within reach, so that I could show it to Caplaun. In analysis you have to drop a little bomb now and then.

"Unfortunately, you didn't understand anything, Studer. That's why I was so annoyed. I suppose Caplaun's death was fated . . .

"Greti, you must sing the sergeant the song, our song . . . as a way of saying goodbye." Dr Laduner smiled, a tired smile, then added softly, "It was the song that made me accept Herbert for analysis . . . Come along to the drawing room, Studer."

It was the strangest concert Studer had ever heard.

The drawing room was cold; the window looked out onto the courtyard, at the back of which was the chimney pointing up into the sky, red as a butcher's thumb. Grey light filtered in through the glass.

Dr Laduner was sitting on the round piano stool, a handwritten sheet of music in front of him. Beside him, erect, stood his wife. Her red dressing-gown had stiff folds. The doctor played the accompaniment quietly, Frau Laduner sang:

At times you get as lonely as can be . . .

And Studer saw the apartment on the first floor, the cigar stubs in the ashtray, the bottle of brandy, the book open on the desk . . . There were withered leaves on the branches of the birch tree outside the window.

It's no use going home to pour yourself
A schnapps, assuming there's some in the house

The kitchen window in O Ward. And Pieterlen standing at the window, staring across at the women's ward, where Irma Wasem was standing at the window looking across at him.

It's no use feeling sorry for yourself . . .

Little Gilgen sitting on the edge of the bed, little Gilgen taking the photo of his wife out of the drawer of the bedside table, then suddenly disappearing . . .

You'd really like to make yourself quite small . . .

Caplaun, Herbert Caplaun had hidden in Gilgen's house. Hidden from his father and his psychiatrist.

260

And then, and then – Studer put his hand over his eyes – the water splashing up in the dull starlight . . .

> Then close your eyes, shut out the world outside
> And be alone . . .

Frau Laduner was silent. A few soft chords. Then it was very quiet in the room.